ENSLAVED

HOPE TARR

"A touching story of salvation and renewal . . ."
— *Best-selling author, Madeline Hunter on* Vanquished

Jewel Imprint: Sapphire
Medallion Press, Inc.
Printed in USA

"VANQUISHED is an emotionally charged story where the drama leaps off the pages. Hadrian and Callie endure so much. Hadrian's past is particularly dark and there are some moments in the story that are heartbreaking to read. My heart went out to them as they struggled to fight the demons of their pasts. In each other's arms, they find a peace and love that neither felt was possible. VANQUISHED is a beautifully written story full of passion and peril."

—*Nannette, Joyfully Reviewed* (www.joyfullyreviewed.com)

2006 BURIED TREASURE by All About Romance
"VANQUISHED is worth searching out. This is a very rich book. The historical background isn't wallpaper, instead we get a real feeling for the historical events of the time period and how they shaped the attitudes of Caledonia Rivers and Hadrian St. Claire. I love the late Victorian and Edwardian period and VANQUISHED really captured the atmosphere of that time. Booklist called it an intelligent, sexy historical romance. I agree totally."

—*All About Romance* (www.likesbooks.com)

"VANQUISHED is a vivid, passionate romance."

—*India Edghill*

"A book to feast upon. Fresh and original. Don't miss this one."

—*Patricia Potter*

DEDICATION:

To my dear friend, Barbara Joy Casana, whose canny wit, all-seeing gaze, and gentle smile have brought peace, clarity, and joy to so very many lives.

Published 2007 by Medallion Press, Inc.

The MEDALLION PRESS LOGO
is a registered tradmark of Medallion Press, Inc.

Names, characters, places, and incidents are the products of the author's imagination or are used fictionally. Any resemblance to actual events, locales, or persons, living or dead, is entirely coincidental.

Printed in the United States of America
Typeset in Adobe Garamond Pro

10 9 8 7 6 5 4 3 2 1
First Edition

ACKNOWLEDGEMENTS:

My sincere gratitude goes out to Helen Rosburg for giving a publishing home to Gavin and Daisy's unique love story, and to Creative Director, Adam Mock, and the rest of the talented team at Medallion Press for once again creating such a splendid package for the book.

I'd also like to acknowledge my "home team," the Fredericksburg, VA friends who, on a daily basis, keep me sane, smiling—and writing—with their laughter, wit, and abiding good nature. Barbara and Johnny Casana, Cheryl Bosch, Clyde Coatney, Kyle and Rebecca Snyder, and Phil and Trista Chapman, I feel so tremendously fortunate to have you all in my life.

Finally, to Rob and Virginia Grogan, publishers of "Front Porch Fredericksburg," my heartfelt thanks for all your friendship, support, and career encouragement over the past six years. It means a lot. Actually, it means everything.

CHAPTER ONE

"A many years ago
When I was young and charming
As some of you may know
I practiced baby-farming."
—GILBERT & SULLIVAN, *HMS Pinafore*

> Roxbury House Orphanage
> Kent, England, 1876

Footfalls bounded up the attic stairs. The three children tensed, breaths bated, gazes flying to the unlatched door. As soon as the last of them, Daisy, had stolen inside, they snuffed out the stub of candle and settled in to wait. Almost a quarter of an hour hence, the fading sunrays admitted through the smudged glass of the one weather-beaten window served as their sole source of light. Dust motes floated like feathers in the still, heavy air. In the artificial hush, the slightest creak of a board or the unsanctioned crack of knuckles or, God

1

forbid, a sneeze seemed to ring out as loudly as the chiming of the famed Bow Bells of which all three occupants had been born within earshot, rendering them forever East Londoners, true-blooded cockneys.

The door opened on a screech, sending a sliver of light slicing through the shadows. Harry Stone poked his silver-blond head inside. "All's clear," he announced in a high whisper, drawing his friends' collective sigh. He crossed the threshold, the lantern he held serving as a spotlight for the lopsided grin that girls, the older ones especially, seemed to find so very irresistible.

Scowling, Patrick O' Rourke—Rourke—popped up from the milk crate he was crouched behind. "Jaysus, Harry, you're late again. This is the third time in a row."

Ducking to avoid the low-hanging eaves, the lanky sixteen year-old drew the door closed behind him. "Is it my fault some of us have work to do?"

The Scot answered with a snort. "Aye, hard labor it must be coaxing the bonny Betsy out of her knickers and into the straw with you."

Making a seat on a stack of old school books, Harry shrugged. The son of a dockside whore from East Cheap, for him sex was a necessary physical function, an activity as inevitable as eating, sleeping, or pissing. "Spying on me again, mate? Well, mind you watch close. You just might learn something."

Rourke snorted though in the dim light his cheeks burned bright as any candle flame. "Och, I've had plenty of girls."

Legs swinging, Harry let out a laugh. "Goats, don't you mean?"

Rourke faced him, fists clenched. "Best close your clapper, Stone, or I'll see it closed for ye."

Crawling out from the underbelly of an old pedestal desk, Gavin Carmichael decided it was time to intervene. At fourteen he possessed neither Harry's golden good looks nor Rourke's brawn and glib tongue, but he had a canny knack for diffusing arguments between friends and foes alike, a trait that had earned him the sobriquet of Saint Gavin. He wasn't entirely certain he fancied being likened to a saint. Saints tended to live short lives of poverty and self-sacrifice only to be broken on wheels like Saint Catherine or beheaded like Saint John the Baptist or burned at the stake like Saint Joan of Arc. The latter fate held a particular horror for him.

"Rourke, Harry, that'll more than do. We've a lady present, after all." He jerked his head to indicate the "lady" in question.

Nine year-old Daisy sat atop a sea chest, skinny legs swinging. She tilted her head of wheat-colored hair to the side and pursed her pretty upside-down mouth, a sign she was working on unraveling life's latest mystery. "But straw's itchy."

Rourke tossed back his head of long auburn hair and hooted with laughter. Swiping a broad-backed hand over watery eyes, he said, "Dinna fash, sweeting. If ever the lovely Betsy has an itch, our mate Harry will be more than happy to scratch it for her."

Wincing, Gavin cleared his throat, a signal that a change of topic was in order. "Ladies or rather lady and gentlemen, I hereby call this twelfth monthly meeting of the Roxbury House Orphans Club to order. Have I a second?"

"Second." Jumping down, Daisy tugged on the skirts of her plain brown school smock.

The foursome settled in to form a circle, huddling cross-legged beneath the eaves. Harry set his offering, a handkerchief full of lemon drops and peppermint sticks pilfered from the kitchen, in the center along with the lantern. Later the booty would be divided among them, though Gavin always gave most of his share to Daisy.

Daisy reached across and tugged at Harry's shirt sleeve. "You're forgetting the best part."

"I am?" Harry hesitated, looking puzzled, and Gavin surmised his friend's mind was still in the stable with the bountiful Betsy.

"The oath, blockhead," Rourke hissed.

"Oh, that. Right-o." Catching Gavin's pointed look, Harry began, "Through thick and thin."

He elbowed Rourke. Rubbing at his poked ribs, the Scot scowled and said, "Forever and ever."

Beaming, Daisy reached across and wrapped her small hand about Gavin's little finger. Smiling into her shining eyes, he dutifully added, "Come what may."

"We'll stay together . . . just like a real family." Breaking hands, Daisy clapped hers together, clearly awash in delight. Their oath was her favorite part of their monthly ritual, especially as she always got to say the finale. "Do real families hold secret meetings in their attic?" she asked of the circle though her gaze rested on Gavin.

As Gavin was the only one among them who'd had a proper family, two parents who were married to each other and a baby sister, Amelia Grace, he was uniquely qualified to answer. Still, he hesitated, emotion threatening to trip his tongue, gaze riveted suddenly on the feeble lantern flame, which seemed to grow into a raging inferno before his eyes. His parents and Amelia Grace had died when their tenement had caught fire, and they were trapped inside. By rights Gavin should have died, too, but at the last minute his mum had pressed a penny into his palm and sent him off to the bakery for a day-old loaf to stretch out the leftover supper stew.

"Gav?" Daisy tugged on his sleeve.

He pulled his gaze from the flame and turned to look at her. Working to overcome the invisible chokehold about his throat and the thickness blanketing his tongue whenever the word "family" was mentioned, he said, "They c-could, I . . . I s-suppose, if they w-wanted to. But no, n-not usually. They're too . . . b-busy w-working."

In truth, he couldn't recall his parents doing much else but work, his mother especially. Even sitting before the hearth in the evenings reading aloud from her small library of cherished books, his mother had kept her nimble, work-roughened hands busy be it making brushes, putting the final "fancywork" finish on ladies clothing, or sewing canvases for hammocks.

Daisy slipped her small hand into his. "Then we're the ones who're better off, aren't we?" She punctuated the statement with a brisk nod and a bright smile as though the riddle of familial relations had been solved at long last.

Of all of them, Daisy had the least experience of what it meant to be part of a family. She'd been left in a laundry basket on the steps of St. Mary-Le-Bow in Cheapside when barely a month old with no legacy beyond the blanket wrapped about her and a roughly scrawled note that read, "Be good to my baby." Whether she'd come to Roxbury House under the auspices of the boys' benefactor, Prime Minister William Gladstone, or by some other means was anyone's guess. Regardless of who had brought her to the Quaker orphanage, it was a far more desirable destination than a parish workhouse or, worse still, one of the so-called baby farms. In the latter, gin-soaked country crones charged desperate young mothers fifteen shillings a month to take over the care of their infants. The money supposedly went for the child's keeping, but more often than not he or she was slowly murdered with feedings of lime-laced milk and sundry other poisons. Many a small, newspaper-bundled body had been found on a country roadside. It was a terrible trade.

"Yes, poppet," Gavin said, grateful she'd escaped such a gruesome fate. With her pale hair, slanted green eyes, and slight built, she reminded him of a wood sprite or an angel depending upon whether she was in a mischievous or reverent mood. "I expect we are."

Daisy divided her gaze among them and said, "Can we act out the story of the pussy cat who wore boots? I like that one best of all."

The other two boys answered with groans, but a warning look from Gavin brought them quickly around. If Rourke wanted Gavin's help with his next history assignment and Harry someone to take over sweeping the horse stalls so he might busy himself with Betsy in the loft, they knew they'd better consent. Before long Harry was acting the part of the king with gusto and Rourke throwing himself into the role of the ogre. That left Gavin to serve as narrator and stage director, the perfect position for him. After nearly a year he knew all the parts by heart and yet he could never be certain when his stammer might crop up.

There was no question but that Daisy would assume the lead role of Puss. Being the center of attention was the entire point of the game, and the cat's cunning and sheer pluck resonated with her Cockney soul. Watching her strut about the dusty floor, an old cavalier's hat falling low over her brow and a moth-eaten mantel of velvet flung about her narrow shoulders, Gavin felt at perfect peace.

"Good show, sweetheart," he called out at the play's

end when she swept off her hat and took her bow. "What a brilliant little actress you are, isn't that so, lads?"

"Aye, that was a crack performance," Harry agreed, tearing off his paper crown as though happy to be free of it.

"A bonnier lassie there's not to be found treading the boards in London or in Edinburgh either, for that matter," Rourke added, for though he'd lived on English soil for most of his life, he always made it a point to give equal due to his birth country.

Obviously transported to grander times and loftier circumstances in the world of make-believe, Daisy curtsied and dimpled and blew kisses to an invisible, adoring crowd. Gavin presented her with the last of the props, a *papier-mâché* rose she liked to drape over her arm and pretend was a full, fresh bouquet.

None of them knew it, but that evening was the last they would ever meet in the attic.

Gavin received the summons to the headmaster's study the next morning before the breakfast bell had even rung. Standing in the hallway waiting to be called within, he felt his stomach knot and his palms sweat. Someone must have discovered the secret attic meetings and reported them, it was the only explanation. The storage space was declared off-limits, but more so than treading on forbidden territory, it was the playacting that would land them in trouble. The Society of Friends, or the Quakers as the sect was commonly known, strove to shun the earthly vanities of fashion, phraseology, and entertainments. Music, dancing, and plays were strictly forbidden. Were the headmaster to discover Daisy as the instigator of their little theater, the brunt of the blame would fall on her slender shoulders. To protect her as well as his other two friends, Gavin was prepared to claim their attic meetings were entirely his idea.

Fortunately for him, the Society of Friends abhorred violence in any form. The canings and birchings and sundry other methods of corporal punishment meted out in the meanest work houses and the finest public schools alike were absent from the orphanage. Discipline usually involved performing additional chores for the good of the group coupled with a meditative exercise meant to bring the offender to an understanding of the source of the selfish or evil impulse that had led him astray.

The study door opened, revealing the headmaster's tall, simply-clad form. Gavin squeezed his folded hands together behind his back and steeled himself to be strong. "You sent for me, sir?"

The headmaster, a man in his forties or thereabouts, nodded and beckoned him inside. "Gavin, a visitor awaits thee."

A visitor? Prime Minister Gladstone, perhaps? Gavin's heart lifted with joyful anticipation. He hadn't set eyes on his benefactor since the night of his rescue a year before and had never had the opportunity to render proper thanks. The fire had made him not only an orphan but also homeless. Frozen, footsore, and fevered, he'd been wandering the East London streets for more than a month living off found coins and scavenged foodstuffs. One particular bitter night, too weary and dispirited to take a single stride more, he'd lain down upon a set of tavern steps and slipped into a fitful, dream-filled sleep.

In his dream there was plenty of stew to go around and instead of being sent off to the baker, he'd stayed behind and become trapped inside the burning tenement building with his family. Flames hemmed them in on all sides, and the low ceiling was about to fall. Black smoke choked his lungs and the very air was too blistering to breathe. Kicking out at her crib, a red-faced Baby Amelia Grace let out a shriek that reached to the burning rafters. Gavin's mother picked up the baby to comfort her but moments away from death, what comfort could she give? Suddenly a dark angel swooped inside the narrow room. Wrapping the four of them in his black-winged embrace, he bore them upward beyond the fire's reach to safety or Heaven, Gavin couldn't be sure which.

He awoke to the scents of bay rum and leather and tobacco swirling about him like a luxuriant olfactory cloud. Strong arms lifted him from the step. He opened his eyes and looked up into the craggy countenance of the angel from his dream, only his savior was no celestial being but a flesh-and-blood man of late middle years. Passing in and out of consciousness, he had a vague recollection of being laid across a tufted leather carriage seat and borne away to a stately townhouse set on a quiet street, a lion's head knocker decorating its black lacquer door. Later he'd learned that his benefactor was Prime Minister William Gladstone and the house to which he'd been brought Number Ten Downing Street. A fortnight later, fever-free and well-fed, he left the ministerial residence and boarded a train bound for Kent—and Roxbury House.

Perspiration pricking his armpits, Gavin looked beyond the headmaster to the tall, broad-shouldered man wearing a top hat and caped greatcoat looking out the window to the vegetable garden. He held his arms behind his back, one gloved hand cinched about the wrist of the other. Prime Minister Gladstone, it had to be!

Gavin held his breath as his "visitor" turned slowly toward him. Mindful to hold his shoulders straight, he looked up, expecting to meet the high forehead and deep-set eyes he remembered from the year before. The jolt of disappointment nearly knocked him to his knees. The fierce face shaded by the hat's beaver brim belonged not to the kindly Prime Minister but to a stranger.

The headmaster joined the visitor at the window. "Friend St. John is thy mother's father. He has been searching for thee all this past year and has come to bear you home."

Panic plowed Gavin in the gut, threatening to turn his bowels to water. His mother had spoken of her father only rarely, but when she had the term "tyrant" had been applied. "But . . . I . . . don't w-want a g-grandfather. I d-don't want to l-leave. I have . . . f-friends . . . here." *I have Daisy.*

Gaze kind, the headmaster shook his crown of closely cropped salt-and-pepper hair. "The Lord has a plan for thee, Gavin, as He does for each of us. Trust it is so and open thyself to the Inner Light."

"Enough!" Mr. St. John crossed the room in two long strides and settled hard hands on Gavin's shoulders, gloved fingers tightening like talons. "We may be strangers, but we share the same blood. I'm your grandfather, and I've had the very devil of a time finding you. Like it or not, I'm taking you back with me to London."

London! Gavin's heart flipped with fear at the mere mention of the capitol city, a place he associated with foul smells and fiendish faces, with cramped corridors and crowded streets, with fire and screams and the sickening stench of charred flesh.

"But I don't w-want to g-go to L-London." *I don't want to go with you.*

Shaking free of the stranger, Gavin backed up toward the door, head filling with brash plans. He'd always been fleet of foot. If called upon to do so, could he run as far as his breath and legs would carry him and then hide out in the hope his grandfather would give up and leave without him?

Mr. St. John's heavy brow lifted and then settled visor-like over gunmetal gray eyes. Looking up into that steely gaze, at once Gavin understood that his grandfather was not the sort of man who would give up—ever.

He advanced on Gavin. "I see you inherited your sire's damnable Irish temper, but you're still a St. John by blood and if I have to beat it into you with a birch and mold you with my own two hands like a cursed lump of clay, you'll live up to your birthright, by God."

The headmaster stepped between them. "Friend St. John, thy grandson has suffered much loss this past year. Can you not at least grant him leave to bid goodbye to his friends? The little girl, Daisy, is as a sister to him."

St. John dismissed the entreaty with a wave. "I'll thank you to remember it's *Mr.* St. John, and while I'm grateful for your keeping my grandson fed and clothed, I'll brook no further meddling. From here on, his future is a family matter that concerns you not. See that he's packed and ready to leave within the hour."

He shouldered his way past them and strode out into the hallway, his retreating footfalls ringing on the flagging.

The headmaster turned to Gavin, his clean-shaven face registering sympathy and, Gavin thought, pity as well. "I know thy grandfather seems a hard man, Gavin, but there is that of God in him as there is within each of us. Put thy earth-bound will aside and trust all will be well."

Trust all will be well? Gavin felt himself torn between hysterical tears and bitter laughter. Had it been the Lord's will for his parents and baby sister to burn up in a fire? Was it divine intervention or happenstance that he alone had been spared because there wasn't enough stew to go around? He didn't like to think of the Creator as a capricious puppet master, and yet if everything that came about did so by God's guiding hand, what other conclusion might he draw?

Gavin felt tears prick his eyes and didn't trouble himself to blink them away. "If I must go with him back to London, then I wish I were dead and lying beside my real family in the churchyard."

The headmaster's eyes widened. "Gavin!" he said, tone harsher than Gavin had ever heard him use before. "Test not the Lord with the making of such an oath."

His face softening, he reached out as if to lay a hand on Gavin's arm, but Gavin was beyond comfort. He jerked away and sped out the door, one thought burning through his brain. *I have to find Daisy.*

He found her in the attic sitting on the dusty floor, head resting on her tented knees. She looked up when he entered and he saw she'd been crying. Had the news traveled so quickly? "I heard you were being adopted."

Damn, he'd wanted to be the one to tell her. Determined not to show her his sorrow, Gavin shook his head. "Not adopted exactly. I have a family after all or at least a

grandfather. He's come to fetch me back to . . . L-London."
Even now that the first shock was fading, he couldn't keep
from stumbling over that one dreaded word.

She sprang to her feet and launched herself at him.
"Gav, take me with you," she begged, wrapping her thin
arms about his legs. "Please, take me. I'll be quiet as a
mouse and good as gold, I swear I will. Your horrid old
grandfather won't even know I'm there."

Gavin felt a warm droplet trickle down his cheek
and disappear into the top of her head of corn silk hair.
"You're always good, Daisy. In fact, you're the best little
girl in the world. As soon as I'm settled, I'll write you to
let you know my direction and how I'm getting on, and
you must practice your letters so you can do the same."

Burying her face against his torso, she shook her
head. "I don't want us to only write. I want us to be
together as we are now."

Gently, very gently, he disengaged her clinging
hands. He reached into his pocket and drew out the
wrapped handkerchief he'd meant to give her later, his
share of the pilfered candy from the night before. He
untied the bundle, snapped off a bite-size piece of peppermint stick, and popped it into her mouth. Gaze on
hers, he set his mind to memorizing every detail of her
dear little face—the wide-set green eyes that angled upward at the corners, the pert little nose that turned up
ever so slightly at the tip, and the adorable "upside down"
mouth with its full top lip—and felt his heart cave in on

15

itself under the weight of so much love and loss.

Crunching the candy, she looked up at him with big soulful eyes. "You won't forget about me, will you, Gav?"

He retied the hankie and pressed it into her palm. "I could never forget you, Daisy, not in a million years. And no matter how long it takes or how hard it is, someday, somehow I'll see we're together again."

Bottom lip trembling, she looked up at him, lashes spangled with tears. "You swear?"

Gavin nodded, the lump in his throat grown so large he could scarcely speak past it. "I swear."

Through thick and thin,
Forever and ever,
Come what may,
We'll stay together . . . just like a real family.

CHAPTER TWO

"Why, how now, *monsieur!* What a life is this,
That your poor friends must woo your company?"
—WILLIAM SHAKESPEARE, Duke Senior,
As You Like It

The Palace Song & Supper Club
Covent Garden, London
Spring 1891

t had been a bad day. Certainly not the very
worst day of Gavin Carmichael's twenty-nine-
year life—the day of the fire occupied that
honor. Neither could it match the trauma of the second worst day of his life, the day his grandfather had
swooped into the headmaster's study at Roxbury House
and taken Gavin away from Daisy and everything else
he held dear. If he was to be precise, and precision was
among the qualities which had landed him among the
ranks of London's top notch barristers despite his young

17

age, he would have to say it was the *third* worst day of his life.

The third worst day and still it felt as though he was skirting the edges of Hell, if not the core of the inferno, than surely one of its outer rings. Ah, yes, Limbo, Dante's First Circle, described his state perfectly. "Abandon all hope, ye who enter here," or so was writ on the gates. Abandoning all hope of ever finding Daisy was precisely what the detective's report, delivered that day, called for him to do.

Despite the prevalence of scarlet in its décor, The Palace wasn't particularly hellish or satanic so much as it was tawdry. One of the new song and supper clubs cropping up like clover throughout the city, it was luxurious in the overblown style reminiscent of the better class of brothels, the columned entrance festooned with plaster garden statues, colored lamps, and gilded trelliswork, none of which served any apparent function beyond adding to the general decorative clutter. Filing inside with his friends Harry and Rourke after a deucedly long wait, Gavin had gathered a general impression of thick carpets, mirror-covered walls, and windows aglow with stained glass. A spiral staircase led downstairs to the auditorium. Rows of white cloth-covered tables faced the semicircular stage hung with crimson and gold curtains, and a gas-fired chandelier reputed to hold 27,000 pieces of cut crystal crowned the coffered ceiling. Yet all the contrived splendor of the place couldn't conceal its basic coarseness anymore than evening tie and tails could transform a butcher into a baronet.

What a snob I've become, Gavin thought, at once guilty and unspeakably sad because it was true and because snobbery, he strongly suspected, was more or less an irreversible state. Even in the midst of it, he couldn't stop the flash fire images from his early childhood from cropping up—his mother's slender, chapped hands; the meanness of the three-room flat the four of them had called home; the bone-penetrating chill that hit like a fist in the face on winter mornings when he crawled out of bed to start up the stove, fingers so cold-stiffened he could scarcely strike the match.

It wasn't until after the fire he'd known how brutal winter could be. Homeless as well as orphaned, he'd made a bed of park benches and the crawl space beneath front steps, cramming crumpled newspapers into his layers of clothes to stave off the wind. He'd been a hair's breadth from freezing to death the night Gladstone discovered him and carried him indoors. With its big, homey kitchen, scrubbed corridors, and lush, green pasturelands, Roxbury House had seemed a seat of opulence and plenty. And yet were he to go back there now, he doubted even it would satisfy his highbrow standards.

That last thought made him well and truly angry, for he hadn't always been this way. No, this puffed up prideful person, this supercilious snob, wasn't really him but rather what the old man, his grandfather had made of him.

You've molded me like a cursed lump of clay, indeed, Grandfather, he said to himself, and then tossed back another mouthful of the dreadful, too-sweet champagne as if it might wash away fifteen years of bitter regret.

Harry, now known as Hadrian St. Claire, leaned over the table toward him. "Gav, are you all right?" To sever ties with his unsavory past, the photographer had taken the new name when he'd set up shop in Parliament Square several years before.

"I'm perfectly fine. Why do you ask?" Gavin replied, not because he was even remotely fine but because in his present circumstances, what else could he possibly say?

Hadrian shrugged but held his gaze. "You looked far away just now." Even when not peering through his camera's eye, his friend could be too observant for comfort, Gavin's at any rate.

Seated to the other side of him, Rourke poured them all more wine. "Aye, the entire purpose of our coming out was for you to set aside your quest for the night at least and have some fun. It's been fifteen years, Gav. Daisy is likely married by now with a family of her own, a real family such as she always wanted, not we ragtag orphan lot. For all we know, she might even be d—"

A scowl from Hadrian cut off the Scot at mid-word, but Gavin knew what he'd meant to say. Dead, Daisy might be dead.

Gavin shook his head. "I can't give up. She's out

there somewhere, I can *feel* her."

Indeed, there'd been times over the years when he'd awakened to the sound of sobbing and known beyond all reason he wasn't dreaming, that Daisy was somewhere out there in the great wide world in deep distress, perhaps even calling out his name. At other times, she'd suddenly appear to him in his dreams, no longer a little girl but a grown woman. A woman who looked up at him with wounded green eyes and a full, trembling mouth. *You swore, Gavin. You bloody well swore.*

For the past year he'd done his level best to find her. Indeed his friends had hinted on more than one occasion that his search bordered on obsession. So be it. He couldn't expect them to understand. Though all four members of the Roxbury House Orphans Club had been famous friends, he and Daisy had shared a special bond, a connection which transcended the physical limitations of time and space.

The detective he'd hired was from one of the top London agencies, but he only managed to track Daisy so far as Dover in the spring of 1877. Apparently she was adopted shortly after Gavin had left Roxbury by a husband and wife acting team, Robert and Florence Lake. The Lakes had been players in a traveling regional theater company that had stopped in Dover for a fortnight's spell. After that, the trail went cold, and the detective held out scant hope it might heat up again.

Rourke held up the folded program hawking the

evening's performances, notably that of its top liner. "If anyone can take your mind off long-lost little girls, it's sure to be this Delilah du Lac. Judging from the artist's sketch, she's a stunner."

Gavin gave the program a half-hearted glance. Earlier when he'd stood in queue beneath the entrance canopy, he had ample time to study the full-size poster displayed on the building's façade. If the promoter could be believed, Mademoiselle du Lac was newly arrived from Paris and possessed an angel's face, a nightingale's voice, and a body befitting the Biblical temptress from whom she'd taken her thoroughly disreputable name. And yet the color drawing of a voluptuous redhead wearing too many feathers and too few clothes had failed to move him.

Still, no one fancied a spoil sport and his two friends had weathered more than their fair share of his dark moods of late. He plucked the cloth-wrapped champagne bottle from the ice bucket and topped off their glasses, determined to be carefree and jolly and boisterous if it was the last act he accomplished on earth.

Raising his champagne flute, he offered a toast. "To Miss Delilah du Lac, may she come onstage and seduce us all with her siren's song."

They touched glasses, his friends answering with "Here, here" and "That's the spirit, man."

Determined to set aside his melancholy, he spent the better part of the next two hours telling Hadrian and Rourke, their white-jacketed waiter, indeed anyone who would listen what a jolly good time he was having. He ordered pease pudding and pigs' trotters because that's what his friends were having, never mind the lobster patties and new potatoes would have suited him far better. After finishing off the champagne, he joined his friends in ordering mugs of bitter stout, followed by a bottle of hock.

But all his studied jocularity was nothing more than a farce, a ruse. His stomach ached, his head ached, and as for his heart, it had never felt emptier. He hazarded a glance to Rourke and then Hadrian, blissfully emptying the dregs of what must be their third bottle of the house swill. With two penny cigars wedged into the corners of their mouths, they looked as though between them they hadn't a care in the world. How he envied them, not Hadrian's skill with a camera or Rourke's knack for turning a few quid into a fortune, but their simple ability to savor the moment and be happy.

Not so simple at all.

No matter how hard he tried, he couldn't seem to throw himself into the spirit of the place, into the spirit of fun, and the actuality was a great deal harder to swallow than a bad supper or bitter beer. As always, the failing, the lack, began and ended with him. Something that once had lived inside him had gone missing and, whatever that something was, he could no more find his way back to it than he could find Daisy. That he'd actually let himself be lulled into thinking he might lose himself in a smoke-filled London supper club struck him

as hopelessly absurd, a cruel jest played upon him by The
Powers That Be.

But not as cruel as being made to endure yet another
lame joke from the pinstripe-suited comic currently strut-
ting about the stage. Turning away from the platform, he
looked about the sea of cloth-covered tables and saw the
real show wasn't taking place on the stage but in the audience—the pugilist with the bulging biceps and shaved
pate flanked by two buxom blondes wearing heavy paint
and plunging necklines whom he presented to the waiter
as his "nieces;" the trio of factory girls gawking at Gavin
and then blushing and giggling at turns once they caught
his eye, their elaborate bonnets stacked with silken flowers, feathers, and in one case, a faux canary with black
button eyes; the dour-faced dockman putting down
his third pitcher of stout and barking to the music hall
chairman to get a move on and bring out Delilah du Lac
straightaway.

Gavin was in full sympathy with him on the latter.
He'd already suffered through a bad burlesque featuring
a gadabout husband who received his comeuppance at
the hands of his clever wife, an Italian performing fan-
tasias by hitting his hammer upon a grisly instrument
constructed of bones; and a middle-aged man dressed
in drag affecting the persona of the pantomime dame,
Widow Twankey. The striking of the chairman's gong
and the shuffling of scenery taking place behind the
drawn velvet curtain announced each new act, which

was invariably billed as the "most amazing," "stupendous," and "splendiferous" mankind had ever beheld.

Another hour crawled by, measured not by clock hands turning but rather by the consumption of yet another pint of beer. Their pitcher dry, there was still no sign of the mysterious Mademoiselle du Lac. The music hall chairman must be a cagey fellow for it was becoming clear he meant to hold back his top-lining performer until the very end of the night, building his audience's anticipation while milking them of the maximum coin. Pulling out his pocket watch, Gavin confirmed it was coming on midnight. Delilah du Lac would have to make due with one fewer admirer this night.

He pushed back his chair and stood. Suddenly the room seemed to be seesawing. Damn, he'd drunk too much. Tomorrow he could look forward to a splitting head and cottony mouth, his just desserts for imbibing too much, staying out too late, and generally pretending to be someone other than who he was.

He gripped the table's edge, hoping no one would notice he was holding on to steady himself. "You'll have to excuse me. I've an early morning briefing to deliver, and I'll do my client no great service if I arrive still asleep." He congratulated himself he'd gotten the words out without slurring too terribly.

Scowling, Hadrian reached for his sleeve. "You can't leave now after we've waited all night. Delilah du Lac is the very reason we're here. She'll be coming on any time now."

"Aye, for once Harry has the right of it," Rourke spoke up, wiping his mouth with the back of his hand. "We've bided this long for a look at the lass and so have a hundred-odd others. To pack the house like this, she must be worth the wait."

Gavin had his doubts. Another tarted-up dance hall girl with dyed hair, heavy paint, and scanty clothing— he'd seen a chorus of them so far that night and there was no reason to believe Delilah du Lac would constitute any measurable improvement on the common, *very* common, theme.

He shook his head, already imagining how good his bed's new mattress would feel beneath his back. "I'll find my own way home. You lads stay on. I'll expect a full accounting of the lady's charms tomorrow. For now, goodnight and—"

"Ladies and gentleman, I give you the Nightingale of Paris, the Muse of Montmartre, the Chanteuse of Calais, the lovely, the sublime, the splendiferous Miss Delilah du Lac." The music hall chairman's voice chimed in as Gavin took his first less than steady step toward the exit doors.

Gavin bit back a groan, hearing the death knell of his early escape in each pompous, overblown syllable. Damn, if he'd only found his resolve a moment sooner. His present choices were reduced to two: be stuck there for the duration of her performance or be abominably rude and walk out in the midst of it. As eager as he was to be on his way, it wasn't in him to be discourteous to a woman even if the woman in question wasn't precisely a lady.

He pulled out his chair and sat back down just as the velvet stage curtain jerked up. The spotlight illuminated a baby-faced pianist seated at a grand piano wearing bright green suspenders and a very tall hat. The light shifted slightly to the left, focusing on the tall, slender young woman standing in silhouette, her one slipper-shod foot propped upon the bench to show off the arc of a perfectly shaped leg. Feathers dressed her cinnamon-colored curls, a bustier hugged her high-sloped bosom, and a flounced striped-skirt rode above her knees. She sent her gloved hand on a slow, salacious slide from ankle to thigh, carrying the skirt hem with her.

"Good evening, gents. Or as we say in Paris, *bonsoir*." She fingered the black garter banding one milk white thigh, and Gavin joined the other male members of the audience in sucking in a collective breath.

Delilah du Lac dropped her slender foot from the bench to the stage floor and turned about to face the audience, and Gavin suddenly understood what all the fuss was about. Unlike the chorus girls he'd seen earlier that night, her face looked porcelain smooth, the features delicate as Dresden china except for her lush lips, her body lithe and long-limbed, her breasts generous without being bovine.

27

"My, my, what fine looking gents we have with us tonight," she remarked, addressing the pianist. "Shall we give 'em a taste of what they came for? Some sugar and spice?" Looking out onto the sea of tables, she raised her voice and asked, "What shall it be first, mates, the sugar—or the spice?"

She punctuated the word *spice* with a shimmy of her hips, and seconds later the audience exploded with calls for, "Spice, spice!"

Smiling, she slid a hand over the pianist's shoulder and said, "You heard 'em, Ralphie. Spice it is."

The pianist answered with an eager nod and laid into the ivories, stroking out the score to popular music hall tune, a saucy number Gavin recognized as "Oh! Mr. Porter." Delilah swept a scarlet boa from the seat, draped it about her slender white throat, and sauntered forward, the cone of limelight following her to the front of the stage. She stopped at the edge, and Gavin caught a whiff of her scent, some spicy mixture of jasmine and mint and musk that somehow managed to rise above the cigar smoke.

Wetting her lips, she sang:

"Oh! Mr. Porter, what shall I do,

I wanted to go to Birmingham, and they've taken me to Crewe,

Take me back to London as quickly as you can

Oh, Mr. Porter what a silly girl am I."

The lyrics were mildly suggestive but not terribly

risqué. Any bourgeois matron or young maid might have sung the same song from the bench of her parlor piano without drawing so much as a raised brow among her guests. It was the bold sensuality of Delilah's delivery that made the song seem so overtly sexual—the steamy look in her slanted eyes, the perfect pucker of those moist red lips, the perfectly timed pauses and suggestive winks that made the most innocent-sounding of words seem fraught with innuendo.

The music shifted to the mellower tune of a number from *The Beggars Opera* and Delilah opened her scarlet slash of mouth to sing, "Can love be controlled by advice? Will Cupid our mothers obey? Though my heart were as frozen as ice, at his flame 'twould have melted away."

Delilah du Lac was obviously well-practiced at playing to her audience. At "heart," she laid her folded hands over her left breast, lifting it so even more of the creamy cleavage slid out of her gown's top. At "flame" she lifted her slender arms above her head and quivered her torso and hips, giving the impression of liquid mercury or dancing fire, her swaying more hypnotic than any hypnotist's pendulum.

Watching her, Gavin was mesmerized. She was obviously a pro at working *it*—the stage, the crowd, him. She was working it—and she was *very* good. So good, in point, he could almost believe she was staring at him particularly, her gaze fixing on his face, her half moon brows lifting, and her stage smile slipping. He stared back, not

29

at her breasts or her legs but directly in her eyes. For a frenzied few seconds, he felt the intensity of her regard like a physical touch, felt the answering hammering of his heart and the unmistakable stirrings of arousal. All at once it was as if he and Delilah du Lac were the only two people in the crowded club, as if the smile returning to her ruby lips was meant for him alone.

Gavin honed his gaze on her mouth, too wide for fashion and yet so sensuously shaped he could well imagine nibbling and licking and tasting the ripe fruit of those full lips for hours on end. Noting how her top lip was a near mirror image of the bottom, he felt something more powerful than lust slam into him.

Recognition.

The last time he'd seen that upside-down mouth it had been smeared with red, too, not with stage paint but with peppermint from the broken off bit of candy stick he'd given her. The sweet had been meant to take away the bitterness of their goodbye.

Daisy? Gavin blinked, half-wondering if the surfeit of drink, cigar smoke, and wishful thinking hadn't conspired to cloud his vision and muddle his memory. The alcohol must be pouring into his bloodstream at a powerful pace because he would swear the woman who was the object of every slack-jawed stare in the place was the grownup incarnation of his childhood friend.

Perspiring profusely, he sat back in his seat and reached up to tug loose his tie. Delilah du Lac. Daisy Lake. *Lac* was the French word for lake, after all. He'd been searching the four corners of England and all this time Daisy must have been in France. What an idiot he was not to have considered the possibility before. As for his detective, he made a mental note to fire the fool on the morrow.

"All right, lads," Delilah—Daisy—called out. "I've given you a taste of spice. Now it's time for a nibble of sweet."

Taking his cue, the pianist slowed the music to a soulful ballad Gavin recognized as "After the Ball." Delilah stood in the center of the cone of limelight singing of love lost due to misplaced pride, and the wistful expression on her face and the familiar crystalline purity of her voice chased away the last of Gavin's doubts. Hers was a woman's voice, not a child's, and one which obviously bore the benefit of years of practice and professional coaching, but even so the similarity was too striking for him to be mistaken.

Delilah and Daisy were two facets of the same woman. The years had transformed her coltish girl's body into that of a woman, but beneath the mask of greasepaint, her heart-shaped face was familiar still, the childish promise of great beauty ripened to full bloom.

He dropped his gaze to her long legs sheathed in black fishnet stockings and was reminded of the rumors his friends had repeated earlier. *Legion of lovers. The Prince of Wales invited her to a very private supper when he was in Paris last. Talent onstage said to come as second*

31

to her talent between the sheets. At the time he'd listened with only half an ear, but now each salacious snippet was a drumbeat echoing in his ears, a razor slashing at his heart.

He glanced between Hadrian and Rourke. What the devil was the matter with them? Didn't they recognize her? Didn't they know?

The ballad ended and apparently it was time for "spice" again. The music picked up pace, a raunchy burlesque number Gavin couldn't begin to name. Delilah strutted up and down the stage in time to the tune, interspersing high, thigh-baring kicks with slow, suggestive bump-and-grinds. Watching her, mouth dry, Gavin felt the sharp poke of an elbow in his side.

He turned to a grinning Rourke. "If she moves even half that well in bed, her reputation will have been well-deserved, aye?"

Steeling his voice to steadiness, he answered, "It's all part of her act, for the benefit of the audience. Offstage I'm certain she's a different person entirely."

The effects of drink were fading, replaced by the headier intoxication of raw, animal lust. He felt as if his every sense vibrated with a previously unknown awareness, a steady-striking pulse point of need, stirrings that Daisy in her present incarnation as Delilah was ridiculously adept at arousing.

Rourke cast him a skeptical look but was wise enough not to argue the point. "I've set my sights on a certain wee heiress. Pocket-size though she is, I suspect once she warms to me Lady Kat will prove far too lusty in bed to leave me time for show girls, even ones who move like . . . *that*."

Show girl. Gavin winced at the word and yet that was exactly what Delilah—Daisy—was.

Hadrian yawned behind the back of his hand. "You'll get no competition from me, either. She's a tasty morsel, but I'm very much missing my bed and my bride."

Rourke snorted. "What he means is Callie would turn him into a castrato if she caught him ogling another woman."

Hadrian didn't deny it. "I'm married and to hear him talk, Rourke is as good as engaged, but there's nothing to keep you from following your fancy."

Rourke nodded his agreement. "Aye, if a fling with a show girl is what it takes to melt your melancholy, go to, man. Go to."

"I've no interest in a fling," Gavin said. Watching a glowing Daisy stroll back over to the piano, he was already busy calculating how he would go about getting her alone.

He didn't mean to keep his friends in the dark indefinitely—she'd been their friend, too—but after a year of combing England looking for her, he felt a private reunion was more than deserved. As soon as the performance was over, he would slip backstage and find his way to her dressing room. Or perhaps he should send their waiter with a note inviting her to join him at his table for a glass of champagne. Yes, yes, that's likely how these things were done. He'd gladly choke down another whole bottle of the dreadful stuff if it meant seeing her alone.

Rourke interrupted his thoughts with a clap on the back. "So, Gav, after all your fashing, aren't you glad we wouldn't take no for an answer and dragged you out anyway?"

Gavin didn't hesitate. "Yes, Patrick. I can honestly say there's no place I'd rather be."

CHAPTER THREE

"The boy I love is up in the gallery,
The boy I love is looking down at me,
There he is, can't you see,
waving with his handkerchief,
As merry as a robin that sings in a tree."
—*The Boy I Love Is Up in the Gallery*,
Music hall song made famous by Marie Lloyd

The song spiraled to a close, and Daisy parked herself by the piano to catch her breath. Draping an arm about the pianist, she called out, "Maestro, for my final number give us a cross between spicy and sweet, if you please."

Each night, her act concluded with her selecting one man from the audience to bring up onstage for her most seductive number. This night's selection would be "A Little of What You Fancy," made popular by music hall legend, Marie Lloyd. Like any song, it was the delivery

35

more than the lyrics that set the tone of the piece. A suggestive smile, a shimmy of shoulders or hips, a subtle inflection of voice could transform the most demure of drawing room melodies into the bawdiest of ballads. It was all in good fun, and the audience ate it up as evidenced by the hefty tips that came her way afterward.

The handsome dark-haired man sitting at one of the front row tables with his friends had caught her eye from the very first. *A real gentleman,* she'd thought, but beyond that he had the look of someone she'd once cherished and lost, Gavin Carmichael, the orphan boy she idolized as a child. For a split second, she actually thought he *was* Gavin before dismissing the notion as fancy fed by wishful thinking and more than a passing resemblance. Taking in his confident carriage, the apparent ease with which he chatted with his tablemates, and the habit he had of looking everyone, including her, squarely in the eye, she told herself he couldn't possibly be the sweet, stammering, slope-shouldered boy of her memory.

Like Gavin, this solemn-eyed man struck her as the serious sort, not one to appreciate being singled out and subjected to a feather boa looped lasso-like about his immaculate shirt collar—which made the prospect of tweaking that aristocratic nose and coaxing a flush into those high-boned cheeks all the more irresistible.

From the orchestra pit, a drum roll sounded, her cue to sashay down the stage stairs and choose her night's "victim." Summoning her most sultry smile, she announced,

"I'll need a volunteer from the audience. Whichever of you fine, strapping gents shall it be, hmm?"

Predictably, hands shot up to the sky along with calls of "Over 'ere, sweet'eart," and "Pick me. *Me!*"

Playing to the crowd, she pursed her painted lips into the pout she knew from experience would turn every man within eyeshot into a randy, raving lunatic. "Oh, my, so many gallants to choose from, my poor head is spinning."

Tapping a finger to the beauty patch beside her mouth, she made a show of scanning the audience, pausing every now and again to hesitate over a pair of pleading eyes or to smile into a flushed face, all the while knowing exactly who she would pick—the dark-haired archangel with the sad, solemn eyes and the beautiful lips. For the span of a single song, she simply had to have him.

"I think it will be . . . *you!*" She stabbed her finger at him and then crooked it, beckoning him onstage.

Looking like a startled stag confronted with a hunter's rifle, for a handful of seconds he stared at her unmoving. One of his grinning friends jabbed him in the side. Coming to, he looked back over his shoulder as if the object of her pointing must be sitting at a table behind him. Daisy hid a smile and silently counted off to five. By "four" he'd turned back to her, expression horrified. Staying in his seat, he jerked his head back and forth and mouthed "no."

He's shy, she thought, followed by, *How delicious.*

After two solid weeks of being ogled by brutes and occasionally pawed by the bolder ones, the prospect of having to coax a man onstage with her was strangely titillating. Watching the mortified flush spread over his high-boned cheeks, she felt a jet of warmth shoot between her thighs and was startled by it. Though her act was overtly sexual, when performing she was very much detached from her body. More often than not, she felt as though she'd left her physical self entirely, as though she were the puppet master pulling the strings behind the scene of a Punch and Judy show, only instead of Punch, the puppet she manipulated was called Delilah. The byplay and banter she kept up with the males in the audience was entirely for show. The allure of her act rested on her ability to convince every man in the room she must be mad for him, but the truth was she never once felt the slightest sexual stirring while onstage—until now.

Heart drumming and palms perspiring, Gavin watched Daisy sashay down the steps, the spotlight following her as she headed straight for him. As much as he wanted to see her, becoming part of her act hadn't been any part of his plan.

She drew up at their table. "*Bonsoir,* gents. Do any of you lads know French? It's the language of love, after all." Even though she addressed the trio as a group, Gavin didn't miss how her eyes never left his face. *God, Daisy.*

Rourke volunteered Gavin to speak any language she fancied and gamely suggested they commence with

Latin. Faces wreathed in grins, he and Hadrian shifted to the side to make room.

Daisy flung her slender arms out to the side and announced to the audience, "I think our handsome friend must be shy. Are you shy, sweetheart?" Gaze locked on Gavin's, she leaned over the table, sending cleavage spilling out the top of her gown, and ran her tongue along the seam of her lips, a slow, deliberate slide that had the heat pooling in his groin. Straightening, she called out to the other tables, "Come on, fellows, this fine young gentleman wants for encouragement. Let's give it to him, shall we?"

A wave of boos and hisses rolled over the room. From the back, someone called out "Pisser" and another more benign voice added, "Lucky bloke," but for the most part Gavin was too caught up in his beautiful tormentor to pay them much heed.

Wrenching his gaze away from her, he pleaded with his friends. "You go, Patrick. You fancy being front and center more than I."

"Not a chance." Rourke reached across and slapped him on the back. "It's your night. It won't kill you to have a bit of fun for once."

Mortified, Gavin swung around to Hadrian. "Harry?"

Hadrian shook his head and then gave him a thumbs-up. "Can't, mate. Callie would have my cock on a platter if she ever found out and even if she didn't,

I've had more than my share of show girls in my bachelor days. Pretend you're in court before the judge and jury, if that helps you. Whatever it takes, go to!"

Gavin started to answer he didn't care to "go to," but instead found himself swallowing a mouthful of feathers. Standing behind his chair, Delilah ran practiced palms over his shoulders and down his shirtfront, stopping barely above the waistband of his trousers. Fingers pointed downward, she brought her mouth over his ear. "Either be a sport and come on stage with me or have me finish out my act here. What's it to be, *chéri?*"

The threat levered Gavin to his feet. Face burning, he submitted to her winding the boa about his neck and then using its tail as a leash to lead him onstage. He mounted the platform amidst raucous applause just as two burly stagehands set down a gilded chair sideways in the spotlight.

"Take a load off, love," she said, shoving both hands against his chest. Falling back into the seat he caught a whiff of the cool, clean scent of peppermint on her breath, her favorite sweet from all those years ago.

Like Delilah seducing Samson or Salome dancing for Herod, she circled him, her swaying movements matching the tempo of the music, her every teasing gesture designed to arouse. Standing in front of him, she slowly peeled off her elbow-high opera gloves finger by finger, the left hand with her teeth, a slow, seductive striptease. Gavin sucked in his breath, hoping his erection wasn't visible to the audience as it must be to her.

She bent over him, grabbing the back of his chair with both hands. Her breasts were a hairsbreadth from his mouth, her green foxfire gaze a burn he felt like a brand on his flesh. In the subdued lighting, her skin, very white and slightly damp, glowed like pearls.

Turning her face to the side, she called out, "I think he likes it, gents. What about you?"

The crowd roared its approval and Gavin more than suspected his wasn't the only hard-on in the room. Coins fell upon the stage floor like hail, one striking Gavin in the outer thigh. Delilah smoothed her hand over the smarting spot and cooed, "Poor baby," loud enough for the audience to hear. The next thing he knew she was in his lap, or rather straddling it, a leg on either side of his chair. Hands braced atop his shoulders, she wiggled her bottom, her sultry smile telling him she was feeling every brick hard inch of him.

All at once, her eyes flashed open and her jaw dropped, taking her smile with it. "Gavin?"

He nodded. His mouth felt too dry for speaking but he managed to mouth the words, "Yes. Yes, it's me."

In that moment, he forgot he was on stage, forgot he was a respected barrister in a compromising, some might say *humiliating* position, a collar of feathers about his neck and a boner tenting his trousers. Feeling as though his blood had turned to molten lava, he threw back his head and fitted his hands to her hips and let her dance in his lap in time to the music.

She pulled back, and he fancied the sudden hitch to her breathing and the trembling of her thighs wasn't part of the act. Now that she saw him for who he was, she was feeling it, too, something so bold and powerful and altogether erotic that surely simple lust must pale in comparison.

The music built to crescendo. Her eyes found his. Looking apologetic if not precisely shame-faced, she whispered, "It's the finale. I'm . . . I'm sorry."

Before he could ask what she was sorry for, she arched back, and he found himself eye-level with her splayed thighs, a sliver of moist pink flesh peeking out of the slit in her silky black drawers. Suddenly she flipped over, somehow managing to execute the somersault without kicking him in the face. Bounding to her feet, she turned to the audience. In one smooth motion, she reached down and pulled the drawstring of her bloomers. The garment felt away in two halves, revealing the scanty black lace thong beneath.

To a man, the crowd surged to its feet. More money fell upon the stage, crumpled pound notes this time amidst catcalls and wolf whistles and thunderous applause. Playing to the applause, she strutted up and down the stage, stopping periodically to bend over and pick up the money, a device to show off her exquisitely tight, milk white bottom.

Hands full, she pranced back to the piano and

dropped the heap of collected coins atop. "Our volunteer has been a proper sport. He deserves something sweet, doesn't he, Ralphie?"

The pianist obliged with a violent nod. "Aye, Miss Du Lac, seems he ought to get somethin' for 'is trouble."

Daisy winked, a broad gesture meant to be seen all the way to the back of the room and strolled back over to Gavin, still seated in the chair. She settled her hands on his shoulders and looked long and deep into his eyes. "Fancy a sweet, love?"

Gav, have you brought me your sweets again this time?

Gavin opened his mouth to answer that no reward was required but before he could, she grabbed him by the shirt collar and crushed her mouth to his. Drowning in a sea of peppermint and applause, Gavin shot up from the chair, wrapped his arms about her slender waist, and lifted her off the ground.

Off into the distance, a male voice yelled out, "That's the way, mate. Give her a good rogering."

The crude remark returned Gavin to reality. He wrenched his mouth away from Daisy's and looked past her to a sea of salivating faces. All at once he remembered where he was and, more importantly, who he was.

"Enough!" He stripped off his evening jacket and threw it about Daisy's shoulders. Staring into her startled eyes, he said, "This is for your own good," and swung her up into his arms.

"Put me down, you bleeding idiot."

Feet flailing and palms pushing against her captor's solid chest, Daisy could scarcely wrap her mind about what had just happened. Victim or volunteer, Gavin had turned the tables on her. He'd seized control of the audience, *her* audience, as well as her physical body, and now her shoulders and torso were locked within the vise of his hard-muscled chest and solid chaining arms.

"Not on your life." Dodging her pummeling, he rushed across the stage with her.

"It may well be my life. If you don't let me finish, we both may be torn to bits."

This once she wasn't exaggerating. Out in the audience, mayhem erupted. Looking back over the shelf of his broad shoulder, she saw tables toppling onto their sides, chairs crashing into walls and mirrors, and patrons fleeing to the exit doors or staying on to engage in bare knuckles brawling. Several angry men tried storming the stage, their bull-necked leader vowing to tear apart the spoilsport limb by limb. Fortunately Gavin's friends were made of sterner stuff than typical London toffs. Leaping up from their seats by the steps, they used their fists to forestall the onslaught.

Daisy whipped her head back around just as a burly stage hand stepped into their path. Fists cocked, he said, "Put 'er down."

Jaw set, Gavin shook his head. "Step aside."

The hand came at them but Gavin deftly blocked the blow and then planted a smacking punch dead center of the man's bulbous nose. The heavier man dropped back, blood spurting.

Gavin reached out his bloodied hand and tugged the stage curtain aside. Ducking through, he twisted his head around to look at her. "Which way?"

Her dressing room was by far the safest spot. "Go to the left and then down the hall. The first door on your right—the one with the star," she added, succumbing to an absurd burst of pride. "But set me down first."

He hesitated and then set her down. She grabbed his hand and hurried him down the musty corridor.

The back of the house was a barebones affair, a dingy warren of narrow, poorly lit corridors. Gas and water pipes ran along the low, stained ceilings and the bare floors were gritty with filth. They drew up to the door of Daisy's dressing room, footfalls pounding behind them. Heart racing, she reached for the knob and pulled, remembering too late how the warped door stuck. The last time she tried opening it, she'd wrenched her shoulder. "Oh, bugger."

The footfalls were closing in, almost upon them. "Stand aside." Gavin reached around her, yanked open the door, and shoved her in ahead of him.

Inside the small room, she threw the bolt, and they fell back against the peeling plasterwork. For the next few seconds, they stood side by side, their rapid-fire breaths the only sound.

Turning his head to look at her, Gavin said, "That was quite a performance." His cynical tone told her he hadn't meant it as a compliment.

Determined not to be cowed—she didn't need his approval, not after all these years—she lifted her chin and said, "Thank you."

She ran her gaze over him searching for similarities to the boy she'd known as well as marking the differences in the man he'd become. He wore his hair shorter than before, but it was still the same thick mass of blue-black waves albeit with a few threads of early gray at the temples. His face was leaner than she remembered it being, his eyes the same intense celestial blue that had always made her think of springtime skies. His mouth seemed thinner or at least less inclined to smiling than she remembered and his nose stood out as more prominent, slightly hawkish, and a bit arrogant even. A few faint lines had found their way into his high forehead and about the corners of his eyes. The ghosts of past cares, she surmised, for he couldn't be more than thirty, if that.

My God, what a beautiful man he's become.

He'd lost her boa in their mad backstage dash. Sweat streamed the sides of his face and plastered his white shirt to a torso that looked to be both lean and well-muscled. And, dear Lord, how tall he'd gotten. Even though she wore high heeled slippers, the top of her head came only to his shoulders. Accustomed to standing at eye-level with Frenchmen, being in such proximity to a man she was forced to look up to, and not any man but Gavin, the hero of her childhood, the love of her young life, had her feeling vulnerable and weak-kneed and altogether out of her element.

The corners of his mouth lifted ever so slightly, showing he hadn't entirely forgotten how to smile. "Through thick and thin, indeed."

Hearing the snippet of their old childhood oath brought her closer to crying than she'd been in years. Her heart's desire landed in her lap only fifteen years too late —cruel, cruel fate. "Gavin, what are you doing here?"

He lifted dark brows. "I thought to ask you the same question." A droplet of sweat splashed the side of his sinewy neck, and she had the absurd notion of catching it on the tip of her tongue.

Pounding fists descended upon the outer door, the rumbling and raised voices calling them back to the present problem. "Miss Du Lac, are you all right? Shall I call for the constable?"

Daisy recognized the voice of the prop man, Danny. She didn't really know him, but he seemed a decent fellow and he sounded more concerned than hostile. She turned to the door and called back, "That won't be necessary, Danny. I had a little misunderstanding with a mate of mine, but it's all straightened out now."

A deeper, disgruntled voice called out, "Make it up with lover boy on your own time, Delilah." Damn, it was the music hall chairman, Sid Seymour, who was also owner of the club. "The front of the house is at sixes and sevens, and I count myself lucky the police commissioner is a mate of mine; otherwise we'd be shut down for disturbing the peace. And mind, any replacements or repairs are coming out of your wages."

Bugger! Daisy chewed on her bottom lip, mentally calculating the damages. Just one of those gaudy, gilded wall mirrors must cost a small fortune—a small fortune to her. At least he wasn't sacking her. That was something, she supposed. Still, at this rate she'd be doing the can-can until she was eighty just to pay it all off. Even if the situation turned out not to be quite that dire, docked wages meant the month would be an especially lean one not only for her but for the dear ones she'd left behind in Paris.

Gavin opened his mouth to answer but Daisy laid a finger over his lips and shook her head, motioning him to silence. Directing her voice to the door, she said, "Sod off, Sid. You've made a mint on me these past two weeks, and don't think I don't know it. For the pittance you're paying me, I might as well sing for my supper at the Grecian Saloon."

The Grecian on City Road was more of a variety saloon than a supper club, according to her promoter, but it drew a good crowd and for the same money she'd only have to do one show an evening, not two.

The threat hit home. "Come out, and we'll talk about it."

Not about to open the door and give Gavin up to the professional bullies she knew Sid would have waiting, she put him off. "Tomorrow, Sid. If you want to see me back here for the matinee performance, I'll need to go home and put up my feet."

She waited until their fading footfalls confirmed they'd turned the corner, and then she swung about to Gavin. Stabbing a finger in his face, she said, "I hope you're happy. I only have another two weeks to finish out my contract here, and thanks to you I'll be lucky to break even. More likely, I'll end up in debt."

For the first time since he carried her offstage, Gavin looked less than sure of himself. "I have every intention of compensating the club for any damages incurred."

Good intentions—whoever had said the road to hell was paved with them must be a wise person—make that wise *woman*, indeed. Daisy had long ago given up on the promises of men. You couldn't feed your family on broken promises or broken dreams either, for that matter.

Needing to put some distance between them, she kicked off her shoes and crossed the narrow room to the metal dressing screen, a small luxury she'd brought with her from France. The folding screen had been a gift from her adoptive parents on her first opening night. Painted with daisies in honor of her name, it brightened the dingy room. Beyond that, it felt important to have something of the familiar about her when virtually everything else felt, if not exactly foreign, then part of a long ago dream.

She slipped behind the cover and shucked off Gavin's evening jacket. Tossing it over the top, she said, "You never did say what brought you here tonight."

Even with the coat off, his scent still clung to her, some combination of bay rum and leather and musk, utterly masculine and thoroughly delicious. Fingers clumsy, she started on the laces of her corset.

He followed her to the front of the screen. "Would you believe I had a fancy for 'a song and a pint,' as they say?"

She let out a low laugh. "No, I wouldn't. If you'll pardon my saying so, you don't strike me as the music hall sort."

Bits of shed feathers sticking to him and sweat soaking through his wrinkled shirt, still there was an air of aristocracy about him, a sense that no matter how dirty he got, he would always be clean.

"Shall I take that as a compliment?"

Their eyes met at the very moment her corset fell away. Breasts swinging free, she took a full, deep breath, her first since that morning. "Take it as you like."

His gaze went to the tops of her bared shoulders, and she smiled to herself. Whether they were old friends reunited or strangers meeting for the first time, whether she was Daisy or Delilah, he wanted her badly. The pisser was that she wanted him, too. Taking advantage of the screen's cover, she brushed her hands over her nipples, imagining his broad-backed hands there instead. Oh, this wasn't fair, this wasn't right. What a gamester God must be. The first man to truly rouse her was the very man she couldn't ever trust herself to have. If only he might be a stranger instead of a former friend who'd hurt her so very badly.

"In that case, would you believe I recently suffered a . . . disappointment, and Harry and Rourke thought I needed some cheering up?"

Her hands stilled on her breasts, her nipples sticking out as straight as darts. "A *romantic* disappointment, you mean?" As soon as the question was out, she despised herself for how desperate she must have made herself seem by asking it.

He didn't answer but his silence and sealed lips were answer enough. *Some woman has hurt him,* she said to herself, annoyed at the irrational stab of jealousy the thought brought about. He wouldn't be the first man to come to a music hall to take his mind off a failed love affair by drinking too much and ogling women's tits and bare legs.

He snagged her gaze and for a full moment Daisy forgot to breathe. Feeling as though she were drowning in a deep blue sea, she heard him say, "Believe it or not, my coming here tonight was pure happenstance—or luck, if you prefer."

The dressing room was scarcely larger than closet-size, and she was naked except for the thong. Even with the partition standing between them, his closeness had a potent, erotic effect. Remembering the wonder-ful warmth and hardness of him beneath her bum, she smoothed a soothing hand over her pubis, parted her inner lips, and slid a testing finger inside.

My God, I'm wet for him. If he came to me now, I'd let him do whatever he wanted. I'd go down on my hands and knees for him on this dirty floor and let him have me any way he fancied.

Face warm, she bent to unsnap her garters. "Those men with you were Rourke and Harry?" She'd been so focused on Gavin at the time she'd given his friends scarcely a glance.

"Yes. They both live in London for the time being. Harry has set up shop as a photographer in Parliament Square and Rourke divides his time between his townhouse in Hanover Square and his castle in the Highlands."

"Rourke has a castle?" She unhooked the right gar-ter and rolled the stocking down, careful not to run the costly silk.

Gavin nodded. "He made a bloody fortune on rail-way shares—several fortunes, actually."

So Patrick had done well for himself. It shouldn't have surprised her. He'd always been a canny chap but a castle, well, that was quite something. "And what do you do—other than sitting about being rich, that is?"

Too late she heard the bitterness in her voice, amazed that after fifteen years his betrayal must still hurt so very much. She'd thought to have gotten over all that long ago, another of the many lies she told herself.

"I'm a barrister, actually."

That startled her. She remembered the blond-haired man at his table, Harry most likely, making mention of judges and juries, but the reference hadn't sunk in at the time nor had she given any thought to what he might do for a living. She assumed he was filthy rich or living on his expectations like most highborn young men.

"Really?"

"Yes, really."

Succumbing to wickedness, she slipped off her black silk panties and tossed them over the screen, laughing aloud when the garment hit its mark on his shoulder. "That's rich. Do barristers make it a habit to drag performers off the stage and punch out stage hands, or is the law only for us common folk?"

A scarlet tide swept over his face, and she suddenly remembered how easy it had been to make him blush when they were children. It was good to see that some things hadn't changed, at least not entirely.

"I can honestly say you're my first abduction."

She smiled in spite of herself. He might have become a bit stiff, more than a bit, but he had a sense of humor at least.

He picked off the garment and handed it back to

her. "I'll wait until you're decent."

Naked, she reached for the black silk wrapper she'd left hanging on the wall peg and slipped it on. She stepped out from behind the screen, still tying the sash. "I'm decent—or at least as decent as I'm likely to get."

He stared, gaze running over her and then snapping back up to her face. Wondering what he found so shocking, she glanced down. The robe didn't reach to the floor but it fell below her knees, covering more than her costume had. Was the vee-shaped neckline what he apparently found so objectionable, then? She hadn't thought it particularly daring, but perhaps she wasn't the best judge of such things?

The spot between her thighs was bloody throbbing, a dull, drubbing ache. Afraid he might read her thoughts on her face as he used to read her when they were children, she moved to her dressing table. Back to him, she picked up the powder muff from its tin and dabbed her perspiring bosom. "So, what is it you wanted to ask me?"

"I suppose I was curious to know where the hell you've been for the past fifteen years."

CHAPTER FOUR

"Marry, I prithee, do, to make sport withal:
but love no man in good earnest; nor no further
in sport neither than with safety of a pure blush
thou mayst in honour come off again."
—WILLIAM SHAKESPEARE, Celia,
As You Like It

Dropping the muff, Daisy turned away from the mirror and shrugged. "France. Paris mostly though I've played the provinces in the off-season a time or two."

Over the years, Gavin had imagined their reunion myriad times but never had he anticipated it would turn out quite like this. Staring after her, he could scarcely credit how bitter she sounded, how brazenly she behaved. Whether she called herself Delilah or Daisy, the woman powdering her bosom and parading her bare legs in front of him was very much a stranger. He felt enough of a fool without revealing the extraordinary lengths he'd gone to this past year in searching for her. By all appearances, she'd no desire to be found, certainly not by him. Even so, after all he had endured to find her, he wasn't about to simply walk away. At least not without first hearing her admit who she was and how she'd come to . . . *this*.

"How the devil did you end up in Paris?"

Standing before the full-length mirror, she pulled the feathers and pins from her hair, grateful for the excuse to face away from him. "I was adopted by an older theatrical couple, Bob and Flora Lake. We went on tour with a regional theatrical company but when the company folded, the Lakes decided Shakespeare was as good as dead and their best chance for scraping out a living acting was to go to Paris and sign on with one of the popular musical review companies."

Gavin stopped short of smacking a hand to his forehead. That explained why the trail had gone cold after Dover.

"So you went from a Quaker orphanage in the Kentish countryside to Paris, the cultural capitol of Europe. Such a change of scene must have entailed quite an adjustment?" He started to ask more—how had she fared in Paris, had she ever thought of him—but her cool-eyed gaze in the mirror had him holding back.

She gave a glacial smile, and he felt the frost of all that composure like a geyser of ice water shooting through his veins. "I suppose so but then again I'm a survivor, Gavin. I've been making adjustments, as you say, all my life." She turned to face him, shaking out her shoulder-length hair. "In my case, being a tomboy helped enormously. Climbing fences and trees with you lads strengthened my legs so I was able to execute the highest kicks of any girl in the chorus."

She hiked up a leg to demonstrate, propping her bare foot on the stool not unlike the stance she'd struck onstage. Gaze riveted on that firm white thigh, Gavin swallowed hard, feeling as if all the air has just been sucked from his lungs while other parts of his anatomy began to thicken and thrum. Growing up, Daisy was the closest person he had to a little sister. The moment he first set eyes on her fifteen years before, he'd been moved to care for and protect her. Beyond that, he scarcely thought about her sex at all. But the long legs he'd seen kicking up a storm onstage and the generous swell of cleavage spilling out from the top of her wrapper reminded him she was very much a grown woman—and a desirable one.

She lowered her leg, the silken dressing gown sliding back into place, and Gavin found himself once more able to breathe. "I've been told I have a fair voice, and so as I grew older, more and more lead parts came my way."

"You have a beautiful voice," he said, both because it was true and because he sensed that male praise devoid of an ulterior sexual motive wasn't something she received all that often.

"Thank you."

She looked down as though suddenly shy, the golden tips of her long lashes brushing the tops of her high-boned cheeks. The demure posture put him in mind of the brash yet sweet girl she'd once been, giving him hope that buried beneath her armor of powder and paint, feathers and silk some kernel of the Daisy he remembered might live on.

She raised her gaze to his face. "I've done some acting, too, in what the Parisians call *opera-comiques*. Of course a theatrical review isn't at all the same as a proper play, but it's something, a credit, or at least I hoped it was." The look of naked yearning on her face wasn't lost on him.

As a barrister, gut feeling frequently served as Gavin's failsafe, especially in cases that ran amok when a key witness suddenly changed his or her story or opposing counsel brought out trumped-up evidence at the final hour. Drawing on instinct, he asked, "Is acting, serious acting, something you're interested in pursuing?"

Daisy's eyes widened, making her look very much as she had when as children he presented her with a lemon drop or peppermint sweet. "It's what I want more than anything, what I feel I was born to do." She hesitated and then confided, "Pursuing an acting career is why I decided to come back to England, to London, in the first place."

She'd come back for her career, not for him. Gavin

knew it was ridiculous to feel hurt and yet he couldn't discount the pain her admission stirred in him. In a perfect world, she would have revealed she'd been searching for him all along as he had her.

"Have you had any auditions?"

She hesitated and then shook her head. "I heard Drury Lane is to open its season with *As You Like It,* but when I went to see about reading for a part, the stage manager turned me away. Apparently I don't come with the proper . . . credentials."

"The theater manager, Sir Augustus Harris, is by way of being an acquaintance of mine. I could have a word with him on your behalf."

He couldn't erase her past any more than he could go back in time and prevent his grandfather from finding him, but Daisy's lack of London contacts was an obstacle he was more than capable of surmounting. He helped their friend, Hadrian, several years before when he'd first come to London and though it had taken some time to build up his business, his Parliament Square photography shop was thriving.

"You know the manager of Drury Lane?"

That seemed to impress her. He fancied she looked at him in a new light. "We're both members of The Garrick." He hesitated, wondering how much explanation the situation warranted. "The Garrick is a private gentlemen's club devoted to providing a meeting place for actors and those with a love of the arts and letters."

Daisy's smile fell. "I know what the Garrick is, Gavin. I'm not a complete simpleton."

Damn, but he was making a hash of this. "Sorry, I didn't mean to imply . . . I only know you've been living abroad and—"

"Living abroad in *Paris*, the cultural capitol of Europe, as you say."

For the first time that evening, he didn't only smile, he *grinned*. "*Touché*. At any rate, someone has to extend that first helping hand. Why not let that person be me, someone you trust, an old friend?"

"Are we friends, Gavin?"

Years ago he would have taken one look at her and known exactly what she was thinking, but now her painted face seemed blank or at least unreadable. "We once were. I'd very much like for us to be so again."

The light in her eyes dimmed. She looked at him warily, or so it seemed. "We haven't seen each other in fifteen years. Why would you go to such trouble for me?"

He hesitated, wanting to answer honestly but disliking dredging up that painful part of his past. "You may not know it, but when we were at Roxbury House, you helped me greatly. Many of the other orphans poked fun at my stammer, but you did everything you could to set me at my ease, drawing me out to take part in games, refusing to simply let me sit on the sidelines and watch. Even managing our little attic theater was a sort of therapy for me. Now that I'm in a position to help you, why not allow me to return the favor?"

Knowing how self-conscious he was of his stammer, which grew worse whenever he was singled out, she had him act as stage manager, a role that had allowed him to remain behind the scenes while still being a part of it all.

She'd understood him as no one else ever had.

Arranging an audition was the very least he was prepared to do for her. He wasn't a social reformer such as William Gladstone, but he could see she badly needed rehabilitating. Since they got back to her dressing room, nearly every bawdy word from her mouth, every brazen behavior had struck him as a cry for help. The stage paint made her look older than her age, four-and-twenty at his last reckoning, and rather hard. He desperately wished she would use one of the many jars of creams and lotions set atop her dressing table to take it off. Once the concealing cake of it was stripped away, he would very much like to lay his hand against her cool, clean cheek.

She shook her head. Beneath the garish greasepaint, she looked like a bewildered child. "I don't know, Gavin. After all these years, I never expected to even see you again let alone be beholden to you. I'm not sure it would feel . . . *right*."

He hadn't anticipated she might turn him down. "You can't really mean to . . . to go on as you are . . . can you?"

She bristled visibly, and he knew at once he'd made a

grave mistake. "And just what's the matter with the way I'm going on as you put it? All things considered, I've taken rather good care of myself and—"

She clamped her mouth closed as she had when as a child she'd been on the verge of blurting out some secret. Wondering what that secret might be, he cautioned himself not to press. Her life until now really wasn't any of his affair no matter how much he might wish it otherwise.

Navigating the landscape of her brash self-sufficiency and stubborn pride was proving a trickier affair than he'd first thought. Giving up on diplomacy, he said, "Dash it, Daisy, you're better than this, and we both know it."

"Am I now?' She pulled open a dressing table drawer and took out a bottle of gin. "Fancy a drink?"

Horrified, he shook his head. No, thank you."

"Suit yourself." She unstoppered the bottle and knocked back a healthy swallow.

That decided it. "Daisy, I want you to leave this place tonight. I want you to come home with me."

"Come home with you!" She whirled about.

"Not only for tonight but for however long you might wish to stay."

The startled look vanished. She pulled another swallow and set the bottle aside. "Are you asking me to move in with you? Why, Gavin, this is all so sudden." Her lips twitched as though suppressing a smile.

Face heating, he hastened to reassure her. "You would be my houseguest. I have a flat near the Inns of Court.

It's spacious, and I'm not there terribly often. You'd have the place more or less to yourself and could come and go as you pleased."

"But I've two more weeks before I finish out the run. If I forfeit on the terms of my contract, Sid can sue me. I doubt he'd bother, but I'm also quite certain I'd never see the money he owes me."

"Let me worry about that. I'm a barrister, mind? Contracts can be broken."

"Even if that's true, I've still got to live, eat, and pay my rent, haven't I? And I've . . . obligations in Paris I can't, I won't abandon."

Obligations. Gavin didn't much care for the sound of that or the fierceness in her voice when she said it, but he reined in his curiosity—jealousy—rather than risk chasing her off. "I'll provide you with a stipend to cover any . . . obligations you may have here or abroad. You've only to tell me how much you require."

"I don't know, I . . . I've never lived with anyone, a man that is."

"Give it a month, then. If you find you simply can't abide me, I'll help you find a fitting lodging of your own."

A lodging he would pay for, she presumed. All this talk of money had Daisy feeling as if a cold draft had entered the room, which was odd because ordinarily a man's offering to settle a sum on her brought about a warm, fuzzy glow. But the man standing before her and as good as offering to take her into keeping wasn't any man. He was Gavin, and the thought of taking money from him in payment or anything else filled her with a sick sense of loss.

And yet the opportunity he was offering her, how could she possibly turn it down, especially when the future was no longer hers alone to consider and hadn't been for a very long time? What for so long had been a dream, and a far-fetched one at that, was transformed into a distinct possibility—and in the span of less than an hour! It was like a dream, a fairytale, a circumstance so fantastic she should be pinching herself to make sure she wasn't really asleep.

One by one, he'd knocked down her objections until there was no other answer to give than yes. "Very well, Gavin, if you're sure you really want to do this. If you're certain I won't be a bother."

"Quite. I'm scarcely home these days. In likelihood, we'll rarely run into one another."

She followed him to the door. "In that case, I accept only I can't come with you tonight. I'd like the chance to smooth things over with Sid, if I can. I owe him that much if nothing more. And it will take me a few days to gather my things."

"At least let me see you home safely."

Home at present was a dingy suite of rooms atop a Jewish bakery in Whitechapel, not the best of neighborhoods, but the rent was cheap and the food was free so long as you didn't mind a steady diet of bread and cake.

She'd struck up a friendship with the baker's wife, who let her have whatever hadn't sold by closing.

She shook her head, not wanting him to see how meanly she lived. "I can manage."

Beyond her pride, she remembered how he suffered from a recurrent nightmare about tenement houses, and empty stew pots, and a baby's cradle surrounded by flames. At Roxbury House, his screams sometimes had traveled all the way to the girls' dormitory at the opposite side of the building. She suspected he avoided setting foot in the East End as a means for holding that particular inner demon at bay, and she didn't want to be the cause for forcing him to face it now.

"I suppose you'll be wanting this back." She handed him his evening jacket.

Taking it from her, he reached into the inside breast pocket and pulled out a stack of his business cards. Handing her one of the cream-colored squares, he said, "Send word when you've given your notice."

He hesitated at the door. All that ale and champagne must be resident in his bloodstream still, for he found himself turning back and reaching out to lift a lock of her hair. The cinnamon thread curled about his forefinger felt warm and impossibly silky. As though sparked to life, it seemed to dance with light—myriad hues of russet and gold compounded to form that single color—red.

But no, it wasn't her hair that was dancing but his

hand. His hand, he noted in some distress, was trembling. "You c-changed it."

He shoved the offending hand inside his coat pocket, wishing the stammer might be as easily dispatched. Though it had barely troubled him earlier in the evening, now that the alcohol was wearing off, it had returned, more pronounced than ever.

She shrugged, sending the robe sliding farther off her shoulder. "Mousy blond is hardly the color for the stage."

He recalled the color as more a cross between wheat and honey, fresh and wholesome, not mousy at all, though he didn't care to correct her.

"You changed yours, too." She reached up her slender hand and picked a feather out of his hair. Brushing it off, she added, "You wear it shorter now."

Oh, that. The blue-black curls used to brush the tops of his shoulders, an unruly mop his grandfather's valet had tamed with a pair of sewing shears and a liberal dressing of macassar oil. Afterward Gavin had stared at his reflection in the cheval dressing glass. Feeling like a shorn sheep on fair day, he'd scarcely recognized himself. Was that when it had begun, when he'd first begun to lose his true self, to disappear?

Her face took on a faraway look. "I remember it brushing your shoulder, the blue-black of a crow's wing and so silky soft I couldn't get enough of threading my fingers through it. In fact, I recall one time you let me brush and braid it though you swore to throttle me if I so much as breathed a word to Harry or Rourke."

I would have let you do anything, absolutely anything. I'd let you do anything to me now. Even back in the day when touching one another had been cloaked in childish innocence, her soft kneading fingers had felt so very good on his scalp.

She reached out her hand to him again and he tensed, wondering where and how she might touch him. "So, Mr. Carmichael, do we have a deal or not?"

Gavin let out the breath he'd been holding back, relieved and disappointed in equal measure. How crass she sounded, how so unlike the sweet, dear girl of his memory. Like him, had that girl also been made to disappear?

Enfolding her slender pink palm in his, he gave the warm flesh the slightest squeeze. "Yes, Miss Lake." Under no circumstances would he address her by her stage name, not now and not ever. "We have a deal."

The dressing room door closed behind Gavin, and Daisy sank down onto the footstool, feeling as if every jot of energy she possessed had been siphoned from her, leaving behind an empty shell, a soulless vacuum.

Had she really just agreed to move in with him? Sleeping with a man was one thing, living under his roof and rule quite another. She hadn't even given Sid her notice and already she felt like a caged canary. No matter how much gilding was on the cage—and Gavin's promise of a generous allowance (a stipend, he'd called it) and free room and board certainly presented a glittering picture— what he was offering her was a cage all the same.

The one-month caveat was her saving grace. Nearly anything might be gotten through if one knew the endpoint in advance, and in this case she wasn't worried about him reneging. Likewise, when he assured her she could come and go as she pleased, she'd believed him. His heavy handedness in carrying her offstage earlier that night seemed out of keeping with his character, which despite the new self-possession and manly confidence didn't seem to have changed in fifteen years. She admitted she'd brought on his brashness herself, goading him far beyond any normal man's endurance. He didn't strike her as the sort of man who would lord his status and power over her as another might. Certainly sharing his bed would be no hardship.

If anything, she was afraid she might like it entirely too much.

Once upon a time, Gavin had been her best friend, her confidant, her hero, but that time was long ago and far away. Though he might wear a matured version of that boy's face, the aristocratic man who'd stood before her with censor undercutting his every perfectly enunciated syllable wasn't the same sweet, accepting boy any more than she was the same starry-eyed adoring girl with whom he'd frolicked in the barns and meadows at Roxbury House.

I could never forget you, Daisy, not in a million years. And no matter how long it takes or how hard it is, someday, somehow I'll see we're together again.

Through thick and thin, indeed! She'd been nine years-old when she'd last seen him that day in the orphanage attic, and she'd believed every word out of his mouth. Once his hoity-toity St. John relations reclaimed him, he'd cut her out of his life as thoroughly as a surgeon might cut out a cancer. He'd never so much as written her a letter or answered one of the many she sent. En route to Dover, she'd exerted the full power of her child's will to persuade the Lakes to stop off in London so she might find him and say goodbye. Eager to win her over, they agreed, if only to placate her.

Even for a nine-year-old seeing a big city for the very first time, locating the St. John residence hadn't been all that hard. The grandfather was a nob, she'd seen that straightaway, and nobs tended to congregate in the city's fashionable West End. By process of elimination, she'd traced Gavin's grandfather to Park Lane. Afterward, it was merely a matter of cajoling her new adoptive parents into chatting up gardeners and sundry household help in order to obtain the exact direction. When she ventured her first trembling knock upon the main door, it was answered by the plum-in-the-mouth butler who informed them "Master Gavin" wasn't "at home" but rather away at school.

Tears blurring her eyes, she'd scrawled her Paris direction on a scrap of paper and left it to be given to him. Once in France, she posted several more letters, this time to him at school, but he never answered with so much as a line. After the second year with still no reply, she'd stopped waiting, stopped hoping altogether. For years now, she planned just what she would say to him, exactly what words she would use, were they ever to meet again. But standing face-to-face with him in the close confines of her dressing room, she hadn't been able to recall a single carefully crafted retort.

When she first realized who he was, the shock had nearly dropped her to her knees.

She was too practical by nature to believe in miracles and too jaded by experience to believe that happenstance could ever work in her favor. She hadn't really expected to meet him again and certainly not in a song and supper club in a seedy section of Covent Garden.

In spite of her stage paint and changed hair color, Gavin had seemed to recognize her from the first. But then even as a boy, he had a canny knack for seeing through façades to a person's very soul, hers especially. She never had been able to pull the wool over his eyes as she had with Harry or Rourke or their teachers.

At Roxbury House, he'd been her friend, her confidant, and surrogate brother. There had never been anything romantic between them. And yet seeing him again had affected her and in a far from sibling sort of way. If she was honest with herself, and that wasn't always the case, she would admit that he'd been the object of her secret fantasies for years now.

She remembered a tall, long-boned boy with the beginnings of broad shoulders, the flesh stretched taut over a fencepost-thin frame. A boy with big, gentle hands and a poet's soul to whom she'd been able to take all her troubles and share all her dreams. The gangly adolescent of her memory had grown into a wholly splendid specimen of man. The subdued suit was the perfect foil for his stark masculine beauty, his broad shoulders owing nothing to a tailor's padding, and the worsted wool of his trousers expertly cut to cinch across narrow hips and taut buttocks. When he'd swept her into his arms and carried her offstage, he handled her as though she weighed little more than the feather boa. In the midst of fighting him, she'd felt how solidly muscled he was, how lean but powerfully built. She considered again how easily he'd subdued her and a sigh slipped from her parted lips.

From the moment she'd seen him sitting so straight-backed and proper at his front row table, she'd wanted to walk up to him and unbutton his suit coat one shiny brass button at a time, slowly slide it off those breathtakingly broad shoulders, and then start to work on the buttons fronting the crisp, white shirt beneath.

And now all at once he was back in her life, ready

and willing to help her achieve her greatest ambition, her heart's desire. He was offering to help her become a serious actress, an opportunity straight out of her dreams, and the answer to a prayer she'd almost given up on ever realizing. She'd be a fool to walk away, wouldn't she? When she accepted the current contract, she hadn't realized The Palace was in the heart of the Covent Garden theater district. To be so close to the theater, the *true* theater, and yet so very far removed from it in all the ways that counted was heart-rending.

Of course, she wasn't a fool, at least not entirely. Though Gavin had been her childhood confidante and protector, her big brother in every way but blood, he was a grown man now. She hadn't missed the telltale tenting of his trousers when she caressed him onstage or how standing inside the dressing room door he seemed to keep finding excuses to touch her. No, the sweet, soulful boy of her memory was a grown man and if her years in France had taught her anything, it was that men were all cut from the same cloth.

She fully expected they'd be sleeping together within the week.

Gavin found Rourke and Harry waiting for him at one of the few tables left standing, an empty whiskey bottle and three shot glasses littering the stained tablecloth. Other than an old African man sweeping the broken glass from the floor, they were the only ones left in the club.

"You waited." Feet crunching on broken bottle glass, Gavin approached. "I wouldn't have blamed you if you'd left."

Harry looked up from dabbing a spirit-soaked cloth on his split knuckles and shot him a wink. "Through thick and thin, mind?"

So, he wasn't the only one of them to remember their old oath. Gavin dragged over a chair and sat down.

Straddling the back of a now three-legged chair, Rourke's bloodied lips broke into a grin. "Christ, Gav, you took long enough. I hope she was worth it."

"Well worth it." Dividing his gaze between his two friends, Gavin announced, "I've found her."

Rourke turned to Harry and rolled his eyes. "One rut with a showgirl and now he fancies himself in love."

Harry shook his head. "If that's the case, we have to take you out more often—on second thought, maybe not." He cast a rueful look downward to his black and blue knuckles, no doubt wondering how he was going to explain them, along with his bruised cheek and torn shirt, to his bride.

Gavin shook his head. "It's not what you're thinking. We spent the time talking."

Rourke jerked his head to Gavin and scowled. "What a bloody waste."

"She's Daisy, *our* Daisy." Reading their worried

looks, he hastened to reassure them. "It's not what you're thinking. I'm not drunk, at least not much, and I'm not delusional, either. Delilah du Lac is Daisy, or rather the stage name she's taken for herself."

His two friends looked flabbergasted, but unlike him they hadn't had the past hour to get used to the idea. "Are you serious?" Hadrian finally asked.

"Are you sure?" Rourke added.

Gavin nodded on both counts. "Quite."

Ever the skeptic of their group, Rourke asked, "In that case, do you mind my asking where the devil she's been keeping herself all this time?"

"Until a fortnight ago, she was living in France with the couple who adopted her. She's come to London to try to make it as an actress—a serious actress. I promised to use whatever influence I have to get her an audition for *As You Like It* at Drury Lane, but first I have to find a way out of the contract she signed. Like as not there's some legal loophole waiting to be uncovered, but I suspect this is one of those situations when out and out bribery will prove more expeditious than the law."

She'd insisted on staying to smooth things over with Sid, as she called it, though the club owner didn't strike Gavin as the sort who was inclined to see reason. Money, or rather bribery, would be his bottom line. He cast his gaze about the room, mentally assessing the damage. At least a quarter of the table and chairs had been reduced to kindling and most of the floor-length mirrors survived as empty frames.

He turned to Rourke, the businessman among them. "What is your reckoning of what replacing this rubbish will cost?"

Harry and Rourke exchanged smiling looks. Harry spoke up and said, "I wouldn't worry about it, if I were you."

Gavin shook his head. He'd given Daisy his word and, by God, he meant to keep it. "I promised to pay for the damage; otherwise the club manager will as good as own her."

Despite the seriousness of the situation, Rourke looked amused. "Dinna fash, I know for a fact no reckoning will be required."

"Are you saying the club manager has decided to forgive the debt?" Having overheard Daisy's charged back-and-forth with the club owner, the slimy Sid hadn't struck him as the forgiving sort.

"Indeed he has," Harry confirmed.

He and Rourke exchanged glances and then burst into laughter. Wondering if they might be drunker than they let on, Gavin asked, "What is so funny?"

Swiping the back of his busted hand over watery eyes, Harry shook his head. "Rourke just bought the place a few minutes ago, lock, stock, and barrel."

CHAPTER FIVE

"I had rather have a fool to make me merry
than experience to make me sad . . ."
—WILLIAM SHAKESPEARE, Rosalind,
As You Like It

Two days later, Gavin sat with Rourke and Hadrian in what until a few days before had served as his study, his formerly feral cat, Mia, stretched out on the arm of his chair. Reaching over to stroke her soft black and white fur, he kept one eye on the wall clock as he listened to his two friends recount the full story of how Rourke had come to be in possession of The Palace.

After leaving Daisy's dressing room door, a furious Sid had stomped to the front of the house, intent on having his bullies drag Gavin's two troublemaking friends out into the alley for a proper beating. Rourke's offer to purchase The Palace outright had forestalled the violence. At first, Sid assumed the Scot was either drunk or bluffing or a bit of both, but when Rourke produced a money clip of 100-pound notes to stand as his surety, along with his business card and signed marker for the balance, which would arrive by bank draft at the week's end, Sid changed his tune. Instead of ordering up a beating, he ordered the contents of the bar be brought out to seal the deal.

"If I can buy a castle in the Highlands, then why not buy a palace in London to go with it?" Rourke asked with a grin. It was an open joke among them that the Scot accumulated property as other men accumulated lint and pocket change.

At present, Gavin's flat was all the property he cared to manage. With the help of his two friends, he'd spent the previous day converting his study into a miniature theatrical school. He'd even gone so far as to box up all but the most necessary of his legal texts and law school tomes to make room on the bookshelves for the dramaturgical library he hastily amassed—comedies and dramas by European masters Shakespeare and Ibsen, Wilde and Pinero, Chekhov and Zola. No Gilbert and Sullivan, though. Musical theater struck him as scarcely a step above the vulgar dance hall burlesques he'd suffered through the other night. Daisy was quite simply too fine to be locked into performing that sort of rubbish, he saw that clearly. Her rehabilitation from dance hall chanteuse to serious actress hinged on making quite certain she saw it, too.

Sipping a glass of whiskey, Rourke shook his auburn head. "Delilah du Lac and our wee Daisy one and the same woman—I can scarcely credit it."

Gavin pulled on his cuffs and stared ahead to the study door. Daisy was due any time and the prospect of seeing her again had him feeling absurdly nervous. She'd solidly refused to let him have any hand in helping her move, swearing she had but little with her. He couldn't say she'd been rude, not exactly, but she had been firm, making it clear she meant to settle her affairs with her promoter without his help. It occurred to him to wonder if such a strident display of independence might be masking some secret something or rather *someone*, she might be hiding from him, but for the time being he resolved to set aside that maddening thought. Even if it were the case and another man was involved, he had no claim upon her—at least not any he might yet enforce.

"Delilah du Lac was a dance hall persona only, a fiction," Gavin replied more strongly than he intended. "Now that Daisy will be pursuing a theatrical career, she'll either use her given name or we'll come up with a more suitable stage name."

Hadrian and Rourke exchanged looks. Without speaking, Hadrian walked over to the sideboard, unstoppered the crystal whiskey decanter, and poured three fingers' worth of the amber-colored alcohol into a glass. Turning about, he offered the drink to Gavin. "Fancy a spot of whiskey to take the edge off?"

Gavin didn't like to think his nervousness was that obvious but apparently it was, to his friends at least. He shook his head. "No, thank you." He wanted to be clear-headed when his "houseguest" arrived.

Hadrian shrugged and sipped his drink. "Our Daisy always did have a fancy to tread the boards, though I dare say she'll find London tame compared to Paris. If even half of the rumors flying about are true, she's experienced her share of living beyond kicking up her heels in the can-can."

The rage rolled over Gavin with the swiftness of a thunderbolt splitting in twain a placid summer sky. "I don't think I care for what you're implying."

Hadrian hesitated, but his gaze never wavered. "I'm not implying anything. I only mean she's sure to have had a protector, perhaps several. Those Paris dance halls may cater to bourgeois families for the early performances, but after the sun goes down over Monmarte, *ooh la la*. The Moulin Rouge is known about Paris as a market for love."

Legion of lovers. The Prince of Wales invited her to a very private supper when he was in Paris last. Talent onstage said to come as second to her talent between the sheets.

Gavin had spent the past few days replaying the

rumors in his mind. As much as he wanted to believe they were gross exaggerations, Daisy's behavior onstage and later in her dressing room certainly bore them out.

Still holding onto the hope that it was all or mostly an act, he snapped, "I wasn't aware you'd been to Paris."

The jibe hit home. Scarlet heat flooded Hadrian's face and his grip on the glass tightened. "You don't have to go abroad to experience life, or recognize it, for that matter. Any woman with Daisy's . . . *attributes* and in that line of work is bound to attract a goodly share of male attention, not all of it unwelcome. Why, just the other day I happened upon a copy of one of Nadar's photographic portraits of Sarah Bernhardt. Now there's an example of a highly successful French actress who started out her er . . . *career* as a courtesan. The French don't seem to attach the same stigma to these arrangements as we English do. Christ, Gavin, with an upbringing like Daisy's, surely you don't expect the girl to be a virgin—do you?"

Gavin shot out of his chair, sending Mia jumping off the armrest and scurrying for cover. Meeting his friend's startled gaze, he said through set teeth, "You're all but implying she's a common whore. Would you care to rescind that remark?"

"Draw it mild, Gav, he dinna mean it like that." Rourke stepped between them and laid a restraining hand on Gavin's arm. Glancing down to the thick fingers curled about his bicep, Gavin realized he'd raised his fist with the full intention of planting it in Harry's face.

Christ, what's gotten into me? Among their trio, he'd always been the placid one, the peacemaker, the sometimes saint, and yet a casual comment about Daisy's all too probable past had him on the verge of coming to blows with one of his two best friends. The situation sounded an inner alarm.

Backing away, he shook off his friend's hold. "Sorry. I don't know what came over me. Seeing her again after all these years, the same and yet so very different, has wreaked havoc with my head. It seems I'm incapable of rational thought."

Hadrian picked up his drink. "No worries, Gav. A woman can do the very devil of a dance through a man's mind. When that boudoir photograph of Callie landed on the newsstands, I wanted to murder every paperboy I could get my hands on even if I was the one who'd taken the blasted picture in the first place. How's that for irrational?"

"Unlike Callie, Daisy apparently has earned her reputation."

Hadrian nodded. "Well, you must admit, she's on her way to being famous, or rather infamous, on two continents—hardly shabby work for an orphan girl born with one foot in the workhouse. I, for one, say good on her."

"Why thank you, mate. I quite agree."

The three men swung about. Daisy stood in the

doorway, a carpet bag dangling from either gloved hand.

Tearing his gaze away from her, Gavin looked between Rourke and Hadrian. Standing at stiff attention, they resembled the Queen's Guard outside Buckingham Palace rather than two friends reuniting with a third. But then Daisy wasn't their Daisy any more but Delilah du Lac, a celebrity whose fame had reached across the Channel. Though Hadrian was besotted with his Callie, and Rourke had set his cap for the lovely if prickly Lady Kat, they were still men with the normal male curiosity.

Gavin's manservant, Jamison, appeared red-faced in the doorway behind her. A sparely built man of fifty-odd, Jamison had been in Gavin's employ since he'd left his grandfather's residence and set up his own five years before. Ordinarily it took a great deal to disrupt the servant's implacable calm, but it seemed Daisy had managed the feat within mere minutes of her arrival. "Please accept my apologies, sir. I asked the lady to wait while I announced her, but the moment I turned my back, she—"

"Hightailed it through the foyer and barged directly in," Daisy finished with a wink. "Truth be told, I've never been terribly good at waiting."

"That's quite all right, Jamison," Gavin said. "If you'll see about some refreshment, we'll take over entertaining Miss Lake."

Dropping her bags inside the door, Daisy swept into the room. Smartly turned out in a princess-cut emerald green carriage dress and matching hat festooned with blond fringe, she looked elegant and imminently respectable albeit more stylish than the typical Englishwoman. With the exception of a telltale tinge of color accentuating the high curve of her cheekbones and wantonly full mouth, she might have passed for a society beauty back from a shopping excursion to Paris. But had he really expected her to show up in broad daylight wearing full stage paint and short striped skirts?

Rourke rushed forward and captured her in a hearty hug, lifting her from the floor. "Why, you're a sight for sore eyes." Setting her down, he held her at arm's length. "I always knew you'd grow into a beauty. Turn about, lass, and let us have a look at you."

Obviously used to being at the center of male attention, she obliged by stepping back and executing a perfect little pirouette *sans* blushing or begging off. "I'm glad to see you haven't changed a jot, Patrick. You're as charming a rogue as you ever were, only far better looking and taller than I recall."

Rourke grinned. His lack of height had been a sore point for him when they were boys. "Aye, you've the right of it, sweeting, only I'm a prosperous rogue these days— what respectable folk call a *businessman*."

Daisy looked suitably impressed, and Gavin saw how her gaze took in the gemstones twinkling from Rourke's earlobe and the little finger of his right hand. Fighting a twinge of jealousy, he explained, "Rourke has done a

83

great deal better by himself than setting up shop. He's what is known as a railway magnate—or 'robber baron' as the Americans fancy saying."

Daisy swiveled her head back to Rourke, who nodded. "Aye, stealing railway shares from under the quality's toffee-covered noses isna all that different from pinching their watches and purses, save the law can't hang you for it nor lock you up, either."

She turned to Hadrian. "And you must be our very own Handsome Harry all grown up. Why, you're just as fine looking as you ever were, only more so I dare say."

He planted a kiss on the proffered cheek but, catching Gavin's gaze, swiftly stepped back. "You've a glib tongue, my girl, but so long as its compliments you're serving up, I'll gladly take them—only the name's Hadrian now. You're not the only one to take a stage name." He punctuated the admission with a wink.

Watching the three of them slip into flirting and teasing with good-natured Cockney ease, Gavin felt very much the outsider. Even though he lived in an East End tenement for his first thirteen years, he'd never been a part of that world, not really. Despite the menial work she'd undertaken, his mother had always borne herself as a lady and had imparted her fine manners and cultured speech to Gavin from the cradle.

Remembering his duty as host, he invited everyone to take seats. "Tea should be along shortly."

Daisy sat on the settee. Smoothing out her skirts,

she gazed at the whiskey glass Hadrian held and said, "I wonder, do you have any sherry or perhaps a nip of that lovely looking whiskey? I could do with a drop."

Gavin winced, but predictably Rourke declared a round of whiskey to be a capital plan. Gavin made a mental note to take up the topic with Daisy at a later time. For the present, rather than embarrass her in front of their friends, he rose and poured out the drinks.

Hadrian grinned. "Still determined to do everything we lads do, I see."

"Indeed, only better." Her drink in hand, she shot him an unladylike wink. "Bottoms up, lads."

The threesome laughed and touched glasses. Gavin sat stiffly, looking on.

The arrival of the tea tray forestalled further awkwardness. To his surprise, Daisy set her drink aside and served them all without being asked, performing the ritual competently, if not expertly.

Cup and saucer balanced on her lap, she asked, "What did you lads think of my act the other night?"

Compliments poured forth from Rourke and Hadrian, but Gavin kept silent, wondering if she wasn't baiting him. Afterward, they chatted about a variety of topics, including the world's first moving picture show, which had debuted in New York City the year before. Hadrian was curious as to what effect, if any, the new medium might have on the future of theater. Not surprisingly, Daisy was a staunch defender of live performance though she admitted to some curiosity to see the former for herself.

The conversation wound down with Gavin contributing nary a word. Hadrian set aside his cup and saucer and rose. "If you'll pardon me, I've promised to fetch my wife home from her office. No doubt she's too knee-deep in paperwork or placard making or some other worthy task to miss me overmuch, but the plain fact is I miss her—damnably."

Rourke popped up beside him. "You've your bride in pocket, but I've yet to bag mine. A wee bird whispered in my ear that a certain wild Kat means to take her filly for a trot about Rotten Row this afternoon, and I've a mind to show up there myself."

Goodbyes were said and their two friends filed out into the foyer. Resuming his seat, the moment Gavin had been dreading and anticipating in equal turns arrived. He and Daisy were alone.

In the bright light of day and without stage paint to mask her, she looked younger than she had the other night, fresh and pretty if not precisely beautiful. Her heart-shaped face was more piquant than classic, the nose adorably turned up at the tip, the jade green eyes arched upward at the edges, a trait she accentuated by lining her eyes.

But it was her mouth that kept drawing him back, filling his head with fantasies about all the ways he might kiss her. He rather thought he would start by brushing ever so lightly over first one corner of her mouth then the other, then move on to trace the tantalizing ribbon of full upper lip with his tongue before teasing her lips apart and deepening the kiss and gliding inside to taste her, really taste her. When the fantasy progressed to where he was twining his fingers through cinnamon-colored tresses, Daisy's bowed head between his thighs and her moist, hot mouth sliding like a velvet vise over his ready hard member, he knew it was time for this cozy *tête-à-tête* to end. It promised to be a long four weeks.

She took a sip of tea and set her cup and saucer aside. "Catch me up on our friends, if you don't mind. Harry, I mean Hadrian, is a newlywed, I take it?"

Forcing his thoughts back to the present, he nodded. "He married the suffragette leader formerly known as Caledonia Rivers almost a year ago. Until then, she was one of the chief spokespersons on behalf of a Parliamentary bill to grant women the right to vote in national elections."

Daisy hesitated. "She sounds a very worthy woman. I wouldn't have imagined our Harry pairing off with such a sobersides, but then I wouldn't have imagined him pairing off with any woman for longer than it took to coax her out of her knickers."

Her frank speech bothered him more than he cared to let on, but beyond that it had him worrying over her future. Celebrating bawdiness had died out with Nell Gwynne and the Restoration and though many of the current actresses in vogue such as the celebrated Sarah Bernhardt weren't born ladies, they were expected to at least act the part.

He noticed she hadn't touched any of the tea treats, a respectable array of bite-sized cakes, scones, and finger sandwiches as well as a bowl of fresh strawberries served with a side dish of clotted cream, the latter a special indulgence in honor of the new arrival. Wondering if she might be one of those women forever worrying over her weight or if the selection simply wasn't to her taste, he asked, "Is the tea all right? Would you care for something else?"

"Oh, no, this is lovely."

As if waiting for his cue, she piled her plate with strawberries and several sandwiches. She peeled off the bread from a sandwich and popped the filling of cucumber, dill, and cream into her mouth.

Chewing, she said, "It sounds as though Rourke's set his cap for an heiress." Gavin admitted he had. "But I thought he was rich already?"

"Lady Kathryn Lindsey's family is top-drawer, although land poor. It's her pedigree he's after, not her purse."

"Top drawer, is she?" Daisy snorted. "That must mean she's squint-eyed and plain."

Making a mental note to add some rudimentary lessons in manners to her program of study, Gavin shook his head. "Hardly. Lady Kat may not be a beauty in the classic sense, but she's comely enough to have sat for Hadrian as a photographer's model as well as possessed of a razor sharp wit—and the tongue to match it. The only fly in the ointment is that so far the lady can't seem to abide him."

Daisy frowned and picked up another sandwich from her plate, giving it like treatment. "Don't tell me the toffee-nosed bitch doesn't think he's good enough for her?"

He winced at the ease with which the vulgarity rolled off her tongue. "If that is indeed the case then for once our friend, Rourke, finds himself in company with a goodly number of London's finest gentlemen."

Popping another cucumber slice into her mouth, she asked, "How so?"

"The lady simply won't have him—or any other man, for that matter. She swears matrimony is the province of fools, and she'd sooner end her days a maid than submit to a man serving as her legally appointed jailor."

He expected her to shake her head, but instead she tilted her face to the side, a faraway look in her eye. "I can't answer to the maid part, but I'd say she has the right of marriage. Most men treat their mistresses a great deal better than they do their wives—and they don't always treat them so very well."

The statement struck him as sadly jaded for one so young, but more to the point, it was obviously a veiled reference to all the men who'd enjoyed her favors, which in turn led him to ponder the depressing question of just how many men that might be.

Turning back to him, she said, "The other day, I didn't think to ask what sort of law you practice. There are different sorts, aren't there?"

Her question surprised him. He wouldn't have imagined his profession would have interested her, but then it was likely she was only humoring him or being polite. "Most of the cases I take on are felony offenses tried in the criminal courts. Assault, theft, embezzlement, offenses against Her Majesty such as counterfeiting and coining with the occasional murder trial tossed in for good measure."

Gaze shining, she said, "How splendid. I'm so proud of you."

He shrugged, the compliment bringing him back to the awkward boy he'd once been. "There's the occasional satisfaction, but for the most part the work is deadly dull—and frustrating. The law isn't class blind by any stretch. Those with the money to do so generally purchase their way out of trouble whereas the poor and working classes are left to suffer the harshest penalties for oftentimes petty crimes driven more by desperation than any appreciable evil." He stopped himself. "Sorry, there I go stepping up on my soapbox again."

She shook her head. "Not at all, but speaking of soap boxes, do you remember that little makeshift stage we set up in the Roxbury House attic?" She punctuated the reminiscence with a soft smile.

Gavin found himself smiling with her. "Indeed, how can I forget? Given what little we had to work with, boards salvaged from milk crates and nary a proper tool in sight, it was a marvel of architectural design. With all the banging that went on, I wonder we were never caught out."

She hesitated and then admitted, "We were. That miserable tattletale Lettie Pinkerton found us out and threatened to go to the headmaster."

"Piggy Pinkerton." Lord, but it had been years since he'd so much as thought of her, indeed of any of the Roxbury House orphans beyond their immediate circle.

She nodded. "Fortunately she proved even fonder of sweets than of tattling. With Harry's smuggling hot cross buns and lemon tart from the kitchen, she must have gained a full stone that last month."

So she hadn't told him quite everything even then.

It wasn't like before but still it was nice, this easy conversation, this sharing of memories, the good ones at least.

She turned her attention to the strawberries and cream, apparently saved for last. "This is good," she said, and licked a dab of clotted cream from the corner of her mouth.

Watching her, Gavin felt as if the temperature in the room had shot up several degrees. "Jamison has the scones and tea cakes brought in from a nearby bakery. You've only to tell him your preferences and he'll purchase accordingly."

Plate balanced on her knees, Daisy regarded him for a long moment. "Did it take getting used to?"

"Did what take getting used to?"

"Being rich. Roxbury House was nice enough, but even there we each had chores to do and lessons to learn. I've never had servants though I considered going into service once."

"I'd think staying put in one place would seem rather dull after the traveling life you've lived." Only after the fact did he admit the statement concealed a question. Could a woman like Daisy ever be content to settle down in one place—with one man?

She shrugged. "A dancer's career is short-lived. Most girls don't make it past thirty. On days when I perform more than one show, at bedtime I wrap my ankles in cloths soaked in mustard seed oil to ease the swelling."

Gavin had never considered that her dubious profession might take such a physical toll. "I had no idea."

She picked up another strawberry and bit into the fruit, juice dribbling down the side of mouth, making her lips look all the more luscious. The telltale tightening in Gavin's groin was a warning that for once he chose not to heed. Reaching across, he caught the juice with the pad of his thumb as he might have done were they children still. Only they weren't children, they were adults, and the flare of heat between them was an undeniable presence in the room. He swiped his digit along the curve of her bottom lip, tracing its contour, wishing he might taste her with his tongue instead.

Drawing back, he cursed himself for an idiot. "I'm sorry. I shouldn't have done that. It won't happen again."

Daisy shook her head, cheeks flushed as though she hadn't stripped for him only the other day. "No, it's me who's sorry. I'm making a mess. I suppose I'm hungrier than I thought."

For the first time it occurred to him her wolfishness might be the result of missed meals rather than rough manners. She was very slender but he assumed that was from the exercise of daily performances.

"Daisy, when was the last time you ate?"

She hesitated, and then reached for another strawberry. "Why, I'm eating now."

"You know what I mean."

She shrugged. "They were supposed to feed us one meal a day at the club but with rehearsals and what not, that didn't always happen. The rooms I let are above a bakery, so I get more than my fill of bread and pastry, but meat and fresh fruit are hard to come by—and cost dear."

So that explained why she picked off the bread from the sandwiches and turned her nose up at the fancy cakes and scones. He'd assumed Paris patisseries had made her finicky, but apparently he'd been wrong about her yet again. After two weeks above a bakery, she must feel as though she was drowning in dough.

Seeking to divert them from the awkwardness he

created, he said, "I've placed an advertisement for an acting instructor in *The Times* as well as several of the more prominent regional papers."

He expected her to be pleased that matters were moving along but she looked anything but. "You think I need acting lessons?" She drew back, cheeks as bright red as though they bore his handprints.

How to answer honestly without offering further offense? Choosing his words with care, he said, "When you read for a part, you have only the one chance. I want to do everything in my power to ensure you're as prepared as possible."

He more than suspected her background in burlesque barely scratched the surface of what she might do. With a bit of coaching, she might make for a solid actress. To her advantage, she was already very much at home on the stage.

She seemed to soften. "I suppose it's no different from voice or dance lessons."

Relieved they'd gotten past the potentially sticky subject so easily, he took a sip of his tea. "Exactly so."

"That only leaves us to hammer out the terms of our arrangement." She unsnapped her reticule and brought out a pencil and pocket-size notebook. Pencil at the ready, she looked up and said, "I've found that before going into keeping, it is by far best to decide the terms in advance."

Aghast, Gavin stared at her. "Into keeping?"

She answered with a brisk nod. "I know it may seem unromantic to write it all down but doing so saves much time and angst for both parties when the time comes to go separate ways. In our case, you've promised me a stipend to cover my er . . . financial obligations as well as to pay for my incidentals. In return, for the month I'm living under your roof, you'll expect to sleep with me, of course."

Gavin felt himself flushing. "On the contrary, I expect no such thing. I didn't propose this arrangement to make you my mistress. As I said the other night, you are to consider yourself my houseguest."

Gaze never lifting from his face, she said, "Are you saying you don't want to sleep with me, Gavin?" He thought she looked a little hurt.

He shifted in his seat, feeling almost as uncomfortable as he had when she'd forced him to be part of her act. "What I may want or not want is beside the point."

Regarding him from beneath raised brows, she pressed, "What is the point, then?"

He felt the dreaded thickening settle into his tongue. "The point is to . . . to comport oneself in a manner that is p-proper and moral and, well, c-correct." Good God, scarcely an hour alone in her company, and he was reduced to the stammering idiot of his youth.

She tossed back her head and laughed. "Dear Lord, Gavin, what a stuffed shirt you've become. It's not as though I'll mind sleeping with you." She slid her gaze over him, and he felt himself warming not only from

95

embarrassment but also from desire. "I rather think I shan't mind it at all."

"Be that as it may, ours is a platonic arrangement."

"Platonic?" She frowned as though puzzling out the word.

"We will be friends, good friends, as we've always been, but I won't press for more."

She seemed to find that funny. "I assure you, Gavin, I've had any number of men call themselves 'my very good friends,' and it's not stopped them from taking me to bed."

He shook his head at her. Really, what else was he to do? "Do you always speak so . . . freely?"

She answered with a blithe smile and a toss of her head. If she caught the censure underlying the question, she was choosing to ignore it. "Unfortunately, not nearly as often as I'd like. The aim of an entertainer is to please, after all. Not just the audience, but also the stage manager, the chorus director, the promoter. Why, even the lighting crew has a say up to a point. It's not often I have the chance to tell someone exactly what I think."

"I see," he said and the odd thing was he did. They might be occupy opposite ends of the social ladder and yet he, too, had made it his lifetime's work to please others, first his grandfather and later his colleagues and clients, judges, and juries, doing his utmost to live up to the St. John legacy.

In truth, he didn't know whether to feel flattered at

how quickly she'd come around to feeling at ease with him—or stung that in the respect category he apparently ranked somewhere between the dustman who swept the stage between performances and the crew of stagehands who cleared and set up the props. He settled on mildly put out.

"In future, should you wish to temper your running commentary with a modicum of courtesy, I won't take it amiss. Pretend I'm someone *important*, if that helps you."

She answered with a mock pout, a look he found at once sultry and adorable. "My, my, aren't we touchy today."

"That would be because *we* have been up and about since dawn unlike some persons who apparently prefer to spend the morning lying abed." The latter was a veiled reference to her insistence she couldn't possibly call on him before noon.

"I'm sure I'm up and about the same amount of time a day as you are only I keep theater hours."

"We're not in the theater at present."

She grinned, the smile unearthing the matching pair of pretty dimples on either side of her softly pointed chin. "Aren't we, now? Haven't you heard, ducks, all the world's a stage?"

CHAPTER SIX

"Ay, now am I in Arden; the more fool I;
when I was at home, I was in a better place:
but travelers must be content."
—WILLIAM SHAKESPEARE, Touchstone,
As You Like It

Later that day, Daisy stood in the center of her rented rooms, the contents of her closet spread out upon the floor at her feet. She'd paid the month's rent in advance and there was no reason not to keep the place until that time. If things with Gavin didn't work out, she would have an escape route, a haven, though at the moment she was very much looking forward to leaving behind the ever present smell of baking.

Packing the rest of the things she meant to bring with her should be easily accomplished. Had Freddie and the Lakes accompanied her, the move across town would have been a far more complicated affair. No matter how many times they'd moved or how short the stay planned, Flora always insisted the trunks be unloaded, the china and furnishings and sundry accoutrements of civilized life all unwrapped and laid out, the clothing unpacked and hung in closets or folded neatly in drawers. By the end of the first day, there wouldn't have been a single storage box or traveling trunk in sight. Dear Flora, she was in so many ways a remarkable woman.

Traveling alone for the first time in her life, Daisy hadn't brought much with her in the way of personal possessions. Beyond her gowns and costumes and cosmetics, all of which counted as tools of the trade, there was the cherished framed photograph of Freddie, an old rag doll she'd had with her forever and had always called Lucille though she couldn't recall why, and the stuffed animal cat Gavin had given her long ago but likely forgot all about by now.

Looking back over her afternoon, she had to admit it had been an extraordinary day. Funny how in life one often went for long patches of time without experiencing any appreciable shift and then all at once something occurred to set the wheel of change in motion and a lifetime might be lived in a single, solitary day.

After the tense tea, Gavin had taken her on the promised tour of his flat. She'd been amazed and, in spite of her resolve not to soften toward him, touched.

He'd given up his private study and made it into a library of plays and other theatrical texts. That someone, a man, had gone to so much trouble for her both humbled and astonished her. For the span of several minutes all she'd been capable of was to stare about her like an idiot, mumbling "Fine, how very fine" when he pointed out the newly stocked bookshelves with their leather bound library of plays.

That he didn't seem to expect to sleep with her both puzzled and offended her. A man refusing sex on the basis of satisfying his scruples was as foreign to her as riding on the backs of elephants rather than horses or choosing chocolate-covered ants over tea biscuits. Barring one or two lovers who from time to time fancied a good whack, she wasn't used to being the sexual aggressor. Men had been chasing after her since she'd put on her first pair of high heels. The oddity of the situation struck her as enormous, but if she were honest with herself, she had to admit the strange circumstances titillated her, too.

Were it in her nature to be content, rather than planning his seduction, she would be counting her blessings that he wanted her in any capacity at all. If not exactly in dire financial straits, she certainly skirted the edge. The jewelry she'd amassed from her more well-heeled lovers had all been sold, the funds used to pay for Bob Lake's medical expenses. Consumption, or tuberculosis as it was coming to be known, was a cruel disease and battling its ravages a costly proposition. Treatment included periodic sojourns at sanatoria where the mountain air was believed to be of great benefit. As a result, she had little enough money to convert into English pounds and even that was nearly gone.

Even so, the move to England was meant to be, she could feel it. Had she remained in Paris, eventually she might have become one of myriad English expatriate artists who stayed past their prime, whiling away her free hours in cafes and pouring her pittance of a salary into absinthe and opium. Now that she was once more on English soil, her fourteen years in Paris lent her considerable cachet. In addition to The Palace, there were innumerable clubs and variety saloons she might have played. It was a lot to give up—but there was much to be gained.

She hadn't exaggerated when she told Gavin a dancer had a short-lived career. Knees ruined and spirits broken, retired dancers might turn to teaching but more often than not they turned to drink. On the other hand, a woman might find employment in the theater the whole of her life. There were always parts such as Lady Macbeth which called for more mature actresses.

Practicality aside, treading the boards in London had been Daisy's dream for as long as she could remember. Even with so many years and so much hurt between them, she couldn't help feeling a wellspring of gratitude whenever she thought of how Gavin had turned his flat, and his life, inside out to please her. Perhaps he was acting out of guilt more so than friendship. Regardless of his motive in helping her, she wasn't about to look a gift horse in the mouth. She remembered how he encouraged her when they'd put on their little plays in the attic of Roxbury House and felt a tear dampen her eye.

Good show, sweetheart . . . What a brilliant little actress you are, isn't that so, lads? Gavin's voice, or rather the younger version of it, echoed inside her head, a ghost of a long ago time and place.

Daisy scraped a hand through her hair, forcing her thoughts back to the present. She couldn't go back in time and change the course of events, no one could, but she was determined to make the most of the future.

After Daisy left to finish packing up her flat, Gavin took his first opportunity to sit down with Sir Augustus. By prior appointment, he met the manager of Drury Lane in the smoking room of The Garrick.

They settled in at a window table with glasses of whiskey. Sipping their drinks, they chatted desultorily for a few minutes about politics as well as the difficulties of keeping a theater such as Drury Lane financially afloat. According to Sir Augustus, the emergence of so many supper clubs and music halls was cutting into his trade.

Hoping to sidestep that dicey subject, Gavin said,

"You must be wondering why I asked you here."

"I must admit to some curiosity on that score," the older man allowed.

Gavin girded himself to begin. He'd never been terribly good at asking for favors, but he reminded himself that this boon was for Daisy, not him. "A dear friend of mine would very much like to audition for your production of *As You Like It.*" Reading his companion's pained look, he hastened to add, "She has considerable experience in the entertainment field in Paris and most recently in London."

Sir Augustus frowned. "Tell me her name. Perhaps I've heard of her."

Gavin hesitated. He bloody detested her stage name and had vowed to himself he would never address her as such. "Her name is Daisy Lake but she goes by the stage name of Delilah du Lac."

"You don't say? I've heard of her to be sure, who hasn't?" he added, and the slight smirk to his smile had Gavin thinking he wasn't only referring to Daisy's reputation for a nightingale's voice and high can-can kicks. "I heard she was playing The Palace before it closed down."

"Quite," Gavin replied. "But she has considerable stage experience beyond that. She was a regular player at the Moulin Rouge." The latter, he hoped, would afford some cachet.

Sir Augustus shook his head. "Be that as it may, in my experience these showgirls are all cut from the same cloth, plenty of dash but thin on substance. I need a seasoned actress for Rosalind, not simply one who looks well in breeches, though that surely doesn't hurt."

Gavin hadn't been thinking of the role of Rosalind for Daisy but rather one of the play's lesser parts. "I assure you, we're not reaching so high as Rosalind for a first play. Even a small speaking role such as that of Hymen would be a start." He stopped himself when he realized he skirted the edge of begging.

"Very well, I'll see she's put on the list. The audition is a fortnight from today. I'll have my secretary send the information 'round to your office. She'll be called upon to recite a monologue from memory. But our casting schedule is tight. We've no time to waste, so mind she comes prepared, Mr. Carmichael."

"She will, Sir Augustus. She really is quite good, and in two weeks from now she'll be even better. I trust you will find yourself pleasantly surprised."

Sir Augustus sent him a skeptical look and held up his empty glass, beckoning the waiter to bring a fresh drink. "I hope so, Mr. Carmichael. I doubt it, but I hope so."

The next morning at breakfast, Daisy tossed the detested elocution manual across the table. "What rubbish this is. I should be reading plays, not stuffy grammar books.

How much longer before I can read for a real part?"

The retired actress who answered Gavin's advertisement came with a strong set of credentials, both regional and London-based. Gavin had asked around at the Garrick and confirmed she'd been quite a name in her day. The only drawback was that she was coming from Surrey and it would take another several days to close up her cottage and otherwise settle her affairs. In the interim, he didn't intend for Daisy to be idle. Time was, after all, of the essence.

At tea the other day, he couldn't help noticing her diction wasn't quite all it could be. She tended to swallow her *h's* and murder her *r's* albeit only in certain words. Perhaps it came from being raised abroad or perhaps she'd always spoken thus and he never noticed before because at the time he, too, had spoken a similar dialect. His grandfather had beaten the Cockney coarseness out of him with a cane and occasionally a strap, but in Daisy's case a softer approach was warranted.

Unfortunately, she detested the elocution manuals he brought home so much that at times he almost thought she might prefer a good flogging. In the course of their afternoon lessons, three so far, Gavin gathered Daisy shared the common human failing of doggedly pursuing perfection in those areas in which she already excelled and skipping over those in which improvement was most needed. She would practice a libretto again and again until she struck each note just so, and yet when it came to smoothing out the cadence of her Cockney-accented English interspersed with the occasional French phrase she was all too willing to throw up her hands and be done with it.

"Have patience, Daisy. Your audition is in two weeks."

"And what of you, Gavin? Are you always patient?" He caught the gleam in her eye yet found himself seriously considering the question.

Was he patient? Most of his colleagues and acquaintances said he had the patience of a saint and yet he took care only his nearest and dearest friends knew of the restlessness roiling beneath that seemingly placid façade.

He still hadn't told her about having hired the detective, and at this point he wasn't sure if he ever would. Really, what was the point? For Daisy, the past seemed to be just that, in the past. She made it clear she'd come to London to pursue acting, not him. That he spent such a large portion of his life wrapped up in finding someone who apparently hadn't wanted to be found made him feel foolish enough as it was.

And yet he couldn't find it in him to be sorry he'd found her again. Who knew but perhaps The Powers That Be had arranged matters so once he saw her settled he might finally move forward with his life. His grandfather had been pestering him for some time to take a wife. As much as he delighted in thwarting the old man in ways large and small, he had to admit he was warming to the idea of having someone to come home to at night, someone with whom he could discuss the day, share supper and, afterward, a bed. Until now he'd been too preoccupied—very well, *obsessed*—with finding Daisy to give any of the pretty young society misses more than a passing glance, but after the agreed-upon month concluded, who knew. However, now that the object of his obsession had resurfaced to demonstrate just how well she'd managed without him, it was time to think to the future, not only Daisy's but his.

"Not patient by nature," he finally admitted, "but I've had to learn the trick of it. Reading the law requires a great deal more standing about than you might imagine." Indeed, between waiting for judges and juries to make their determinations, he sometimes felt as though he spent half of most days on his feet and the other half on his bum.

"To hear you talk, you must not like it much."

He shrugged. "It's what I do. I suppose I haven't given liking it all that much thought."

"Maybe you should." She planted her forearms on the table and leaned toward him, reminding him of the other night at The Palace when she had practically crawled across his table. "You don't strike me as being very happy, not even a little happy. In point, you seem rather tense."

He stiffened, feeling as if a mirror had been held up close to his face. "As you don't know me, you aren't in a position to make judgments about my mental state."

Rather than argue the point, she said, "Then tell me something about yourself, something personal."

"Daisy, we're at table. This is neither the time nor place."

Pretending not to hear him, she said, "Very well, then, I'll start."

"Daisy, I don't want to—"

"Would it shock you to hear that the evening you came to my dressing room at The Palace, I touched myself behind the dressing screen?"

"Yes, as a matter of fact, it would. It *does*."

"I was wet for you before you carried me offstage, and once we were alone together in my dressing room, I realized how very wet I was. I'm wet now, in fact."

"Daisy!"

"What, you don't believe me? I can show you, if you like." She made as if to push her chair back from the table.

"No!"

"Take me to your room, then, to your bed. Or you can take me right here atop the table if you prefer. On second thought, we might give poor old Jamison quite a start were he to walk in, so perhaps your bed would be the better spot after all."

"I'm not taking you to bed or anywhere else. I'm off to the office. Finish your breakfast and your lesson."

She frowned. "I'm not a child, Gavin, to be told to eat my porridge while it's warm and brush my teeth before bed."

"Then stop acting like one and—"

"A tart? Or perhaps you were thinking more along the lines of slut, slattern, whore?"

He shoved away from the table and stood, his British reserve at odds with his flushed face and the bulge in his trousers. Seeing the latter made Daisy smile as well as hope. She was getting to him. It was only a matter of time.

"I don't know why you insist on debasing yourself every bloody time we're alone together, nor do I presently have time or inclination to find out. By the by, I'll be dining at my club this evening, so perhaps you'll study your elocution manual as well as your audition lines."

Watching him stalk from the room, Daisy picked up her teacup, using the rim to hide what she felt sure must be a decidedly Delilah-like smile. *You can't put me off forever, Gavin. You may think you can, but you can't. Sooner or later you'll give in and I'll have you.*

And after I've given you pleasure such as you've never known before and aren't likely to ever know again, I'll walk away and leave you without a line just as once you did me.

CHAPTER SEVEN

"But, O, how bitter a thing it is to look into
happiness through another man's eyes!"
—WILLIAM SHAKESPEARE, Orlando,
As You Like It

> Week One:

Daisy spent the following week reading the script for *As You Like It* inside and out, studying the sundry other great works of dramaturgy Gavin had amassed in his library, and practicing her diction. In between tasks, she made time to become better acquainted with the other woman in Gavin's life, his cat, Mia. The feline had been wary of her at first, but Daisy had always had a great fondness for cats. She quickly discerned that Mia liked to sleep in the sun spot at the bottom of Gavin's bed. Stroking the cat's soft fur, she summoned a soothing voice and explained she wasn't out to steal Gavin away, only to borrow him. As for the province of the bed, while she certainly planned on visiting, by no means would she be spending the night. In light of that, surely they could work out some mutually beneficial arrangement? The heart-to-heart, sweetened with some nibbles of poached salmon purloined from the kitchen when Jamison's back was turned, had the desired effect. Mia stopped hissing every time Daisy entered the room and on one occasion even consented to curl up alongside her on the sofa seat.

Even if bribery was involved, it felt good to have made a friend.

In the course of the past week, Daisy had been amazed by the late hours Gavin kept. When he wasn't seeing clients at his office or called to court, he divided his time between The Garrick and his fencing club. Even though she still kept theater hours, she was frequently in bed long before he came home at night. She couldn't shake the feeling he was deliberately avoiding her.

Otherwise, their arrangement was working out famously. So far Gavin had been scrupulous about honoring the terms. Other than Jamison, who moved about silent as a ghost, she had the flat to herself during the day and most of the night. If she ran short of money, she'd only to mention as much to her benefactor and more appeared as if by magic. If she wanted to leave the flat for a walk or some other outing, she was free to do so. Her gilded cage was proving to be no cage at all. She had nothing of which to complain and much for which to be grateful—and yet she frequently felt lonely. She missed her dear ones dreadfully and the excitement and activity of her old stage life to a lesser degree. More and more of late, though, she found herself missing Gavin. When they were children at Roxbury House, they'd been inseparable. Now that she lived under his roof, she scarcely saw him. The week before he made it plain he didn't mean to sleep with her. She was almost to the point of believing he only thought of her as a friend.

Harry's impromptu noonday visit was a welcome surprise indeed.

Daisy stepped back from the door so he could enter. "Harry, how lovely to see you, but I'm afraid Gavin isn't at home. I don't expect him for hours, if at all."

Handing her his hat, he admitted, "Actually, it's you I've come to see. We haven't had much of a chance to catch up since you've been back. That is, if you're not too busy?"

"Hardly." She rolled her eyes. "Gavin has me reading one bloody elocution manual after another. If I have to recite 'The rain in Spain falls mainly in the plain' one more time, I'm sure to go stark raving."

He threw back his head and laughed. "In that case, I'll think of my dropping by as a well-timed rescue mission."

"Yes, please do." She caught sight of Jamison's graying head poking out from the pantry. "Thanks, Jamison, but I can manage my mate, Harry, without help."

Entering the alcove, the servant stared at her aghast. "But miss—"

"No buts, ducks." Shooing him off with a wink, she commandeered Harry's arm and ushered him into the parlor. Sundry plays and scripts were scattered about the floor and furniture. She'd never been particularly tidy and, now that she had space to spread out, she took advantage of it.

"Sorry," she said, moving a copy of *Othello* off the sofa cushion so he might sit. "I'm sure my mess must be driving Gavin mad. Perhaps that's the real reason he's so rarely at home."

Sitting, Harry shook his silver-blond head. "I doubt it. As much as he loves making order of chaos, I'm sure it's other matters that keep him away."

"Work, you mean?" She realized she was fishing and Gavin's absences must hurt her pride more than she might care to admit.

He hesitated before answering, "Well, one doesn't become a leading London barrister by being a shirker—a photographer, perhaps, but never a barrister." He shot her a wink.

Settling into a chair across from him, she said, "Dear Harry, you haven't changed a jot. I feel as though fifteen years have fallen away, and at any moment you'll draw out that hankie of sweets. Oh, speaking of refreshment, I suppose I should have asked Jamison to bring us some tea. I'm learning that's what one apparently does in this country when visitors call during the afternoon."

She started up, but he held up a hand to forestall her. "Don't, at least not on my account. I'm not a visitor but an old friend, and afternoon tea has never been a custom I've slavishly observed. I'd love a whiskey, though, if you have it."

She smiled. "Thanks to Rourke, we've a steady supply of scotch laid in. In fact, I'm amazed there's anything left to drink in Scotland."

She poured out the drinks, a small one for herself, and they settled in.

Swirling the amber liquid about in his glass, Harry said, "You and Gav and to a lesser extent Rourke were like wolf cubs traveling in a pack. I always felt a bit of an outsider. Looking back, I think that was why I always arrived late to our monthly attic meetings. You all complained, Rourke especially, and yet you never once started without me. Having you all wait on me, well, I suppose it made me feel special, as though you cared."

She wished she might talk to Gavin like this. He kept his thoughts and feelings locked inside. "Oh, Harry, of course we cared. I'm sorry I never knew you felt that way."

He shrugged. "It was no one's fault, just the nature of our circumstances. You three were all younger and still eligible for adoption whereas I was the hired help, and grateful to be so, I might add. After a winter living off rotted vegetables and whatever other leavings I could scrounge from the market in Covent Garden, Roxbury House seemed like Heaven, the kitchen especially."

Daisy nodded, recalling the wonderful smells of the pies and tarts and loaves of bread the cook had turned out daily by the dozen. "Roxbury House was the only home I'd ever known, the longest I ever lived any place. Once the Lakes adopted me, we rarely stayed put longer than a few months."

He leaned forward. "You've seen a great deal of the world. Growing up in Paris must have been exciting. Callie and I mean to go as soon as she can break away."

She shrugged. Having spent so much of her life in Paris, she saw it as simply another big city not entirely different from London. "The city is beautiful in parts, less so in others. We lived for the longest time in the Jewish quarter in a flat on the Rue des Rosiers. It was a third the size of these rooms and not nearly so grand, but there was the loveliest patisserie just around the corner and the baker used to give me the leftover challah bread to take home at the end of each day. Most places are what you make of them, I suppose."

"Being at the center of things must have afforded you a great many opportunities as a performer. The running joke is that the Prince of Wales spends more time in Paris than he does in London, mostly in music halls consorting with can-can girls. Oh, Daisy, forgive me. That didn't come out right."

There it was again, her past rearing its ugly head. Even catching up with an old friend, she couldn't escape it. "No need to be sorry, that's what I am, or at least what I was until recently."

What she didn't say was that she'd spent a less than memorable night with England's heir, Bertie, as he was known among his familiars. By the time they got into bed, he'd been too much in his cups to do more than fondle her, but he presented her with a handsome gift afterward all the same.

"Daisy, I assure you, I'd be the very last to judge you. If you only knew the things I've done, or come close to doing in the service of getting on in life . . . Well, never mind that, it's a sordid story best kept for another day, but suffice it to say sometimes The Powers That Be give even we reprobates a second chance in the form of a pure-hearted person who loves us enough to see us for who we might be rather than who we are."

"You're speaking of your wife, aren't you?" At his nod, she said, "I hope I get the chance to meet her some day, though I wouldn't want to impose myself or put her in the awkward position of having to receive me. I understand from Gavin she's active politically."

Hadrian nodded. "Until recently, she led the London arm of the British women's suffrage movement. She's stepped aside but continues to do much good work from behind the scenes, not only to advance women's liberty but also the plight of London's poor. As for imposing

yourself, that's rubbish. Callie is the most compassion-
ate and open-minded of women. She's managed to look
beyond my black reputation, thoroughly well-deserved
in case you've any doubt."

"It's different for men. A man is allowed, even encouraged to experiment sexually, whereas a woman who
openly takes a lover is outcast." She hoped she didn't
sound as bitter as she felt.

Grinning, he shook his head. "You and Callie already have a great deal more in common than you may
think. It sounds exactly like something she would say."

"In that case, I shall very much look forward to
making her acquaintance. I'll even promise to be on my
best behavior so as not to embarrass Gavin."

At the mention of their mutual friend, Harry so-
bered. "He cares for you very much, you know. He
always has, only before he saw you as a little sister in
want of protecting. Now that you've found each other
again, I rather think he's the one in danger of having his
heart trod upon."

Ah, so they'd got 'round to the point of his impromptu visit. "You're worried I'm not good enough for
him, that I'll hurt him?" It wasn't really a question.

He snorted. "Not good enough? Hardly. If you're
looking for someone to help you come up with all the reasons why it can't ever work out for the pair of you, then
I'm afraid you're talking to the wrong person. Callie is a
lady born and but one step removed from qualifying as

a living saint. She could have done far better for herself than a former pickpocket and whoreson, but for whatever reason, she chose me, and I'm thankful every day she did."

"What are you saying?"

"If you truly care for Gavin, don't allow differences in money or station or petty opinion stand in the way of your being happy together. But if you're just out to have a bit of fun and then be off, he isn't the man for you."

She shook her head. "I'm not the sort of woman who settles down to domesticity. Oh, I could put up a jolly good front for a while, I'm an actress after all, but eventually I'd let my guard slip and show how much I hated it all, and before it was over we'd end up hating one another, too. I couldn't bear that."

"Gavin doesn't strike me as the sort who'd expect to come home at night and find you waiting with his pipe and slippers. All I'm saying is don't toy with him, Daisy. He's far too fine to be used that way. If it's a plaything you want, a casual dalliance, there's no shortage of scoundrels in London who'd be delighted to accommodate you. I should know. Before I fell in love with Callie, I was the very worst of them."

He wasn't telling her anything she hadn't discovered already. On the crossover voyage, the ship's captain had invited her to dine privately in his cabin and once in London, Sid, the owner of The Palace had propositioned her before the ink on her contact had fully dried.

For whatever reason, including no particular reason at all, she turned them both down. Even so, all Harry's preaching about love and marriage was sinking her spirits if only because the picture he was painting seemed so very staid and conventional, so very deadly dull. As the old saw went, variety was the spice of life. It was grand to see Harry so happy and content, and yet though she didn't care to be a spoiler, the cynic in her had to resist mentioning he and his Callie were newlyweds still.

Rather than dampen his bliss, she said, "The French have a very different view on love and marriage. Not all lovers are meant to marry or stay together the whole of their lives, for that matter, and yet those sorts of light liaisons can be valuable all the same."

He cocked a sandy-colored brow and studied her for an uncomfortably long moment. Finally he said, "Is that really what you're looking for from your life, another *light liaison*?" When she didn't answer, he went on, "Falling in love with the person who completes you and having that person love you in return is the most extraordinary experience in the world. Trust the word of someone who's had more sexual exploits than he cares to count—there's nothing that comes near to matching the experience of true love, nothing at all."

After Harry left, Daisy took herself out for a good long

walk to mull matters over. Several hours later, she found herself standing in the midst of Covent Garden Market. Harry had mentioned the market time and again when they were children, describing the fruit and flower vendors, the butchers and bakers and fishmongers in great detail. After his bringing it up again that day, she was curious to see it for herself.

Thanks to Gavin, for the first time in her life she might purchase whatever she wished without worry. As it turned out, there wasn't a thing she could think of needing.

Restless, she meandered through the covered market building, divided into five sections: the Row area, the Flower Market, the Russell Street area, the Floral Hall, and the Charter Market. Harry hadn't exaggerated. The place was enormous. Strolling along the aisles of stalls, she stopped to make a series of small purchases for her dear ones back in France—a package of dried figs, apricots, and pineapple for Freddie, a new pocket knife for Papa Lake, who'd taken to whittling now that he had to spend so much time resting, and a shiny copper kettle for Flora who, as far as Daisy knew, still made do with hers though the spout had been broken for nearly a year.

Wrapped purchases in hand, she was thinking of heading for home when from across the aisle an old gypsy woman hailed her. "How now, dearie, why so sad? Come over to Mother and let me read your future. With your pretty face, it's sure to be rosy indeed."

Daisy didn't believe in divination and a gray-haired

old woman in a loose fitting robe festooned with stars and wearing a great many odd-looking necklaces and rings didn't strike her as a particularly exotic sight. There'd been fortune tellers aplenty who set up their tables on the banks of the Seine. One or two had even shared the tricks of their trade, and she'd discerned that more than reading tarot cards or the lines in a patron's palm, a good fortune teller was adept at reading human nature.

Even so, Harry's visit had left her feeling lonely as well as lost. She wanted Gavin but she wanted him on her terms. Why couldn't he simply let go of his high-minded principles and be her lover as any other man would?

Giving in to impulse, she crossed the aisle to the old woman.

Seated behind the cloth-covered stall covered in pouches of dried herbs, mysterious vials of murky liquids, and decks of tarot cards for sale, the woman looked up at her through rheumy eyes. "What's the trouble, dearie?"

Daisy hesitated and then thought, *Oh, bugger it, why not? It's only a bit of fun, after all.* Leaning in, she confided, "There's a friend of mine, a man, whom I've just met again after many years apart, fifteen years in fact."

The crone whistled. "Fifteen years is a long time to be separated from the one you love."

"I didn't say I love him!" Realizing she'd all but shouted, Daisy dropped her voice and admitted, "But I do fancy him a lot and, well, I believe he feels the same about me. I'd like for us to be lovers."

The crone shrugged her thin shoulders. Casting her gaze across the aisle as though searching for her next mark, she said, "It all sounds grand. What's the trouble, then?"

"He's very stubborn and he won't let himself come near me for fear of seducing me which is absurd because . . . well, because I've been with other men."

The woman shrugged her thin shoulders, and Daisy suspected there was little of life she hadn't seen or heard. "A pretty piece like you can't manage your man, pshaw on that." The gypsy turned her head to the side and spat. "Now be a good girl and cross Mother's palm with sixpence, and I'll give you my failsafe charm for bringing your young man around to your bed."

Daisy hesitated, heartily doubting that dousing herself or Gavin with some vile smelling love potion or wearing an amulet of toad piss about her throat would be of any help. She took a step back, thinking to make her excuses and move on.

As if sensing her imminent flight, the gypsy caught at her wrist. "You drive a hard bargain, dearie. Make it a groat, then, but be quick about it."

Justifying the four pence expenditure as no more than she would have spent if she'd bought a bit of ribbon or lace for herself, Daisy opened her purse, picked out the silver piece, and dropped it into the crone's outstretched claw.

The gypsy tucked the money in a leather pouch at her side. Settling back in her chair, she folded her bony arms about her chest and looked Daisy up and down for a long moment as if taking her measure. "The very next evening you have the chance to get him alone, serve him up a good strong drink and afterward a fine hot meal with some oysters to start. Rub his neck and his shoulders and ask after his day. If you can't land him in your bed after that, come back here and find me, and I'll give you your money back. I swear it on Hecate's name."

Daisy stared at her. "Are you saying all I need do is serve him supper?" Could it really be that simple?

The gypsy broke into a broad grin of broken and missing teeth. "The way to a man's heart is through his stomach, dearie. That trick's as old as Eve."

CHAPTER EIGHT

"We that are true lovers run into strange capers;
but as all is mortal in nature, so is all nature
in love mortal in folly.
—William Shakespeare, Touchstone,
As You Like It

The mantel clock struck its ninth note when Gavin walked through the door of the flat later that evening. Earlier Daisy had sent a message by way of his secretary asking for the pleasure of his company and saying she had something she wished to show him. Assuming she wanted help running through her lines or perhaps to recite her monologue for him, he'd made a special point of coming home. In truth, he was too tired and dispirited to bother with dining at his club. He felt like a physician who'd just pronounced his patient dead, only Jem Baker wasn't past his pain but at the very start of it. As much as he tried telling himself he'd done everything legally and humanly possible by the boy, he couldn't help wondering if he might have done more or, barring more, better certainly.

The evidence against Jem was irrefutable as he'd not only been caught in the act of housebreaking but confessed to the crime. Gavin had appealed to the judge for leniency based on the lad's tender age of fourteen and the fact he'd been forced into thievery by his father, a career criminal. Even so, the sentence had been harsh: one year of solitary confinement followed by three years of hard labor in an adult prison. When Jem emerged, he would almost certainly do so as a hardened criminal. There would be no William Gladstone and no sojourn at Roxbury House to save him.

Daisy emerged from the library as he was setting his briefcase down by the door. "I was practicing Jacques' monologue from *As You Like It*. I heard footsteps outside in the hallway and thought it might be you. At least I hoped so," she added. Slanting him a warm-eyed gaze, she looked the slightest bit flushed.

"Where is Jamison? It's not a Wednesday, is it?" On Wednesdays the manservant took the day off to visit his elderly mother.

"No, but I gave him the evening off. I hope you don't mind."

He started to ask why but stopped himself when he

realized he truly didn't care. Daisy was there, that was all that mattered. For the time being, everyone else in the world seemed unnecessary somehow, superfluous. Wearing a simple but lovely pale green silk gown that brought out the deep emerald of her eyes and her pretty hair pinned into a loose knot at her nape, she was like a drink of water to a thirst-parched man.

"How lovely you look," he said both because it was true and because he desperately needed to say something, anything, to break the tense silence that invariably fell between them at moments such as this. Moments when the shadows and the stillness and the silence seemed to swirl about them like an Avalonian mist, whispering all sorts of forbidden possibilities for how the evening might play out.

Her sympathetic gaze settled over his face. "You look tired. Was it a trying day?"

"Indeed." In the midst of shucking off his coat, he briefly recounted the day's tragic turn of events.

When he finished, she said, "Knowing you, you did everything humanly possible and beyond to save him."

She stepped behind him, her scent filling his head with fantasies of all the ways it could be good between them. Her hands settled over his shoulders and then slid slowly downward, taking his coat sleeves with her, chiseling away at his self-control as surely as if she wielded a sculptor's tools. He knew he'd only to lean back a little, and he would feel her breasts brush against his back, a bittersweet temptation. *God, Daisy.*

Her deft touch quickly freed him of the garment, but her hands felt so wonderful he found himself wishing it might take longer. Just a handful of seconds, and yet it was the closest to paradise he'd come in such a very long time.

She moved back, and though the spell wasn't entirely broken, he could breathe again. "There, that has to be better?"

He started to answer then realizing it wasn't really a question, settled on a mute nod. It seemed to satisfy her. Smiling, she turned away to hang the garment on the hall tree, and he indulged in the silent pleasure of watching her, the elegant curve of her spine, the trim waist that cinched in just so, the perfectly proportioned hips and lush bottom that didn't require a bustle's padding.

She swung around so swiftly it took him off guard. "Fancy a drink before dinner?"

Ordinarily he didn't partake at home, but it had been a bloody bad day, and even though he'd left work behind him until the morrow at least, the tension and the damnable sense of failure stayed with him, weighing heavily on his shoulders, his soul, his mind. If nothing else, a stiff drink would purchase him the release of sleep and on a night such as this, when his body was exhausted but his mind was racing with "what ifs," somnolence was as close to peace as he might come.

He followed her into the parlor. "A glass of scotch

would be most welcome."

She walked over to the decanter on the sideboard and poured three-fingers into a glass. Crossing back over to him, she handed him the drink with a soft smile.

He took it from her, their fingertips brushing ever so briefly, making him imagine what a simple thing it would be to press her pretty pink palm to his lips. "Thank you." He hesitated and then asked, "Are you joining me?"

The image of her swigging gin from the bottle in her dressing room still haunted him, but over the past week he'd seen no evidence that she was a closet drinker or much of a drinker at all. If he didn't know better, he could almost believe she staged the scene on purpose to shock him.

She shook her head. "I found a lovely Cote du Rhone in the market today. The wine seller recommended it as an accompaniment to the rack of lamb. I'll wait for dinner."

Taking a seat in the armchair, he snapped up his head. "We're having rack of lamb?"

Looking pleased with herself, she nodded. "Indeed we are and roasted potatoes and braised beans with almonds—and lemon tart for desert if you've room left. Oh, and we're starting with oysters, but don't worry, they're fresh. I just bought them from the market this afternoon."

"I'm not worried." He glanced into the dining room where the table was set for two, a brace of candles and a centerpiece of fresh field flowers occupying the center. "You've been busy."

She nodded. "I went to Covent Garden Market, the one Harry was always regaling us with stories of, remember?"

He did. "You didn't encounter any pickpockets, I hope," he asked with a wink, feeling better by the moment.

She shook her head. "No pickpockets, only an old gypsy woman."

"Did she tell you anything interesting?"

She hesitated and then shrugged. "Not really. The usual rubbish about fame, fortune . . . true love."

At her casual dismissal of the latter, Gavin felt his mood dip, a dull sadness that had nothing to do with Jem tugging at his heart. Daisy wasn't a marrying woman, she'd made that abundantly clear, and even if she were to change her mind, how the devil might matters ever work out between them, a charismatic actress and a stodgy barrister? Could there possibly be a more star-crossed pair in all of London?

She hesitated, smile slipping. "I should confess that though I did shop at the market, I used some of the money you left me and sent out for the supper. I hope that's all right."

"Even better. I'd much rather spend the evening talking with you than watching you slave over a hot stove."

That seemed to amuse her. Gaze sliding over him, she said, "You never know, Gavin. You just might enjoy watching me . . . *slave*." Before he could think how to answer that, she added, "Oh, look, you're empty."

He followed her glance down to the glass in his hand. Damn, if he hadn't drained it. Rourke had been bringing him scotch whiskey for two years now, but he couldn't recall it ever slipping down quite so smoothly. Before he could answer yes or no, she was drawing the glass from his grasp.

A minute or so later, he had a fresh drink in his hand. "I'll see about setting out dinner," she said, slipping into the other room.

An hour later, the remains of the meal and the half-finished bottle of wine sat between them. Gavin set his cutlery on the side of his plate and looked up, a sleepy sense of satisfaction settling over him.

"That was delicious, far better than anything served up at my club. Thank you." As a matter of fact, he couldn't remember the last time he'd supped at his own table. Excellent though the food had been, it was his charming dinner companion who made the evening special.

Daisy smiled, the candlelight casting a soft glow over her face, making her eyes seem even larger, her lips more lush. "I'm glad you enjoyed it. I enjoyed serving you."

She pushed back from the table and rose. He started to follow her up, but she motioned for him to stay seated. Stepping behind his chair, she laid her hands on his shoulders. "You need a massage."

He started to refuse but the firm pressure of her hands felt wonderful, his will woefully weak. His stiffened muscles had loosened considerably, the alcohol a pleasant warmth coursing through his veins, the meal a satisfying weight filling his belly, and Daisy's slender, capable hands kneading the knots from his neck and shoulders a slice of heaven on earth.

She leaned in and laid cool lips against his nape. "I want you, Gavin. I want us to make love. Is that so very bad of me? Can't you set aside those high-minded scruples of yours for once and give in? You might even find you like it. I know I will."

Like it, indeed. He was more than half mad for her. Even so, he shook his head. "This will never work."

"It will if only you'll let it."

She slid a warm hand down the front of him and settled her palm on the inside of his thigh. He'd been hard for her since he sat down to supper and relied on the table to hide him, but there was no hiding now.

"Switch off that famous brain of yours, and let me show you how good it can between us?" She rolled her hand over the bulge of his erection, the heat from her palm searing through his trouser wool.

He was on his feet, whipping about, sending the chair crashing onto its side. "Oh, God, Daisy, you feel so good, so bloody good against me."

"Don't tell me, Gav. Show me."

Sliding his hands into her soft hair, he bent his head and took her beautiful upside-down mouth in the kiss he'd been fantasizing about for the past week. She tasted of mint from the jelly she served with the lamb intermingled with the spiciness of the wine they'd drunk. Moaning, she shifted beneath his hands, his erection pressing into her soft belly.

She lifted her right leg and braced her foot on the table's edge, her inner thigh sliding over his hip. She didn't need to ask. He knew exactly what she wanted from him.

He slid his hand up her limb from ankle to thigh, marveling at how her flesh could be at once so firm and so silken. She wasn't wearing panties. Between her thighs, damp curls brushed his palm. Her slit was wet and warm and fragrant with musk. For a split second, he wanted nothing more than to bury his face in that sweet, fragrant spot and tongue her until she was no longer the one in control, until he was the master rather than her all too willing slave. He sank one finger inside her and drank in her answering moan.

She wrenched her mouth away and looked up at him, eyes feral and expression stark with need. Her beautiful, bruised mouth opened on a single word. "Please."

It had been a long time since Gavin had been with a woman, but he fancied he still remembered what to do. He slipped his finger inside her again at the same time he slid his tongue between her parted lips. Imagining how later he would bury his face between her open thighs and tongue her until she came, he kissed the corners of her mouth, the dimple at the side, the pulse point behind her ear. He lifted his head and looked down at her. Seeing the raw desire written on her face, her passion-drugged eyes, he felt a heady rush of masculine pride.

He drew his hand away, and she let out a whimper of protest. Her frantic fingers found the flap of his trousers. "Oh, Gavin, I can't wait any longer. I have to have you this once if never again."

This once if never again.

The remark snapped Gavin back to the present as surely as a dousing of cold water. He dropped his hands to his sides and backed away from her. "Daisy, we can't do this."

"Why not?" She looked as though he'd slapped her. "Don't you want me?"

He saw the hurt shadowing her face and hastened to reassure her. "Want you, Daisy? I'm on fire for you. You're the embodiment of every fantasy I've ever had as well as those I dared not consciously entertain—until now. Be that as it may, I won't take you like this. I want you for always, not just for the night."

Hearing how he wanted her must have made her feel on firmer footing because she summoned her Delilah smile and took a step toward him. "We can do it as many times and as many ways as can be fit into the next three weeks, how's that?" She reached for his waistband.

He pushed her hand away. "Stop it."

In the dim light of candles, he saw the flare of anger in her eyes. "And if I don't care to stop, why should I? Why should either of us? We're not children any more.

We're adults. We can please ourselves as we like."

He dragged a hand through his hair. "We're friends, good friends. I brought you here to help you, not to make you my mistress."

She shrugged as though it was all merely semantics. "Whether you call me your mistress or your friend, you want me, Gavin. I know you do."

He knew better than to deny it. "It's not that simple."

"It is. You make things too hard by half for yourself and for me. I want you, Gavin. I've wanted you ever since I was old enough to understand what wanting someone, a man, meant. Life is bloody short, or at least it can be, and if it's in our power to grasp a little happiness while we may, then why the bloody hell not? There's no one we need answer to and afterward, well, it doesn't have to mean anything."

He'd come close, so very close to giving in, but her last statement reminded him why it was so very important he stay strong. Daisy had to learn that sex was neither a weapon nor a bartering tool but a gift—a precious gift.

He shook his head and turned away. "That's the very thing, sweetheart. It does for me."

Hours later Daisy lay awake, replaying the foiled seduction in her mind and touching herself in the bed. Gavin must think her a trollop and why shouldn't he when she played the part of the whore to perfection? The truth was she was a good deal more at home seducing men than being friends with them. Attempts at the latter invariably landed her in someone's bed anyway, so why not skip all the pretending and get on with the main event?

Only Gavin wasn't like the men she'd known in France. He wasn't like any man she'd ever known before. Whether Frenchmen or British expatriates, they'd wanted something from her, sex in varying degrees. Whether it was several good whacks on the bum before calling it a night or a full-on fuck, afterward not a single one had shown the slightest interest in her feelings, her opinions, and most especially not her dreams. Gavin always treated her as a person, a friend, an equal. Since she admitted she always wanted to be an actress, he'd done his utmost to make that dream come true for her. If she had a jot of decency, she'd accept his friendship for the gift it was and learn not to ask for more than he was willing to give.

Only she wanted more from him than friendship, and her mounting frustration was beginning to give their encounters a definite edge. Remembering the taste and texture of his mouth moving over hers, the perfect pressure of his warm palm and probing fingers, she slid a soothing hand between her thighs. Gavin had the most beautiful hands, broad-backed and long-fingered. Watching him do the simplest of tasks such as buttering his breakfast toast or fiddling with his fountain pen frequently brought her close to coming. Imagining he touched her now, she closed her eyes and circled her clitoris with a single damp digit.

But self-stimulation was a poor substitute for the weight of a flesh-and-blood man pressing you into the mattress in the most delicious of ways. The problem, hers at any rate, was that she didn't want just any man. She wanted Gavin and after tonight she knew he wanted her, too.

What she hadn't counted on was his stubbornness, his seemingly unbreakable power of will. He was easily the most self-disciplined person she'd ever known and while that was likely a virtue more often than not, she'd had her fill. She'd be mad as a March hare if he didn't give in soon.

She came, muffling her moan in the back of her hand. Afterward, she slipped into sleep. The dream was vividly erotic, engrossingly intense. She and Gavin were in bed together. For whatever reason, perhaps none at all, she knew it was their first time. Whose bed it was or where they were wasn't clear, but the mattress was goose down, soft yet firm, and there were a great lot of fluffy white sheets. Gavin lay propped against the banked pillows, chest bare and the sheet riding low on his waist. Straddling him, she made a point of kissing him in all the places he liked best. She couldn't wait to go down on him.

"Oh, Gavin," she murmured, still entrenched in sleep,

the increasingly violent sounds forming the backdrop of her dream. "Oh, *chéri*, let me make it good for you."

Another cry, this one low and guttural, tore forth from his throat. Like that of a wild animal caught in a hunter's snare, this wasn't the sound of male satisfaction but one of deep pain and hopeless despair.

Daisy bolted upright, her sex drenched and quivering. The cries weren't coming from inside her head but rather from the other end of the hallway. Awake now, she recalled the nightmares Gavin had suffered while at Roxbury House and threw her legs over the side of the bed.

Naked, she fumbled in the darkness for her wrapper. She found it draped it over the footboard and pulled it on, cinching the silk sash on her way out the door. Even in the midst of undertaking a rescue mission, her body couldn't seem to settle, pubis pulsing and nipples swelling as if stroked by unseen hands.

She padded down the hallway to Gavin's door. Until now she'd never so much as peeked inside. She reached out, hesitated, and then made up her mind and wrapped her knuckles smartly on the wood paneling. No answer. He must be in a deep sleep. She started to turn back when from within another wail sounded, catching at her heart. She remembered the nightmares he had as a boy and wondered if this might be the same one or if the sad sights he saw as a barrister were fresh fodder for a heart and mind overburdened by compassion. Either way, she had to save him, she had to help, even if it was only for one night.

His door wasn't locked. The cut glass knob slipped in her damp palm. She hesitated, one foot hovering over the threshold. Before when she entered a man's bedroom, it was always by invitation or at least a strongly worded hint. But the room she was about to enter unbidden was Gavin's bedroom, forbidden territory. After tonight, that must be especially true.

She stepped inside and pulled the door softly closed behind her. "Gav, it's me."

The bedside lamp had been left burning. On the table beside it a book lay open along with a pair of wire-framed spectacles she'd never seen him wear. He must have fallen asleep reading.

Gavin lay thrashing in the center of the bed, pulverizing a pillow between his clenched hands. Broad shouldered and leanly built, his arms were corded with muscle, his belly beautifully flat. Her gaze snagged on the sheet riding low on his waist. As in her dream, he wasn't wearing a nightshirt or sleepwear of any sort, and the sweat sheathing his lean, muscled torso had her forgetting to breathe.

She crossed to the bed and reached for the pillow. "Gavin, it's only a dream. You're—"

Before she could get the rest out, he reared up. Grabbing hard hold of her, he hauled her onto her back and came down on top of her, pinning her to the bed. "Let me loose, you bloody fucker. Let me loose!"

"Gavin, stop! It's me. It's Daisy."

"Daisy?"

Her name seemed to penetrate the fog of the nightmare. His hold on her slackened and his hands fell away. His eyes flashed open. "Oh, God, Daisy, are you all right? Have I hurt you?"

He helped her up and she sat, rubbing her wrists. No doubt there would be bruising on the morrow, but for the moment she was fine and so was he. "I'm all right. You were dreaming. I tried knocking, but you didn't hear me. Was it the fire dream, the one you used to have at Roxbury House?"

He raked a hand through his damp hair and looked over at her with haunted eyes. "It's like a damned devil's curse, a coiled snake that lies in wait to spring into my path just when I've told myself I've finally gotten beyond it, that I've made some sort of peace with the past. I'll go for months at a time without incident and then suddenly it comes upon me for no apparent reason—the same, always the same." He dug the heels of his hands into his eyes. "Christ, I'm coming on thirty. You'd think after all this time I'd be able to put the past behind me and get on with my life."

A life she knew couldn't include the likes of her, at least not in any meaningful way no matter what Harry might have said. Swallowing against the lump building at the back of her throat, she suggested, "Maybe if we walk through it together, scene by scene if you can bear it, I can help?"

He hesitated and then nodded. "I suppose it couldn't hurt." Leaning back against the headboard, he squeezed closed his eyes. "I'm standing outside by the fire truck helpless to do anything but watch the bloody building burn. The air is thick with smoke. I can taste it inside my mouth, feel it burning my nostrils and choking my throat. Inside the tenement, a baby, my sister, is shrieking. I want to go to her, to all of them, but a neighbor man who managed to get out in time grabs hold of me. There's a terrific roar and then a crash, the roof giving way. Afterward, a sort of unnatural hush falls and I can hear every single sound in the throbbing in my head— the crackling of the dying flames, the blare of sirens in the distance, the rush of water from the fireman's hose. And still the bloody bastard won't set me loose."

Tears pushed against the backs of Daisy's eyes. He was entirely too good a person to be in such perpetual torment. After all the years, it simply wasn't fair. "Is that who you shout at so? You never would say when we were children."

He scraped both hands through his hair, pushing it back where it had fallen over his brow. "Yes. He came up behind me and braced my arms behind my back in a deadlock hold. No matter how hard I cried, how much I pleaded or threatened, he just held onto me that much tighter."

"He saved your life, then?"

He nodded. "Not that I ever thanked him for it. All I wanted was to go to them, if not to save them then to be with them at the end. If I had the strength, I would have knocked him to the ground and run headfirst into the flames."

"If he let you loose, you'd have died as well and that would have been the world's very great loss—and mine." A world without Gavin in it—she couldn't begin to wrap her mind about such an empty state of being.

He turned to look at her, shaking his head. "God, how weak you must think me."

He was always so hard on himself, she couldn't bear it. "Gavin Carmichael, you are the farthest thing from weak a person can be. Don't you see losing your family shaped you as surely as a blacksmith's fire forges metal, formed you into the brilliant barrister and good, kind man you are?"

Without thinking, she laid her head on his shoulder and turned her face into his chest, the coarse hair teasing her cheek, his heart a comforting thrumming beneath her ear. She wasn't accustomed to being held by a man. Actually, she'd shunned such intimacy the whole of her adult life. But leaning into Gavin's solid warmth, reaping the benefit of his heat and strength and maleness, she could see how a woman might be tempted to make a habit of it.

Instead of pushing her away, he wrapped his arm about her. "That boy headed for gaol, I suspect he finds my sterling reputation and supposed legal brilliance cold comfort now he's watching the world go by through prison cell bars."

She looked up at him, gaze rueful and jaw hard-set, and shook her head. "Oh, Gavin, ever since I've known you, you've been saving things—birds with broken wings, one-eyed cats." *Me, most especially me.* "But you can't save them all, no one can, though already you've saved so many and done so very much good, not only for strangers but also friends." At his puzzled look, she explained, "When Harry—sorry, I meant to say Hadrian —stopped by the other day, he told me about how you helped him set up shop as a photographer."

He shook his head as though helping a friend turn his life around was a matter of course. Seeing him thus, so hollow eyed and dispirited, it was all she could do to keep from leaning in and kissing away the cares from that world-weary brow—but of course he wouldn't want kisses, not hers at any rate.

He shrugged. "I made some introductions on his behalf to get the thing going, but it was the merit of his work that made a success of it."

"According to him, you did a great deal more than that. He didn't so much as have the funds for a proper suit of clothes let alone the tin to let a studio off of Parliament Square."

"Hadrian has been known to exaggerate."

She reached up and brushed the damp hair back

from his brow. "As certain other persons have been known to be overmodest. Only look at all you're doing for me. In giving me this chance, you're saving my life, in a way. Even if I fail to win a place in the company, at least I can look back and say I gave it a proper try."

He looked down at her for a long moment. "You won't fail, Daisy. The other day when you were reciting Jacques' soliloquy from *As You Like It,* you didn't see me, but I was there watching just outside the study door. You're wonderfully talented, really you are."

She looked away. Gavin's praise was worth more to her than the applause of an entire audience.

"For whatever small contribution my so-called help turns out to be, better to say I'm only repaying an old debt in part, not in full."

She tensed against him. "What debt could you possibly owe me?" Could he finally mean to admit he ignored her many letters?

"You must know you're the one who brought me back to life, coaxed me into talking and being with people again even if I did have that cursed stammer. The way you used to look at me, I felt as though . . . as though I were ten feet tall."

She relaxed against him, her cantering heart resuming a more regular rhythm. The middle of the night alone together in his room was neither the time nor place to address the subject of how deeply his cutting her out of his life had hurt her.

"Helping you gave me something to do. It was the first time I ever felt as if I could be good at something."

"You're talented at a great many things—singing, dancing, and acting."

"And let us not forget taking off my clothes."

Grimacing, he opened his mouth as if to say something and then closed it.

Now that she knew he was all right, things had returned to normal between them or at least as normal as they might be, Daisy felt sleep weighting her eyelids. Before she might succumb and fall asleep in his arms, she pushed up to go.

Swinging her legs over the side of the mattress, she turned back to look at him. "Gav?"

Already half asleep himself, he cracked open an eye. "Yes, Daisy?"

"About earlier tonight, are we friends still?"

A peaceful smile played about his lips. "Yes, Daisy, we're friends."

CHAPTER NINE

"The more pity, that fools may not speak
wisely what wise men do foolishly."
—WILLIAM SHAKESPEARE, Touchstone,
As You Like It

Week Two:

The day of Daisy's audition at Drury Lane was upon her before she knew it. The first half of the agreed-upon month with Gavin had sped by. Never before in her life had time passed so swiftly.

Standing on the theater steps amidst a fine spring drizzle, she waved to the hansom cab carrying Gavin away. Seeing the conveyance turn the corner and disappear, her heart dropped. Perhaps she should have relented and let him come in with her as he offered to do, but then she would have risked shocking him yet again.

Granted, she wasn't averse to doing her utmost to bring out his blushes in the privacy of his flat, but she also was sensible to the fact that the glittering world she was about to enter belonged to him. If anyone was to wither with disappointment or die of shame, let it be her.

Her greatest fear wasn't that she would fail to win a part but that failure would mean disappointing Gavin. Over the past two weeks, he'd made her dream his. While it was comforting to have a partner in her venture, she worried about letting him down.

Keeping her cloak wrapped snugly about her, she took a deep breath and stepped inside the colonnaded entrance. Inside the theater lobby, she followed the signs to the auditorium. Standing beneath the vaulted ceiling hung with crystal cut electric chandeliers and facing the raised stage, the theater seemed enormous to her, much bigger than she would have supposed from the outside. Gavin had told her Drury Lane seated more than three thousand, but until now she hadn't pictured just how big that must be. Even the Moulin Rouge, the most prestigious house she ever played, seemed small in comparison.

The stage manager who turned her away weeks before walked up to her. Expression harried, he didn't seem to recognize her, which was all to the good. Clipboard in hand, he gestured to the clutch of a dozen or so women congregating in the corner near the stage steps. "Stand over there with the others and be quick about it. We're running behind."

Daisy did as she was told. The chatter stopped when she approached and a tall, elegant blonde heading up the queue broke off conversation with her line mate and turned to Daisy.

"Nice cloak," she said in a carrying voice, her deep-set dark eyes sliding over Daisy from head to toe. "It reminds me of one I passed on to my maid just last month." A collective chuckle rose up and every woman in line turned to stare.

Daisy felt stinging heat settle into her cheeks, but rather than shrink into her cloak and try to make herself as small as possible, she forced her shoulders back and her chin up. "Why, thank you. And might I return the compliment by remarking on what a fine-looking frock you're wearing. Surely I've never before seen a woman your age carry off a youthful fashion half so well."

Color flooded the blonde's face, confirming Daisy's guess she must be thirty or perhaps past it. After that, she turned about and gave Daisy her back, which suited Daisy well enough. At least the byplay had distracted her from her nervousness. By the time the call came to queue up, she was feeling almost her old self.

The stage manager offered an upside down hat from which each woman was to reach inside the crown and draw out a number. Daisy reached inside and pulled out a folded slip. Hoping she would either be last or first—coming in the middle of anything was never good—she unfolded the paper and looked down—and felt her blood turn to ice. Theater folk tended to be a superstitious lot, but other than one or two rituals she observed prior to a performance, Daisy prided herself on being free of most of the silliness—until now. Thirteen was a deucedly unlucky number, one associated with all manner of ill omens.

"Ladies, when we call your number, walk to the center of the stage, state your name and then wait for your cue to begin. You each have three minutes after which you are to make your bow and exit stage left."

The stage manager took his seat in the front row. Beside him were two other men, including a smartly dressed man of forty-odd whom Daisy suspected was the theater manager, Sir Augustus. Though she had never before met him, Gavin's description of the acclaimed actor, impresario, and dramatist fit the seated gentleman to a T.

One by one, the other actresses were called up, starting with the tall blonde. She'd chosen a bit from *Othello* where Desdemona pleads with her jealous husband to see reason. Though Daisy thought her rendition was a touch overdone, her bearing and stage voice obviously bespoke of experience and formal training. Watching the others file on one by one, she admitted they were all quite good in varying degrees and obviously at their ease in a theater of this magnitude.

Number twelve filed offstage, and it was Daisy's turn. Blood from her pounding heart rushed her temples and she felt as if an ocean were crashing about inside her ears. Perspiration broke out on her forehead and under her arms and her hands, which had warmed since she'd come inside, felt like cakes of ice.

Scowling, the stage manager lifted his bull horn and called out again, "Number thirteen—that's you, Miss Lake."

She hadn't had an attack of stage fright in years, and she'd come close to forgetting what a miserable and incapacitating state it was. Aware every eye in the auditorium was trained on her, Daisy mounted the stage steps, also aware that breathing suddenly had become an activity she had to think about rather than do naturally.

She stepped off the last step and walked to the center of the stage, feeling as if her legs had turned to jelly. *Breathe, Daisy, just breathe.*

From the front seats below, one of the men barked, "Do get on with it, Miss Lake. We haven't all day."

She summoned a mental picture of Gavin's face as he looked when he'd fallen to sleep the week before, peaceful and nightmare free. She willed her racing heart to slow and her hitched breathing to relax. Smiling, she looked out onto the stage and directly into Sir Augustus's mildly curious eyes.

"Daisy Lake."

She stepped up to the front of the stage and slowly, very slowly, unfastened the front of her cloak. Holding the men's gazes, Sir Augustus's especially, she gave a shimmy of her shoulders, sending the garment sliding off to the floor. A collective gasp echoed through the small audience.

Drinking in the power of it, Daisy took a deep breath and began, "All the world's a stage and all the men and women merely players . . ."

The Garrick was fast filling up when that afternoon Gavin walked up the steps leading to the club's Italianate façade. Standing in the crowded foyer amidst his fellow members, he waited a full five minutes before one of the circulating porters materialized to take his hat and coat. Saturdays were popular club days for any number of reasons. The unabashedly masculine environment provided a sanctuary for husbands seeking refuge from house guests and sundry social obligations imposed by the feminine world.

He found Hadrian in the smoking room. Seated in a faded wingchair by the window, he looked up from the front page of *The Times* when Gavin approached.

"Sorry I'm late. I dropped Daisy off at Drury Lane on my way. Today is her audition."

Taking his seat in a leather armchair that had seen better days, Gavin flagged a waiter and ordered coffee for them both.

"No worries. As always, I made myself at home as

you can see." Grinning, Hadrian indicated the glass of whiskey he'd been sipping.

The two men shared a chuckle. Though the Garrick was likely the least stuffy of the London gentlemen's clubs, the bylaws mandated that members abide by a certain code of conduct. As in other clubs, the old black balling system operated in full force. Whether he styled himself as Hadrian or went by his real name, Harry, his friend had created quite a scandal the year before by publicly announcing he was the bastard of an East End prostitute. That he sacrificed himself to expose the villainous Member of Parliament who hired him to take a damning photograph of Callie, then the president of the London Women's Suffrage Society, and thereby ensure the defeat of the suffrage bill coming before Parliament, was considered to be a tertiary point. Regardless of the nobility of his motive, sons of whores were quite simply not "clubbable." Though Gavin held a seat on the board of directors, it wasn't in his power to alter the membership bylaws to admit his friend. Even so, he wasn't above using his legal mind to find the means to get around them. In the present case, it meant inviting Hadrian to join him as his guest every bloody chance he got. Except for voting rights, the photographer enjoyed all the privileges of club membership without having to pay the exorbitant fee.

Hadrian folded the newspaper and replaced it on the leather-top table. "How are you and Daisy getting on?"

"I beg your pardon?"

"The acting lessons, do you fancy she's showing improvement?"

Oh, that. Paranoia must be getting the better of him because for a moment Gavin felt like a guilty person working to cover for himself on the trial stand.

The coffee arrived. Gavin took a sip of the strong black brew before answering, "She ran through her audition monologue with me the other night, and she really is quite good."

"I never doubted it. I still remember her crack rendition of Puss-in-Boots, after all."

Hadrian grinned and Gavin joined him though in truth he felt as nervous as if he were the one auditioning before the theater manager and director of Drury Lane. For the past two decades, serious drama had fallen out of fashion, prompting one former lease holder to exclaim, "Shakespeare spells ruin, and Byron bankruptcy." Fortunately, *As You Like It* was one of the best loved of the Shakespearean comedies. Given Daisy's background in burlesque, Gavin reasoned the farcical play with its layers of innuendo and myriad mistaken identities should allow her to showcase her strengths. His main worry was that stage fright might get the better of her. When he dropped her off at the theater entrance, she looked to be on tenterhooks.

Hadrian added a second lump of sugar to his coffee and stirred the spoon. "What do you make of her chances for a part?"

"She has a fine sense of comic timing and her enunciation is vastly improved since working with the acting coach." The latter, a retired actress from Bath, had been nothing short of a godsend. "Wishful thinking aside, I'd say she has a real chance at winning the part of Audrey."

"Audrey? I'd ask you to refresh my memory but as I've never read Shakespeare, or much else beyond photography books and newspapers, you'll have to explain."

"*As You Like It* is a comedy. The majority of scenes take place in the pastoral setting of The Forest of Arden. Audrey is the female rustic clown of the piece. It's a small role but a speaking part. She might also make a fine Phebe, the proud shepherdess who falls in love with Rosalind when she's disguised as a boy—Ganymede."

"Rosalind?"

Gavin took another sip of his coffee and then clarified, "The female lead."

"What about Daisy as Rosalind?"

Gavin almost choked on the strong brew. "Rosalind carries the play. The director will surely go with an established actress."

"You don't think Daisy has a shot at least?"

It was a reasonable enough question and yet Gavin didn't entirely care for his friend's tone. "She still has a lot to learn about how things are done in a proper playhouse. Drury Lane is no dance hall after all."

Hadrian opened his mouth as if to say more, but

the waiter returned with the silver coffee pot and a tray of biscuits.

Gavin waited for him to top off their cups before broaching the subject that had been weighing on his mind. "Daisy mentioned your dropping by the other week. I'm sorry I missed you."

"Actually, I came to see her. I thought we two needed a catch-up chat. I hope you don't mind."

"Mind, why should I?" Gavin asked and yet for whatever reason, perhaps none at all, he felt himself bristling. "May I ask what you two spoke about or is it private?"

Hadrian looked him squarely in the eye and admitted, "I told her if she was looking for a light-o'-love only, you weren't the man, but if she were willing to entertain something more, something deeper, she couldn't find a finer fellow than you. Was I mistaken?"

Gavin shook his head. "I suppose I should thank you for the ringing endorsement, but Daisy and I are just friends. My helping her is no different than my helping you when you first came to London." What a whopper of a lie that was.

Hadrian didn't hesitate to call him on it. "The hell it is. You're in love with her."

Gavin sat his cup and saucer down with a bang. Was he truly that transparent? "If I was in love with her, and I'm not saying I am, I wouldn't know which woman that might be. At times I see glimpses of the girl we all remember but at other times she insists she's Delilah, not

Daisy. It's as if she relishes the role of the hard-bitten tart, not to mention seizing on every opportunity she can to shock me."

Hadrian sent him a sage smile. "Harboring a dual identity is a means of hiding. I can say so from experience. You tell yourself you're hiding from others, from the world, but the truth is the only person you're hiding from is yourself. Give her time, Gavin. This is all new to her. Even though she's used to living in a large city, London can be a very daunting place. In time she may come around."

In time. She only promised him a month and the first half was spent already. "Even if she should come around, I'm not at all sure what I can reasonably offer her."

"Aren't you? You might start with your heart—and your name."

"Marriage." Gavin let the word stand.

Hadrian nodded. "I'm the last man you'd ever expect to hear say so, but marriage to the right person is the nearest thing to bliss on earth."

Gavin looked at him and shook his head. "So speaks the newlywed."

Hadrian paused in biting into his biscuit and shook his head. "Daisy said as much the other day. What a cynical pair you've become."

The problem, from Gavin's standpoint, was they weren't a pair at all. Nor had Daisy given any indication she wanted more from him than a fleeting physical affair.

Even if she were willing to let him be more to her than a casual lover, what more might he be? Given the vastly different social strata they occupied, it was difficult to envision on what plane they might exist as a couple, let alone as man and wife. Had he been left to finish out his youth at Roxbury House rather than been reclaimed and placed in the gilded prison known as "good society," there would be no problem at all. As it was, he was a prominent barrister as well as heir to one of England's finer if not precisely top drawer families, and Daisy was a former showgirl who aspired to be an actress. What kind of life could he reasonably expect to offer her? It was a conundrum for which his supposed brilliant legal mind had yet to come up with a solution. Until he could, he was more than willing to let the topic die.

Apparently Hadrian wasn't. "You used to be the romantic among us, the true believer. What's happened to you, Gav?"

Life had happened to him. For him, love and loss always seemed to go hand-in-hand. If there was any lesson hidden amidst all the pain it was that once you committed your heart, once you loved something or someone, the Universe swept in and stole your happiness straightaway. Gavin opened his mouth to say as much when he caught sight of Sir Augustus Harris, manager of the Drury Lane Theatre, making brisk strides in his direction.

"Sir Augustus, this is a pleasant surprise." Surprised indeed, he rose to shake the older man's hand, wondering

whether the theater manager's early appearance boded
well or ill for Daisy's audition. From what little he
gleaned of the behind-the-scenes of theatrical life, casting try-outs typically took hours, with call-backs extend-
ing into the following day or more.

Introductions made the rounds and Gavin gestured
to the vacant wing chair in their circle. "Join us, won't
you?"

"I don't mind if I do."

The waiter returned and additional coffee and biscuits were brought for the newcomer. Sir Augustus
selected a lemon biscuit and ordered a glass of port to
accompany his coffee.

When they settled in once more, Gavin said, "I want
to thank you for including Miss Lake in your audition
this afternoon. I trust she did not disappoint?"

Sir Augustus brushed biscuit crumbs from his beard.
He washed the last bite of the cookie down with a mouthful of port before answering, "Quite the contrary, her
reading was stellar and her delivery most . . . *unique.*"

Wondering what he meant by the latter, Gavin took
his cue from the theater manager's smiling face and relaxed back into his seat. He hadn't realized until now he
had quite literally been sitting on its edge. "You cannot
know how happy I am to hear it. Do you think you might
find a speaking part for her, then? I was just telling Mr.
St. Claire I thought she'd make an admirable Audrey."
He caught Harry's eye and wondered if he should say

more or if perhaps he'd already said too much.

Sir Augustus stared at him for a long moment. He took another sip of port and Gavin thought, *For the love of God, get on with it*. "My dear Mr. Carmichael, your protégée would be wasted on such a paltry part."

Daisy's try-out must have gone off well then. Gavin mentally reviewed the play's cast of characters. Would Sir Augustus offer her the somewhat meatier part of Phebe, or perhaps Hymen?" The latter role was a walk-on in the final scene, but still it was a speaking part and, as the goddess came on at the finale of the play, theater goers might be more apt to remember her.

Sir Augustus slapped his thigh as though Gavin had said something droll. Knocking back the rest of his port, he shook his head. "On the contrary, Mr. Carmichael, I have found her."

"Found who, sir?" Gavin and Hadrian exchanged glances. *He's drunk*, Gavin thought. *It's the only explanation*. Turning to Sir Augustus, he admitted, "Sorry, sir, but I don't follow you."

A grin wreathed the theater manager's face from ear to ear. "Your protégée, Miss Lake, *is* Rosalind!"

When Gavin returned home from the club, Daisy was waiting for him at the flat door. Cheeks flushed and eyes beaming, she threw herself at him before he even got the door closed. "Oh, Gav, I have the most wonderful, the most amazing news."

Having her pressed against him was bittersweet torment and yet he couldn't find the will to set her aside and move away. She wore only her black silk wrapper with no corset underneath and through the slippery fabric her skin all but scorched his fingertips. He braced his hands along her supple sides, for the moment content just to hold her.

He pressed a kiss to her forehead, the sort of chaste embrace he might have given her were they children still, surrogate siblings, though her body brushing against his brought out feelings that were anything but brotherly. "Congratulations, Rosalind."

She pulled back and looked up at him, expression registering surprise and perhaps a bit of disappointment. Damn, he should have let her tell him in her own way and time. "You knew? Oh, but Gavin, how could you? It all came about scarcely two hours ago."

"London is a small town, sweetheart." Sweetheart— how easily the old endearment rolled off his tongue when she was looking up at him as she was doing now, gaze soft and open, not veiled and distrustful as it all too often was. "Besides that, Sir Augustus is a member of the Garrick, if you'll recall. He came in while Harry and I were having coffee all but bursting with the news."

"Oh, Gavin, do you really think I can do it? Do you really think I'm that good?" In her excitement, she laid her hands atop his shoulders, and he couldn't help thinking how easy it would be to lift her off her feet and into his arms as he had that first night at the supper club, only this time instead of rushing her back to her dressing room he would have very much liked to have carried her to his bed.

He hesitated, heartily hoping Sir Augustus wasn't setting her up to fail by burdening her with too weighty a role for her first part. But what was done was done and the happiness shining forth from her eyes was cause enough for celebration. "Sir Augustus obviously thinks so and he's a far better judge than I." The heat pooling in his groin confirmed it was time to let go. Holding her at arm's length, he said, "A celebration is in order, Miss Lake. You've only to name your fancy. Consider your wish to be my command."

She hesitated, drawing her bottom lip between her pretty top teeth, and Gavin felt a sharp tug in the vicinity of his groin. "If we were in Paris, I could easily come up with at least a half dozen spots within a short stroll, but I don't know London yet. Well, at least not beyond supper clubs, and truly I'd rather not go there."

She would get no argument from him on that score. Dropping his hands to his sides, he said, "We don't have to decide just yet. Go dress and we'll decide from there on."

She flew toward the bedroom door. Halfway there, she turned about. "Gavin?"

"Yes."

"Can there be champagne? Not the dreadful pink kind they served up at The Palace but real French champagne?"

"Sweetheart, if it means seeing you smile as you're doing now, I'd buy you French champagne sufficient to fill the Thames."

CHAPTER TEN

"If the scorn of your bright eyne
Have power to raise such love in mine,
Alack, in me what strange effect
Would they work in mild aspect!"
—WILLIAM SHAKESPEARE, Rosalind,
As You Like It

By the time Daisy was dressed to go, it was still light outside and the weather had settled into a fine evening. In no rush to eat, they found themselves strolling along Brook Street in the West End of town. Gavin told her Rourke's townhouse was nearby in Hanover Square.

"That's not Rourke's, is it?" She paused to point to the Palladian façade of a large red brick mansion.

Gavin smiled. Seeing the city through Daisy's eyes was proving to be a magical experience. In high spirits after her audition, she was eager to take in as many new sites as she might.

"That's the Claridge Hotel. It's something of a London institution."

She mounted the front steps and peered inside the long window to the chandelier-lit lobby. Turning back to Gavin, she said, "It looks very grand. Can we go in?"

He hesitated. If he took her inside, he would likely encounter half a dozen people he knew. Even so, it wasn't as if it was a crime to be seen dining *à deux* with an old friend, even if that friend wasn't old at all but rather a dazzling young actress with a bright future and a notorious past.

She turned back to him, smile dimming. "Forgive me, I wasn't thinking. If it's fashionable, that means you're likely to see people you know and then you'd have to explain me."

If she was testing him, he was determined to pass, to prove to not only her but to himself he wasn't such a snob after all. "Nonsense," he said, seeking to reassure himself as much as her, wishing he might feel as unfettered and gay as he hoped he sounded. "I should be proud to be seen in your company and more than happy to introduce you to anyone we might meet." He extended his arm and, taking it, Daisy followed him up the marble steps.

The hotel's tearoom was crowded when they entered but there were still vacant tables. The *maitre d'* walked up to them and asked, "Have you a reservation?"

Gavin turned around, and the man's face flushed a vivid scarlet. "Mr. Carmichael, forgive me, I didn't realize it was you. I'll be most happy to seat you and the young lady immediately."

Once they were seated at a window table overlooking a most pleasant view, Gavin ordered a bottle of the finest champagne and the waiter went to fetch it, leaving two menus behind. Daisy was too busy remarking on her surroundings to focus on selecting her food.

"Oh, Gavin, this is so lovely, so elegant. And yet it feels odd to be sitting at a table and ordering rather then being onstage. In Paris, my friends and I used to meet at cafes sometimes for a *café au lait* or a glass of wine, but I've never sat in a real restaurant before, not as a patron, at any rate. I . . . I rather like it."

He smiled over at her, ashamed for having hesitated about bringing her in. "You might as well become accustomed to it, sweeting, because as a leading actress this is what your future holds. By the by, Sir Augustus mentioned your recitation was most unique."

She hesitated and then admitted, "Instead of dressing in street clothes to audition, I wore a flesh-colored body stocking. I wanted to play on Jacques's reference to life coming full circle from birth to death."

So that explained her death grip on her cloak that afternoon. She hadn't wanted him to see what she wore under it—or rather *didn't* wear. In retrospect, he was glad she hadn't apprised him of her plan because he likely would have tried talking her out of it. He suspected there was a lesson involved, but at present he was in too good a mood to risk pondering it.

Instead he smiled over at her and said, "Well, that certainly qualifies as unique."

Relaxing back into her chair, she studied the menu. As Gavin's guest, she'd been given the ladies menu, of course. The Claridge was a stickler about such things.

Leaning over to him, she whispered, "Gavin, there aren't any prices."

He hid a smile. "No matter. Order what you like."

He wanted her to become comfortable with dining out, but mostly he wanted her to become comfortable with the notion of being with him, not just for the month but for the foreseeable future or better yet for all time. Holding himself back from making love to her the night before numbered among the most difficult things he'd ever done, but he still hadn't given up on winning her over in the end.

Harry's words from earlier that day rang through his head like the chiming of Big Ben. *Marriage to the right person is the nearest thing to bliss on earth.*

He glanced across the room to signal the waiter they were ready to order when his gaze connected with that of Isabel Duncan, and he felt his smile drop as though the corners of his mouth were weighted with stones. Bloody hell! Of all the people he might have encountered, did it have to be her? The woman was a notorious gossip but worse than that she'd set her cap for him. Everyone—his grandfather, the Duncans, and Isabel herself—thought they should marry—everyone, that is to say, but him. She had a perfunctory prettiness about her and yet she held no appeal for him at all, not because she was lacking in looks but rather lacking in soul.

The one time he allowed himself be cajoled into calling on her, they'd gone for a stroll in Hyde Park. At Isabel's insistence, they stepped off the main path, ostensibly to examine the roses, though Gavin suspected her true intention was to trap him into kissing her. The approach of a beggar child had saved him from an embarrassing situation. Isabel had shrieked at the boy for accidentally brushing against her skirts. Though Gavin took care to treat her courteously during their subsequent encounters—and given the small, elite social circle in which they both traveled, he encountered her far more frequently than he would have liked—he refused to ever call on her again.

The one saving grace was that she was seated across from a young man whom Gavin didn't recognize but heartily hoped was her beau. Who knew, but perhaps his luck would hold and she'd miss seeing him entirely.

Across the room taking tea with her escort, a blubbery

young baronet she'd not the slightest intention of marrying, Isabel looked from Gavin to the cinnamon-haired creature seated too close for comfort beside him and felt a stab of powerful, piercing dislike.

She'd sooner perish than admit it, but she'd been angling for Gavin for nearly a year now—and a year in the life of a young woman skirting the line between debutante and old maid counted as a considerable period of time. She'd planned her strategy like a trophy hunter stalking some elusive African prey, taking care to put herself in Gavin's path whenever possible and making careful note of his preferences in food, entertainment, and even politics. But no matter how many tiresome facts she crammed into her head concerning the forced resignation of Prince Bismarck in Germany or British imperial policy in South Africa, he never exhibited more toward her than a vague politeness.

His attitude toward his dining companion was a far different affair. Watching him over the top of her teacup, she didn't miss the warm glow in his eyes when he looked at his dining companion, bending his ear to her indecently sensual mouth as though whatever she had to say was of the utmost interest.

Unable to bear it any longer, she turned to her escort and demanded, "Who is that woman with Gavin Carmichael?"

Popping a piece of whitebait into his mouth, he twisted his head to look in the indicated direction.

Turning back to their table, his plain face wore a silly smile. "That's Delilah du Lac. Fancy that."

"A Frenchwoman," Isabel hissed, horrified to think of her potential place being usurped by a foreigner. Really, was there no such thing as national pride?

"English, actually, though she's lived in France for years. She's an actress in the musical reviews. I read somewhere she was playing a supper club in Covent Garden a few weeks ago. Imagine us seeing her here."

"Take me over there. I want to say hello."

"But our food will go cold." He cast a rueful look to the substantial repast their waiter had recently laid out.

Isabel was already on her feet, leaving him no choice but to rise as well and accompany her. "Nonsense. We'll only be a minute."

For appearance's sake, she took his arm and steered them across the room. Stopped at Gavin's table, she looked down and said, "Why, Gavin, what a pleasant surprise."

"Isabel." She didn't miss the pained look that crossed his face before he set aside his napkin and rose.

Glancing at Daisy, she said, "Aren't you going to introduce me to your . . . lady friend?"

Looking supremely uncomfortable, he hesitated. "Isabel, allow me to present Miss Daisy Lake. Daisy, Miss Isabel Duncan."

The two women eyed one another, Isabel making a mental note of the showgirl's offstage name. "You're an actress in one of those musical reviews, aren't you, only you go by another name, a *stage name*—isn't that what you people call it?"

"You're Delilah du Lac, aren't you?" Isabel's escort piped up.

The actress shifted in her seat. "Yes, or rather I was. Now I'm pursuing a theatrical career."

Gavin spoke up, "Actually we're celebrating. Daisy's just been given the part of Rosalind in *As You Like It*."

That took Isabel aback. "Surely not the production Drury Lane is putting on?"

"As a matter of fact, yes," Daisy answered. Rising from the table, she said, "If you'll excuse me, I have to visit the ladies'."

How vulgar, Isabel thought. Not about to let her rival march off in triumph, Isabel said, "I'll go with you."

Leaving the two men staring after them, they filed through the dining room. "The ladies' retiring room is just down that side hall," Isabel informed her. "I don't suppose you've been here before to know where it is." Out of the corner of her eye, she glimpsed the Lake woman's flushed face and smiled to herself.

Once inside, they went their separate ways, meeting up again at the washstand. Isabel walked up as Daisy reached over to take the towel the attendant, a young Irish girl, held out. "Thank you," she said with a smile, obviously too ill-bred to know one never directly addressed lesser servants if it could be helped.

Standing before the gilded wall mirror, Isabel made

a show of powdering her nose. "You should know that Gavin and I have an understanding."

Daisy regarded her in the glass, a deep flush riding her cheekbones. "Excuse me?"

"We're to be married," Isabel said. It was a bald lie but then whoever had said that all was fair in love and war certainly had the right of it. "It's been arranged between our families for ages."

"I see." To Isabel's delight, the bitch looked as though she might puke in the washbasin.

"No worries." Isabel reached up to pat a light brown curl into place, feeling better with every passing moment. "I'm a modern girl. I understand men like Gavin must have their bit of fun and flirt before they settle. The two of you, well, it doesn't have to mean anything and in Gavin's case I'm quite certain it won't."

It doesn't have to mean anything. Daisy had said those exact words to Gavin the previous night, but only now did she understand why he looked so hurt.

Smiling, Isabel took a step back from the mirror. "I'm so very glad we had this little heart-to-heart. I should be getting back to my escort. Toodolu."

Feeling as if the champagne she'd drunk might come up at any minute, Daisy leaned over the washstand and splashed cool water onto her burning cheeks. To think she'd been worried that Gavin might become too serious, that at the end of their agreed-upon month, he might balk at letting her go and all along he'd been using her. Using her as every other man in her life had done.

She found Gavin sitting alone at their table. Catching sight of her, he rose and held out her chair. "Is everything all right?"

Heart in her throat, she slipped into the satin-covered seat. "Of course, why do you ask?"

He shrugged. "You and Isabel disappeared for some time."

Their waiter chose that moment to roll by the dessert cart. Turning to Daisy, Gavin said, "If you fancy chocolate, you can't go amiss ordering the mousse."

She shook her head, for once not remotely tempted by the sweet. "I don't care for anything more, thank you." Catching Isabel's smug smile from across the room, she added, "Can we please just go home?"

***

Isabel slipped back into her seat. When the dessert cart was presented, she decided to save worrying about her waistline for another day and ordered the lemon tart *and* the chocolate mousse. Settling in to savor the sweets, it occurred to her that if she couldn't have her happiness in the form of Gavin Carmichael, at the very least she could share her misery.

Delilah du Lac, or Daisy Lake, showgirl or actress, whatever else the woman was, she was a poacher, a thief.

The bitch deserved whatever mischief came her way.

Gavin thought Daisy unnaturally quiet on the carriage ride home. They'd started the evening in such high spirits, but with Isabel's arrival the tempo of their celebration had taken a decided downturn. Wondering what might have passed between the two women, he asked Daisy if anything was the matter not once but several times. Each time, she answered with a tight-lipped "no" and a shake of her head. Finally she'd turned way from him to stare out the window though the darkened streets didn't afford much in the way of a view.

Once inside his flat, however, it was a different story entirely. They barely crossed the threshold when Daisy slammed her reticule down atop the marble-topped hallway table, so hard Gavin was amazed the impact didn't send glass beads flying.

"What the devil was that about?" he asked, reaching for her wrapper.

Pulling away, she yanked it off herself. "What the devil, indeed? You and Miss Pinch-Face seem to be on mighty chummy terms. When I excused myself to go to the ladies', I'd half a mind to find my own way back here, not that I flatter myself you would have noticed."

"Daisy, you're being absurd. Isabel and I have known each other for ages. Her father and my grandfather have gone grouse hunting together in Scotland every year for the past twenty-odd."

She answered with a huff. "Someone has gone hunting all right, only her quarry isn't any game bird—unless you count a certain blue-eyed peacock."

That got his attention. "If you're implying what I think you are, you really are being absurd."

"Am I now? Pity you weren't standing before one of those many full-length mirrors so you might have seen how you preened. And she fawned all over you, the perfect peahen."

For a moment Gavin could only stare at her. Could it be Daisy was jealous of Isabel Duncan? She certainly sounded so. Isabel was a passably pretty girl though she'd never particularly appealed to him. Certainly she couldn't come close to matching Daisy's flamboyant good looks. If there was a rivalry afoot, and it seemed as there was, it couldn't be over appearances. It must be over . . . him.

The realization struck him like the proverbial thunderbolt from above, and he had to make a conscious effort to tamp down his sudden soaring sense of satisfaction. These past weeks he'd been working to make her see him as someone more than a mentor she felt obliged to repay with soulless sex, and all it had taken to turn the tide was another woman showing interest in him. Jealousy, it was such a sublimely simple yet tried-and-true tactic, why hadn't he thought of it before? For the first time in their acquaintance, he would have been most happy to walk up to Isabel Duncan and plant a smacking kiss on her thin, pallid lips.

Deciding to let her stew a while longer, he said, "What do you mean?"

"That milksop debutante has set her cap for you, as if you didn't know."

He forced a shrug and asked, "And what if she has? Unlike certain persons, Isabel is most certainly a marrying woman."

That took her aback, he could tell. She opened her mouth as if to answer and then clamped it closed again.

"Quiet now, are we? You've as good as told me you're not the sort of woman who willingly links her future to that of any man for long, certainly not for life. We all haven't the luxury of living so footloose and fancy free, you know. Being a free spirit is all well and good for you actors, but for a barrister, bachelorhood beyond a certain age is a definite liability."

"Gavin, what are you saying?"

He couldn't be sure, there was only the light from the gas wall sconces to rely upon, but he thought he caught her bottom lip trembling. "Only that I'm coming on thirty. At some point, I'll have to give serious thought to settling down."

She arched a brow. "At some point or soon?"

He shrugged. "That all depends on circumstances, I suppose."

Arms crossed, she tapped a foot on the floor. "Don't

be coy, Gavin. Do you mean to wed that whey-faced bitch or don't you?"

"If not Isabel, then I suppose I shall wed someone like her. Will you mind terribly?"

For once no glib reply or saucy retort rolled off her tongue. In the dim light of the single tabletop lamp, her eyes looked unusually bright.

She shook her head. "I'm tired. I've drunk too much champagne and my head aches. I'm going to bed." She turned to go to the hallway leading to her room.

"Daisy, wait." He came up behind her, covering the tops of her shoulders with his hands. How small she felt, how fragile. He leaned close, his cheek brushing against the softness of her hair. "You've not answered my question. Would you mind if I married?" When she was silent still, he turned her slowly about. Lifting her chin on the edge of his hand, he saw the tears streaking her cheeks and felt his heart lift with hope. "Daisy, what's this? Why tears on what was to be such a happy night?" He reached out and caught a fat droplet on the pad of his thumb.

"Marry who the devil you want and may you both be damned!" She tore away from him.

He bounded after her. "Daisy!" A few weeks before, he would have been mortified to think his manservant might have overheard them, but now he couldn't find it in himself to give a damn.

He caught up with her at her bedroom door before

she could slam it in his face. Tears sparkling on her lashes like snowflakes and body aquiver, she rounded on him. "Yes, yes I'll mind. I'll mind terribly. Seeing you walk down a church aisle, or anywhere else for that matter, will tear at my heart, but because we're friends, I'll find a way to smile and bear it. There, you've won your precious confession and made me cry. Happy now?"

He shook his head, feeling as if his heart were overflowing with tenderness. "Not so happy. I don't want to be the cause of your tears, Daisy. I want to be the cause of your smiles. Dearest Daisy, I want to make you smile, to make you happy. Won't you give me leave to try?"

CHAPTER ELEVEN

"Come, woo me, woo me, for now I am in a
holiday humour and like enough to consent."
—WILLIAM SHAKESPEARE, Rosalind,
As You Like It

Behind the closed bedroom door, Gavin and Daisy
stood facing each other by the bed, their clothes a
collective pool at their feet.

Daisy had undressed many a man, but she'd never
had a lover who came close to matching Gavin's male
beauty. His waist was narrow, his buttocks tight, and
his legs long and well-muscled. For a night, this night,
he belonged entirely to her.

His gaze ran over her and she felt the touch of those
blue eyes like a physical caress. "You're beautiful."

She stared up into his eyes. "You make me feel beautiful. You always have."

He touched her cheek with gentle fingers. "Your powder and paint, you washed them off after your audition, didn't you?"

Removing the cosmetics had been a calculated act on her part, a small test of her courage. Cosmetics were one more prop in the ongoing charade, a mask, a concealing cocoon. She wanted to come to Gavin fresh, new—clean. If only her past might be so easily scoured away.

His gaze brushed over her breasts. He looked back up at her, a sort of awe shining from his eyes. "May I touch you there?"

If any other man had asked such a question, she would have laughed outright. Touching each other intimately was, after all, the entire point of going to bed. But this was Gavin, dear, sweet, honorable Gavin. And knowing what he was, *who* he was, she understood he wasn't asking permission to touch her body so much as her soul.

She couldn't give him her soul any more than she could give him her virginity—impossible to give what she no longer possessed. But for one night, this night, she could give him what he most wanted. She could banish Delilah du Lac to the wings and call Daisy Lake to front and center stage. For one night she would be the sweet, unspoiled girl who lived on in his memory. She could give him that much at least, precious little when she owed him so very much more.

Instead of answering with a laugh or cheeky retort, she looked into his beautiful, solemn eyes and for once spoke from her heart instead of her head. "If you don't touch me, I think I'll die," she whispered because suddenly it felt as if they were, if not exactly in a church, some other sacred place.

"Don't speak of dying when we've so much to live for."

His hands were cold if not exactly shaking. When he touched her nipples with his thumbs, they budded on contact. She shivered, and he started to pull away.

She caught at his hand, holding it to her. "No, don't. Please. I like it. I want you to." *I want you.*

Bolder now, he bent his head and lapped at her nipples, then drew one tight bud into his mouth and suckled, the pull of his mouth bringing the ache between her thighs to crescendo.

"Oh, Gavin." Arching against him, she slid her hands into his hair, the blue-black waves as soft as she remembered.

They fell back on the bed, Gavin coming down on top of her. She wrapped her legs about his waist, loving the rock hard feel of him pressing against her belly. "I'm not a virgin, you know." She said it with a smile but she felt, if not exactly sad, a little wistful.

She'd lost her virginity at the age of fourteen to a Parisian stagehand with a head of tousled black curls and blue eyes that reminded her of Gavin's. Since then, she'd amassed quite a repertoire of sexual tricks, positions and acts calculated to not only seduce but enslave. Before the night was over, she fully intended to use every one of them to make, if not love, than at the very least magic.

"I didn't think you were." He slid his hand over her hip as if learning the landscape of her body, the feel and shape of her.

"You don't mind about me having . . . having been with other men?" She shifted on her bottom and spread her steepled legs wider, a silent signal for him to touch and taste her wherever he wished.

He shook his head. "Delilah du Lac's lovers are said to number a legion. I shouldn't like to think I'm competing with an entire legion." When she didn't reply, he added, "But nor would I necessarily want to be your first, the one to hurt you." His stroking hand moved to the inside of her thigh, his palm warm now and his touch sure and knowing.

"You wouldn't have hurt me. You would have been gentle with me just as you always were, as you are now." Indeed, no lover before had ever touched her with such tenderness, such . . . reverence.

"You deserve to be shown only gentleness."

He bent his head and trailed kisses over her neck, her breasts, and her belly. Coming to her thighs, he kissed the tops and then the insides and then slid a hand between, finding her with his fingers.

"You're so beautiful there, so beautiful and wet." He

spread her inner lips and covered her with his mouth, sending pleasure rippling through her. Lifting his head, he said, "Show me how to touch you. It's important," he added when she still didn't answer.

She opened her eyes and met his stark gaze. Holding it, she reached down and touched her clitoris. "There. I want you to stroke and kiss and suckle me just there." She circled the hard nubbin, her finger slipping in slickness.

His head disappeared between her thighs. He teased her with the tip of his tongue, striking the sensitive spot again and again, the warm tingling in her lower belly and sex building to a hot, rhythmic ache.

The orgasm hit her fast, hard, furious. When she stopped shaking and opened her eyes, she found Gavin braced over her, watching her face. "I can't wait any longer."

She moved her head back and forth on the pillow. "Don't wait. I don't want you to wait. I want you now."

His maleness slid down her belly. He was long and hard, thick and beautifully shaped. She felt the pressure of him against her belly, and the liquid ache of her body's rapidly rising response.

He rose above her, a hand braced on either side of her head. "God help me, Daisy, I want you so much."

"I want you, too, Gavin. She raised herself up on her forearms and lifted her buttocks off the mattress to meet him.

He entered her in a single thrust. Daisy clenched

her legs about his waist, hips lifting to meet him stroke for stroke, milking his member with her inner muscles.

His blue eyes flashed open. "Oh, God, Daisy." A final thrust brought him to climax. Body shaking, he collapsed atop her. Stroking his sweat-filmed back and running her hands along his sinewy sides, Daisy allowed she'd never felt quite so content in all her days.

So this is what it means to be perfectly, blissfully happy, she thought and then ruined it in the next breath by wondering how soon it would be snatched away.

Sleep, when it finally came, did so in snatches. Even slumbering, they reached for each other, legs twining, bottoms bumping, mouths meeting. Around dawn, Gavin awoke to Daisy's slender hand grasping his cock. Gently disengaging her fingers, he eased her onto her back and braced himself atop her. She let out a little moan and spread her legs for him, arching her back in silent supplication though her eyes were still closed. She was still more asleep than awake and yet as wholly aware of him as he was of her, he was certain of it.

Reaching down between them, he dipped a finger into her slickness and brought the digit to his lips, savoring her smell, her taste, her tightness, every remarkable sensation.

"So wet, so sweet."

A taste of her wasn't nearly enough to satisfy—why settle for a nibble when he might have the whole feast? He slid down the length of her until his head was level with her thighs. Spreading her open with his fingers, he bent his head to her sex and ran his tongue from the hood of her clitoris to her slit, a slow, velvet sweep.

Her eyes flashed open, a blaze of green foxfire that warmed his soul and all the rest of him. "Yes, Gavin, oh, yes."

She smelled and tasted like new spring grass, damp with dew and succulently tender. He licked her again, laving her clitoris with the tip of his tongue. Shifting her hips, she reached down and ran urgent fingers through his hair, pulling him closer still.

"Don't stop. Please don't stop."

"Oh, sweetheart, stopping is the very last thing on my mind." Indeed, now he knew what she liked, how to please her, he couldn't fathom wanting to do anything but.

He positioned himself over her and slid into her in one sweet, slow thrust that set her body quivering like a bow-string. She gripped her legs tight about his waist, a sweet vise from which he had no thought or need to escape. A few more thrusts had her coming, the rhythmic throbbing of her inner muscles bringing him to the brink. Even in the throes of it, he remembered his duty and withdrew. The final contraction hit him deep, hard. He squeezed his eyes shut and spilled his seed onto the sheet.

"God, Daisy!"

He collapsed onto his side, the cool press of the covers a welcome balm to his flushed flesh.

"Gavin, are you all right?" Daisy rested her hand on his shoulder.

He opened his eyes and turned over to look at her, hair splayed over the pillow and cheeks wearing the faintest trace of a flush, the loveliest of sights. "I'd say I'm a great deal better than all right, but then I just finished making love with Daisy Lake, the most sublime woman in the world."

He'd never known it was possible to feel this wholly, perfectly happy. He wished he might stop time long enough to bottle this moment, a perfect, golden memory he might take out over the years and relive at will.

If only life worked that way.

"Sublime, am I? I don't know about that, but I'm glad you like me, warts and all." Her tone was teasing but, in the dim light, he caught her studying him.

Hearing the open question in her voice, he hastened to reassure her. "I don't see any warts, only these—kisses from the moon." He ran the knuckles of one hand down the smattering of small, pale white scars on her flat and otherwise perfect abdomen, glad she wasn't entirely flawless. The small blemishes reminded him she was human, after all.

He felt her stiffen and stilled his hand. Gaze searching her face, he asked, "What is it, sweetheart?"

She shrugged, but the clouds in her eyes told him she was hiding something. "I suppose I'm like a cat. I don't much care for having my stomach stroked."

"Sorry." He drew his hand away, wondering what bad experience she might have had and whether or not she would ever trust him enough to tell him about it.

She sent him a quick, tense smile and reached for his retreating hand, laying it atop her mons. "All my other parts are fair game, however."

He smiled though something in her manner had shifted, setting him on his guard. Stroking her, he said, "So I've discovered. I'd be surprised to learn you harbored a single shy bone in the whole of that beautiful body of yours." In point, he was finding he loved how open and free she was, how entirely unfettered by inhibitions or false feelings both in and out of bed. Mere weeks ago he'd thought to if not bend her will, at least bring her about to a more conventional way of behaving, but now the prospect of altering anything about her struck him as the height of arrogance.

He laid a staying hand over one creamy shoulder. "By the by, I've no intention of marrying Isabel Duncan." He leaned over and ran his lips along the curve of her neck. "I far prefer this, *you*, just as you are."

She tilted her head back, leaning into him. "I'll never be that sort of woman, a proper English lady."

Gavin brushed his mouth over her ear. Pleased when she shivered, he slid an arm about her waist, drawing her back against him, and whispered, "I don't want a proper English lady. I want you just as you are."

She shifted to face him. "How can I be sure of that?"

"If anyone should be feeling unsure, I rather say it's me. If you'll recall, I was the one with the cold hands—and feet."

That softened her. "Oh, Gavin." She brought his palm to her lips. "Cold or warm, shaking or steady, yours are the hands I want touching me."

It was the closest to an admission of caring she'd come so far. Moved, Gavin kissed the tip of her nose. "I'm glad to hear you say so because you're the only woman I can imagine touching this way."

Her smile fell, her eyes taking on that icy glaze he hoped their lovemaking might have thawed. "You oughtn't to say such things."

She tried turning away again, but he caught her cheek in his hand. "The bald truth is you've ruined me for other women, Miss Lake. Ruined me entirely, and I'm very much afraid the damage you've wrought is irreparable. However shall I punish you?" He took his time, pretending to consider, giving her a chance to warm to the game. "Ah, yes, I could always lash these lovely slender wrists of yours to the bedposts, I suppose. Of course, if I did that, I would be deprived of your hands. And you have very talented hands, my darling, very clever fingers. Have you ever considered playing the piano?"

She looked up at him and laughed, the ice melting from her eyes, leaving them once again warm and glowing, and he knew that for the time at least he'd won her back from the darkness, back to him. "I'd rather play you, Mr. Carmichael. Your instrument may be in want of a bit of fine tuning, but all in all it's *coming* along quite nicely."

Daisy wasn't much of a believer in living by rules but there was one rule she prided herself on following as though it was carved in stone: never ever under any circumstance let a man hold you after sex. Letting a man hold you meant letting him inside not just your body but your head and quite possibly your heart. It was simply best not to go down that path. For that reason, Daisy had always held firm that none of her lovers should spend the night. Whether a man finished with her in an hour or fucked her straight through to dawn, after giving him a few minutes to recover his faculties, she handed him his trousers and pointed him to the door.

But this time was different, this time was a first. This time her lover was Gavin, and the thought of sending him back to his own bed was something she simply couldn't bring herself to do. It felt so very good, so very right to have him hold her, to trail her fingers down the length of his beautiful back and plant small, nuzzling kisses on his brow, the slope of his shoulder, even the tip of his aristocratic nose. And his lips . . . Dear Lord but she couldn't get enough of kissing him, first one corner of his mouth and then the other, the smooth seam, the sexy indentation cleaving his firm chin. Kissing Gavin was akin to taking that first draught from a cool mountain stream, impossible to quench the raging thirst with one sip or even two.

He cracked open an eye and looked over at her. "Penny for your thoughts."

She'd thought him asleep. Startled, she jerked her head from the pillow of his shoulder. "I was just thinking how warm you are, like a furnace." That much was the truth, although of course there was so very much more she might have said, including how dangerously easy it would be for her to get used to this, to having him in her bed and in her life.

"Is that a good thing or a bad thing?" The smile in his voice told her he knew what her answer would be and simply wanted to hear her say it.

"A good thing for me as I'm always cold."

He lifted his head from the pillow. "You're not ill, are you?"

"Oh, heavens, no, I'm healthy as a horse and always have been. It's only . . ."

"Tell me, won't you? You used to tell me everything when we were young."

Back then she'd confided in him completely, but

fifteen years was such a very long time ago. Deciding she could trust him this much at least, she said, "The first winter we were in Paris, it snowed so that the opera house where the Lakes worked closed its doors until the thaw. No performances meant none of the players were paid, and it wasn't long before we ran out of the funds for fuel. It was so cold inside our flat that my fingertips burned even though I wore mittens. Ever since, I can't abide the slightest chill, at least not without complaining bitterly. If I have my way, I'll keep the stove burning well into spring."

He slid an arm about her, drawing her back against the heat of his chest. "Oh, darling, I'll keep you safe and warm for as long as you let me."

Wrapped about him, Daisy tried to recapture her earlier ease only she couldn't seem to settle. Her thoughts kept circling back to the feral kitten she found in the alley behind their Paris flat, coaxed inside, and tamed so he came when called and took food out of her hand. Puss, she'd called him, after the Puss n' Boots character she so loved acting out at Roxbury House. The Lakes had insisted she release Puss when it came time to move on. He was an alley cat, after all, and would fend just fine on his own. The day before they left, she'd found him laid alongside their busy street, apparently struck dead by a passing carriage. Domestication had dulled the poor creature's wits so he could no longer shift for himself. Daisy had cried all the way from Paris to Reims, but the experience had taught her a valuable lesson.

Letting someone tame you and keep you safe and warm—in the end, there was a heavy price to be paid.

Gavin left her late that morning with a languorous kiss and the promise to do his utmost to hasten home for supper before she had to leave for her first rehearsal. Alone once more, Daisy's first clue something was different, something was wrong, came when upon rising she found herself putting off her bath because bathing meant washing away Gavin's scent. Ordinarily after a night of sweaty, acrobatic sex, she couldn't wait to wash. Even after emerging from the copper-lined tub, she kept coming back to the bed, snatching up swatches of the tumbled sheets and rubbing them against her cheek, inhaling deeply, closing her eyes and reliving every moment of their beautiful night together—how right he smelled, how wonderfully good he tasted.

Pathetic, Daisy, well and truly pathetic.

And yet she couldn't help feeling that more so than any bath making love with Gavin had somehow washed her clean.

Like the flames of the Great Fire which once had devoured

the capital city in four days and three nights, rumor soon spread throughout the London clubs, soirees, and sundry ladies "at-homes" that Gavin Carmichael, heretofore respectable barrister, heir to the St. John legacy, and frustratingly elusive bachelor, had taken an actress into keeping—and not any actress but the scandalous Parisian showgirl, Delilah du Lac. Gavin wasn't oblivious to the rumor, nor did he have to puzzle over its source. Since encountering her at the Claridge Hotel, Isabel Duncan obviously had been brisk and busy spreading her venom. It occasioned him no great surprise when later that week his grandfather stormed inside his dining room while he was sitting down to breakfast.

Ignoring him, St. John barked, "What the devil do you think you're about?"

Gavin set down his cutlery on the edge of his plate and replied, "At present I'm about breakfast. Would you care to join me?"

He counted himself fortunate Daisy hadn't yet come downstairs. Given the hours she kept, she likely wouldn't be up and about for another hour or more. He gestured to an empty chair. "Won't you sit down and have some breakfast?"

"Dash it, boy, don't play games with me. You know full well what I mean. By now, anyone in London who isn't wholly deaf, dumb, and blind knows you've taken an actress into keeping."

Rather than deny it, Gavin said, "Miss Lake is an

old friend. We spent more than a year together at Roxbury—"

"How many times do I have to tell you not to mention the name of that infernal place in my presence?"

Gavin promised himself that this time he would remain calm and collected, treat the present situation as
if it were a legal case and his grandfather the opposing
counsel. Yet the old man possessed a canny knack for
penetrating his armor to get at his most vulnerable places—and then twisting the knife for good measure.

He shot up from his seat. "Bloody fortunate for me
a certain gentleman named William Gladstone bore me
to that *infernal place;* otherwise I might be dead ere now
or worse, one of those poor charity wretches who live one
misstep away from the gallows."

The black scowl riding Maximilian St. John's brow
had terrified Gavin as a boy, but now the primary response it prompted was a deep-seated dislike. "Had your
mother been a dutiful daughter and married where she
should have, you would have been born in comfort and
safety."

Comfort and safety—Daisy's coming back into his
life had shown him how very much more there was to
feel from life than that. "My mother married for love as
I shall. For love, grandfather, or not at all."

"And I suppose you fancy yourself in love with this
. . . this *actress?*" Actress, the old man all but spat out
the word.

This time Gavin had the prudence not to answer, only met the question with silence and a straight on stare. Daisy was adamant that a proper future together was out of the question but were she to change her mind, might he consider marrying her after all? Until now, he'd relegated the prospect of any permanence between them to the realm of fantasy but, if given the opportunity to have more with her, would he find the courage to take it?

His silence seemed to siphon most of the energy from his grandfather's tirade. Gaze going to the door, he shook his head. "Young men will sow their wild oats and if you fancy doing so in your bachelorhood, I suppose I can't fault you for it overmuch. Truth be told, when I first heard the news, I was half relieved to find you were human after all. Keep your doxy so long as she amuses you, but for your family's sake as well as your own, leave off parading her about in public."

"Miss Lake isn't my doxy, and I resent you speaking of her as such."

His grandfather lifted one salt-and-pepper brow. "If not your mistress, then what precisely is the gal to you?"

What was Daisy to him? A lover who swore she would not fall in love with him? A childhood friend who guarded her secrets with the same ferocity with which a society mama guarded her debutante daughter's maidenhead? A protégée who more often than not was more teacher than pupil? How he missed those bygone days when she trusted him so completely she hadn't thought

twice before pouring out all the sad little secrets stored
in her soul. He'd been her friend, her confidant, and
her hero back then. They'd been too young to think of
physical love at the time, but had they stayed on at Roxbury House rather than her whisked away to France and
him shipped off to boarding school, he'd no doubt they
would have become lovers in time.

"I've answered that already. She's a friend, a very
dear friend."

"Friend, you say." His grandfather lifted a brow.
"Well, well, my boy, that's not what we called 'em in my
day, but I suppose it will serve."

Apparently Isabel Duncan's mischief making wasn't lim-
ited to gossip mongering.

Daisy received the summons from the London Vigilance Committee as one might receive a royal command.
She was to report to the Committee's board the next day
at five o'clock in the evening. The hearing would be held
in the Great Room at Caxton Hall in Westminster. The
charge: that her prior music hall performances contained
"lewd and lascivious acts" which threatened the public
morality and therefore made her unfit to be a player in
the company of a theater that had once held the royal
patent for producing "legitimate drama" in London.

The plaintiff was none other than Isabel Duncan.

Daisy received the missive while in rehearsal at Drury Lane. She lost no time in seeking out Sir Augustus. She found him in the manager's office pouring over the accounts ledger. He looked up, smiling when she entered. "Why, Daisy, this is a pleasant surprise."

"Not so pleasant for me." She handed him the summons so he could read it himself.

Looking up, his face was nearly as pale as the vellum sheet. "Dear God, what next?"

Taking it back from him, she asked, "What does this mean? Surely any ruling by this so-called Vigilance Committee isn't enforceable? Why waste time answering to a great lot of hypocrites? I've a mind to simply ignore it."

Grim-faced, the theater manager shook his head. "I'm afraid it's not that simple, m'dear. If you ignore them, they will organize a boycott of the play. Your career will be over before it has begun and the play will be called upon to close. No, you must answer the summons and find a way to ensure you're exonerated of the charge. Perhaps you could speak to that clever barrister chap, Mr. Carmichael, and see what he recommends? I don't like to think of replacing you but for the good of the theater, if I must, I must."

Daisy entered the assembly rooms at Caxton Hall, Gavin

by her side. Combing through the crowd, which must number several hundred, she wasn't really surprised to see Isabel Duncan sitting front and center of the packed auditorium. Isabel sent a smirk her way and then settled back in her seat.

Gavin squeezed her hand. "Don't let her rattle you."

"How can I help it? I feel as though she has not only my career but the fate of Drury Lane in her palm."

The seven-member committee of men and women sat about a square table except for the chairman who stood behind the podium, gavel at the ready. He called out, "Miss Daisy Lake, approach the platform, if you please."

Daisy leaned into Gavin and whispered, "Wish me luck."

"Just remember, you're not alone. I'm here."

She sent him a grateful smile. "Thank you." Leaving him to take his seat, she walked down the aisle of chairs and mounted the platform steps.

"For the record, please confirm that you are Daisy Lake also known as Delilah du Lac."

"Yes, I am she." She carried herself with great dignity, Gavin thought.

Balding and sour-faced, the chairman lost no time in calling the session to order. "The character of Dame Twankey was part of the variety show performance at The Palace, was it not?"

Wondering what a female impersonator's comic bit had to do with her, Daisy nodded. "Yes, that is true."

"Would it surprise you to know that the actor, or rather impersonator, who fills that role is homosexual?"

Daisy took a deep breath. How different London was from Paris where acceptance of a spectrum of sexual preferences and lifestyles was widespread. She thought for a moment and then answered, "*As You Like It,* much admired among Shakespeare's comedies, has the heroine, Rosalind, dressed in drag for most of the play. She even takes Ganymede as her alias, a veiled reference to a gelded horse or castrated young man. In Shakespeare's time, as I'm sure you know, women were prohibited from acting onstage. Rosalind would have been played by a young man affecting to be a young woman disguised as a young man. Is that truly so different from the present day pantomime dames?"

Good show, Daisy. Sitting out in the audience, Gavin felt his chest swell with pride.

The chairman moved on to the next question. "Miss Lake, in your previous variety hall act, you took Delilah du Lac as your stage name."

"Yes, I did."

"Doesn't the name Delilah, the Biblical temptress who brings Samson to ruin, strike you as an overly suggestive name to take for the stage?"

Daisy appeared to give the question serious thought. Tapping a finger against the side of her cheek as she had when Gavin had first seen her onstage at the supper club, it was obvious to him she was playing to the crowd. "I suppose I wanted to *suggest* that people should have a good time."

Titters traveled through the hall. Gavin tensed. *Have a care, Daisy.*

Several more questions were asked and each time Daisy answered with wit, aplomb, and honesty. Gavin had never been more proud of anyone in his life. To answer the charge of whether her act qualified as "lewd and lascivious" she was asked to sing a song from her supper club repertoire. Remembering the seductive heat of that performance, Gavin held his breath. Even dressed demurely, he didn't see how she could possibly carry it off.

"I should like to sing two songs, actually." There was a piano onstage. Facing out to the audience, she asked, "Does anyone here play?"

When no hands went up, Gavin reluctantly raised his. "I play a little."

Smiling, she beckoned him up onstage, putting him in mind of that first night at The Palace. What a long time ago that seemed.

Opening the portfolio she'd brought along, she handed him the sheet music. "This one first," she said, pointing to the score for a naughty number, "A Little of What You Fancy."

"Are you certain?" he asked.

She nodded. Flipping through, she marked her second selection. "Play this one last." It was the imminently respectable drawing room ballad, "Come into the Garden,

Maud."

Hoping she had a method to her apparent madness, Gavin took the sheet music and slipped behind the piano. Taking a deep breath, he began to play the raunchy burlesque number she selected.

She sang the racy song standing wooden as a statue and with a perfectly straight face. Afterward, she sang the ballad in such a seductive manner that, glancing out onto the audience, Gavin saw several men pull out handkerchiefs and mop their dripping brows.

The staid audience exploded in a fit of clapping. Smiling, Daisy dipped into a curtsy.

"You've made your point, Miss Lake." The chairman knocked his gavel, calling for order. "The complaint against Miss Daisy Lake is hereby dismissed."

CHAPTER TWELVE

"O, thou didst then ne'er love so heartily!
If thou remember'st not the slightest folly
That ever love did make thee run into,
Thou hast not loved . . . "
—WILLIAM SHAKESPEARE, Silvius,
As You Like It

Week Three:

With the Vigilance Committee business behind them, Gavin felt in a celebratory mood. His flat lay within walking distance of his office at the Inns of Court. When his client's trial was canceled at the last minute, he set his course for home, hoping he'd find a certain cinnamon-haired actress indoors. He didn't think Daisy had a rehearsal today. Even better it was Wednesday, the day Jamison took the train to Richmond to visit his ailing mother. He and Daisy would have the flat to themselves. They needn't confine themselves to the bedchambers but could make love in any room they pleased. The circumstances were perfectly aligned for a rainy afternoon spent in the most pleasant of ways. Only a fool would pass up such an opportunity.

That wasn't to say he didn't have stacks of legal briefs, depositions, and sundry client files gathering dust on his desk, for certainly he did. No matter how many hours he put in, there seemed to be an endless stream of lost souls in need of defending. But since Daisy's reentry into his life, work no longer occupied the epicenter of his universe. He was coming to suspect he used reading the law as a means for avoiding living altogether.

But such weighty introspections were best kept for another time and place, not when any minute now he would have a warm, willing woman in his arms. He entered the flat, stopping only long enough to shake out his umbrella and set his briefcase down inside the door. "Daisy, darling, I'm home."

He stripped off his soaked outer coat and tossed it over the back of a chair, too impatient to bother with hanging it up. When she still hadn't emerged to greet him, he went room to room calling her name. The last room he came to was hers. She still kept actor's hours, which meant she liked to stay up well into the night and then sleep well into the morning. On those days when a session with her acting coach or some other commitment forced her to rise early with the rest of the workaday world, she sometimes took a rest in the afternoon.

Wondering if she might be napping now, imagining the myriad ways he might go about waking her, he felt himself growing hard. He gave the perfunctory knock and when she didn't answer went inside anyway.

The room, including the unmade bed, was empty, leaving him to face the fact that fortune had not favored him as he'd hoped. It was a rare day he could break away and come home and the one time he had she'd gone out on some errand or appointment. Ah, well, that was life. A brisk walk back in the chilling drizzle would take care of the desire weighing between his legs, at least for the time being. Though he missed out on "lunch," there was always supper to which he might look forward, or rather the interval afterward. On second thought, hang supper. Who needed beefsteak and jacket potatoes when one could dine on ambrosia of sweet lips and silken skin?

Wondering if a perpetual state of lust wasn't bringing his brain to a state of mushy rot, he turned to go. He hesitated at the door, oddly unwilling to leave just yet. She'd occupied the room only a few weeks, and yet its four walls bore the indelible imprint of her presence as if she'd been its inmate for a year or more. Breathing in her scent, he found himself loath to leave. He must be far gone in love indeed for he found himself roaming the room, touching the things she recently touched— her pillow, which still bore the imprint of her head, the chased silver hand mirror and brush on her dresser, the latter's bristles threaded with a few cinnamon-colored strands of her hair, a dog-eared copy of *As You Like It* with her notes to herself scribbled in the margins. Wondering how she was coming along, he reached down to pick up the play when his gaze alighted on a folded sheet of cream-colored vellum covered with what looked to be the beginnings of a letter. He spotted the Paris direction and his heart fell.

A few weeks before he would have found the strength to let the thing lie where it was and leave the room. But that was before. Having Daisy in his life had taught him how susceptible he was to temptation in all its many forms. He picked up the letter and sat down with it on the edge of the bed.

My dearest darling Freddie,

London is a large, crowded city like Paris and yet so very unlike Paris I would risk running out of ink and paper if I attempted to write down all the many differences. People behave very properly here and even the nicer ones are more than a bit stiff. God willing, you will see it for yourself soon enough. In the meantime, my heart yearns to hear news of you. I want to know every thing you've been thinking and doing since I left you. The other day I counted and realized more than a month had passed since I last held you in my arms, and yet it feels like a year.

The letter, or at least what was so far written of it, ended there. Still it was enough to tell him that whoever Freddie was, he held Daisy's heart in the palm of his hand. Balling the missive into a tight fist, Gavin cursed himself for a fool. He'd been going about with his head in the clouds as if he were the love struck swain, Silvius, in that damned Shakespearean play Daisy was studying, and yet by her own admission she'd been counting the days until she could be with her Freddie again—and free of him. Should he really be surprised? Reviewing her recent behavior, not only the things she'd said and done but more importantly those she hadn't, he decided not. She as good as admitted the rumors about her didn't lie, that she'd been with men in France and not only a few. Not once had she made him so much as a single promise. Far from it, she was the one who insisted on limiting the terms of their living arrangement to one month in the first place. Now he knew why. Her lover was coming from Paris to join her and once their reunion was a *fait accompli*, she would have no more need of him. She would walk out of his life with nary a backward glance.

Possibly the worst part of the whole dismal affair was that Daisy hadn't lied to him, not really. Any lying that had taken place was by him. From the moment they'd shaken hands on their "arrangement," he'd done little else but deceive himself that once the agreed-upon month was past, he would have won her over. The passion between them had gone a long way in fermenting the lie. Even now when he was holding the black-and-white proof in his hand, he still couldn't wrap his mind about the humbling truth that she was already making plans to leave him for another man.

But there was one bittersweet pleasure left to him—confronting her and tossing the evidence of her duplicity back in her face. Wherever it was she'd gone off to, she had to return home eventually, and when she did she would find him ready and waiting. Who knew but if his acting abilities held out—and all lawyers had a touch of the thespian in them—he might try making her believe that he didn't give a damn, that he, too, was looking forward to being free.

If only he might convince himself as well.

When Daisy walked in from rehearsal late that afternoon, Gavin was sitting on the serpentine-backed parlor sofa apparently waiting for her. Despite the drizzling weather, she was in a fine mood. The run-through had gone splendidly and afterward she'd even done some shopping. When she came upon the blue felt bonnet trimmed with a black velvet band displayed in the window of a Mayfair millinery, she thought, *Freddie will adore this,* and that had settled it.

And now she'd come home to find Gavin waiting. She hadn't even slipped off her cloak and already she was wet for him. Anticipating several hours of uninterrupted lovemaking, she set the bandbox down and came over to kiss him. "What a lovely surprise."

He pulled back. "It's been quite a day for surprises

all around." He slammed his half-finished drink down on the table and stood.

Taking in his hard gaze, set jaw, and caustic tone, she gathered he was in a mood. "Gavin, whatever is the matter?"

"Who the devil is Freddie? Or should I say your 'dearest darling Freddie'?"

"I . . . I don't know what you're talking about," she lied, though not very convincingly. The tremble in her voice must be a dead giveaway.

Not wanting to meet his eye, she dropped her gaze and spotted the crumpled vellum in his fist. It took her a handful of seconds before it dawned on her just what it was he held. He'd found her half-finished letter to Freddie, the one it had never occurred to her to hide.

She lifted her chin and forced her gaze up to his, confident her face must appear as angry as his. "That is my private post. You had no right to read it, even less to rifle my room."

"I wasn't rifling your room. I came home early to make love to you. When you didn't answer my knock, I thought you must be napping and went inside, hoping to surprise you. Instead, I was the one who received the surprise in coming across this." He raked his gaze over her as though she were some creature, some *monster,* whose heinous motives he could scarcely fathom. "My God, Daisy, it wasn't as though you went to the trouble, or some might say the *decency* of hiding it."

"I didn't think I had to." She pinned him with a pointed look as though he were the one of them in the wrong.

In typical female fashion, she'd somehow managed to turn the tables on him and put him on the defensive—so much for his supposedly brilliant legal brain. When dealing with Daisy, soft emotion, not flinty logic, seemed to rule the day.

"I wouldn't have found the bloody thing if you hadn't left it sitting out with your script." Even with the evidence of her subterfuge in hand, it felt important she not think he stooped to going through her things. "I could almost believe you meant for me to find it and catch you out."

The barb hit home. Cheeks as bright pink as if he had slapped her, she said, "I don't have to justify my life to you, Gavin, or anyone else. As for our arrangement, I mean to pay you back every farthing you've spent on the acting lessons and the books and, well, all of it. It will take me a while, years I expect, but some day I will repay you."

Good God, she must be a cold-blooded creature to bring up the terms of their arrangement at a time such as this. She'd stolen his heart. Compared to that, what did he care for a few hundred pounds?

"I don't want money from you. Whatever help I've given you has been out of . . . friendship." He almost said love but stopped himself before he did and made himself look even more of a fool.

She shook her head, mouth pressed into a firm line. "I don't want you to think of me as your mistress or yourself as my keeper. Whatever we've done together in bed, whatever pleasure I've given you, I've done so of my own free will. I want you to think of our time together as a gift, not a business arrangement."

"I believe the fashionable term is 'protector' and I thought, hoped, to be more to you than that. What we had was never a business arrangement, not to me, but it hardly matters now. You and this . . . Freddie . . . have you some sort of understanding?" He despised himself for asking, and yet he quite simply had to know.

She shifted her gaze away. "I suppose you could call it that."

"What would you call it?"

She whipped her head about and met his gaze head on. "Love, Gavin. I call it love."

"I see. You love this . . . Freddie. And yet you let me make love to you. No, not let me, seduced me, made me so mad for you I'm all but your slave. What was the point of it all?"

She had the effrontery to shrug. "A month is a long time to sleep alone. I wanted you. You wanted me. If we choose to barter our bodies, why shouldn't we? We're both adults. Where's the harm?"

"Damn it, Daisy, when I came to your bed, it wasn't just to fuck you. It was to make love. I thought we were making love." *I thought we were falling in love. At least I was.*

"Men and women share their bodies all the time without involving love. Matters go off a good deal more smoothly without adding messy emotions to the mix, or so I've always found."

The latter allusion to all the other men in her life wasn't lost on him. Whoever Freddie was, he was hardly her first lover and, the steamy letter aside, Gavin was coming to think he wouldn't be her last, either.

Hurt beyond his wildest imagining, he rounded on her. "What are you so bloody afraid of? That we might be happy together, that I might actually love you?"

The questions rattled her, he could tell. She backed away, not because she was frightened of him—she must know by now he'd never harm her—but because he suddenly must have become a mirror for all the things about herself she didn't want to see.

"That's ridiculous. I'm not afraid of anything."

"Then prove it. Let me come with you when you tell this Freddie of yours it's over between you."

She shook her head, expression resolute. "I'm sorry, Gavin, truly I am. Hurting you was the very last thing I set out to do. You've been good to me. More than good, you've been the soul of generosity. I'm very grateful—"

He cut her off with a wave of his hand. "I'm not interested in your gratitude."

"I wish things might have turned out differently, but

I'm afraid it's too late. This time together will always be very special to me. If you believe nothing else, I hope you'll believe that."

A sudden fear seized him, for it sounded as if she meant to end things between them, not in another week, but then and there. That he might never again know the magic of touching her, tasting her, looking into her beautiful eyes and watching her come was almost more loss than even he could bear.

Anger was, if not an escape, a temporary refuge from the raw, bloody hurt. "I don't know why I should believe anything you say. Since we met again, virtually every word from your mouth has been a bald lie. And I swallowed them all, every bloody one, but then, you see, I wanted so very much to believe in you, in the possibility of us. And you made me believe. You didn't need those acting lessons after all. You're a natural actress or a born liar, take your pick. I'm supposed to be a rather smart fellow, and yet I started to believe we might have a chance at some sort of future together. But then you're very good, Daisy, not only the consummate actress but also a top-tier whore. Keep the money. You've more than earned it."

Faced with her open-mouthed stare, he felt as if there wasn't enough air in the flat to sustain the both of them. Though the room was on the chilly side, he was sweating as if the four walls were ablaze. "Stay or go as you please, it's your call." He brushed past her and headed for the door.

She took a halting step in his direction. "Gav, wait, don't go off, not like this."

He whirled on her. "Don't you ever call me that again, do you understand?" He stabbed a finger into the air to punctuate the point, vaguely aware that sweat had broken out all over his body. "Calling me familiar is a privilege of friendship. You, Miss Lake, no longer have that right."

He tore his coat from the back of a chair and walked out the door, letting it slam behind him.

Later that evening, Daisy sat tucked up in a quilt on the carpet in Gavin's study, settled in to wait. Sooner or later Gavin would have to come home and when he did she meant for them to talk. The younger, more impulsive Daisy would have packed her bags and left that very night, but at twenty-four she was getting too old for such offstage theatrics, or at least she liked to think so. Even though the Whitechapel flat was hers for another week, she wasn't foolish enough to venture forth in the infamous criminal district alone past dark with luggage in hand. But more than any practical considerations, she didn't really want to leave with their quarrel still burning like a red hot brand in her brain. Perhaps once Gavin came home from wherever he'd stormed off to, they might talk things over rationally and afterward part as friends?

She left the study door ajar on purpose so she'd be sure to hear him when he came in. Instead of a key turning in the lock, she heard the ubiquitous clearing of a throat she'd come to associate with household servants. A moment later, Jamison poked his silvered head inside. "Will you require anything further, Miss Daisy? I took the liberty of keeping your dinner warm. Shall I bring it to you before I retire?"

Even if he was only performing his servant's duty, he really was a very dear man. "No, thank you, Jamison," she said, forcing a smile. "I shall be fine until morning." Her stomach was too queasy with nerves to think about eating. At any rate, she'd grown accustomed to sitting down to supper with Gavin. Dining was but one of the many things she would miss sharing with him once she'd gone. The admission prompted a hitch in her heart.

He nodded and backed out into the hallway. "Very good, miss. Goodnight then."

"Goodnight."

The short interchange was fraught with meaning. The elocution practice sessions, torturous as they had been, had paid off, yet one more thing about which Gavin had been in the right. Anyone overhearing her say, "No, thank you, Jamison, I shall be fine until morning," might have mistaken her for a lady. Beyond her cultured tone, what astonished her most was how comfortable she felt in the role of mistress of the manor, or in the present case, mistress of the flat. Gavin's flat had come to feel entirely too much like a home, her home as well as his.

She pulled the blanket tighter about her and took another sip of the small sherry she'd poured. Gavin was a creature of habit, and no matter what hour he returned, the study would be his first stop. They would have their chat in a calmer frame of mind and tomorrow she would see about moving her things back to the Whitechapel flat and starting the search for a nicer place. It was better this way, really it was.

And yet if this was truly better, why did she feel so very badly?

Fencing had been Gavin's solace since his grandfather brought him back to London fifteen years before. The twice weekly lessons were one of the few aspects of his gentlemanly training in which he took actual pleasure, one of the few domains where he felt as though he could fulfill his grandfather's expectations and still be himself. The sport provided a vigorous physical workout while requiring a sense of timing, strategic thinking and, above all, self-control. Prior to Daisy and he becoming lovers, the sessions had provided a desperately needed release, the surest means of salvaging his sanity—or what was left of it.

When earlier that evening he stormed out of his flat, instead of drowning his sorrows in drink, he headed for his fencing club. Part gymnasium and part gathering spot, the London Fencing Club kept liberal hours to accommodate its members' varying needs and schedules. There was a small, informal sitting room where one might take refreshment after a match, and a telephone for guests' use. Gavin hesitated and then rang up Rourke, reaching his butler instead. The Scot wasn't in at present, but the butler promised to relay Gavin's message inviting him down.

Rourke must have sensed Gavin needed more than a sparring partner, for Gavin had just emerged from the changing room when the Scot strolled in. "I'm more of a wrestler, mind, but I'll do my level best not to disappoint."

Gavin sent him a grateful smile. "Thank you."

Ten minutes later, they faced each other in the fencing gallery, each attired in the requisite wire mesh mask, gloves, padded jacket, and white breeches and wielding foiled swords. It was the dinner hour, and they had the room to themselves.

Standing the requisite number of paces apart, Gavin lifted his foil, the tip hovering about Rourke's. *"En garde."*

A newcomer to the sport, Rourke couldn't come close to matching Gavin's skill, but he was a natural athlete and over the past year he'd picked up the basics easily enough. He was more than able to handle himself in a friendly sparring session.

Only Gavin wasn't feeling in a particularly friendly humor. He was out for blood, Freddie's blood. In the absence of knowing that supreme satisfaction, he meant to make his friend sweat out every second. They had the safeties on their swords and wore the full complement of protective gear. In such controlled circumstance, where was the harm in pretending?

They advanced and retreated, slashed and parried back and forth across the empty gallery, Gavin mounting an unforgiving assault.

"You must have had a pisser of a day," Rourke called out between labored breaths.

"You've no idea," Gavin shouted back and then lunged forward, aiming for the heart.

The next few minutes were reduced to clashing steel and heaving breaths punctuated with the occasional grunt or oath. Sweat streamed Gavin's face and neck, seeping through his white shirt into his padded doublet. Though he couldn't see his friend's face beneath the concealing mask, he knew Rourke would be in a similar state. At this point, he ordinarily backed off and gave the novice a chance to recover. Only in his mind it wasn't Rourke he was fighting but Daisy's lover, the faithless, feckless Freddie, nameless except for the absurd nickname. Gavin had never hated a fellow human being more.

Envisioning a fair-faced Adonis with a head of

honey-colored curls, he easily parried Rourke's clumsy thrust and then went in for the kill, the point of his blunted sword stabbing into the left side of the Scot's chest. Even with the safety on, such a blow would leave his friend with one hell of a bruise.

"Jaysus, Gav, have a care."

"Sorry," he said, though in reality he was too far gone to feel much of anything beyond an irrational anger, a heated hatred.

Men and women share their bodies all the time without involving love. Matters go off a good deal more smoothly without adding messy emotions to the mix, or so I've always found.

Daisy's callous declaration interspersed with the sounds of their sword play echoed in his ears. Of all the things she'd said to him earlier, hearing that their making love meant absolutely nothing to her hurt the very worst.

He went on full attack, thrusting ever harder and faster until he had Rourke backed into a corner. "Gav, what the devil's got into you, man? Leave off. It's just a practice match, for Christ's sake."

Too far gone to heed reason, Gavin went in for the kill. At the last minute, Rourke turned to the side, deflecting the blow and sending Gavin's sword stabbing air. Committed to the attack as he was, the momentum carried Gavin forward. He caught a flash of steel coming toward him and the next thing he knew, pain seared his left shoulder. Holding onto his sword, he staggered back.

"Gav, it was an accident, I swear it."

He slammed into the plaster wall, vaguely wondering why a bruise should hurt that much. A spangle of stars danced before his eyes. His knees buckled, sinking him as though he stepped upon quicksand.

He opened his eyes to find Rourke kneeling over him, his arm beneath Gavin's head the sole anchor in a suddenly topsy-turvy world. Visor up, the Scot's tanned face dripped with sweat. "The bloody foil slipped. Are you all right? Speak to me, man."

Gavin shook his head. So many questions and focusing on any one suddenly seemed to require a Herculean effort. He tried for a shrug, and the pain that small movement brought about would have sent him to his knees were he still standing.

Gavin moistened his dry lips. "It was my fault. I wouldn't leave off. Can't be as bad as it looks. Just a scratch, I'm sure."

Rourke's grim face told him it must look bad indeed. "You're bleeding like a stuck pig. I assume there's a surgeon on the premises?"

Gavin managed a nod, his head feeling as heavy as a stack of stones. Jaw clenched, he looked down and saw a scarlet stain spreading over the left side of his white doublet.

Unclenching Gavin's fingers from the sword hilt, Rourke gently drew away the weapon and set it safely on its side. "Stay here and try not to move. I'll go and fetch the doctor."

"Get me home, Rourke. I want to go home."

He started to add "home to Daisy" when a shaft of white hot pain shot into his shoulder, stealing his breath and his will. The next thing he knew, his friend's retreating form faded to black along with the rest of the empty room.

CHAPTER THIRTEEN

"Thou seest we are not all alone unhappy:
This wide and universal theater
Presents more woeful pageants than the scene
Wherein we play it."
—WILLIAM SHAKESPEARE, Duke Senior,
As You Like It

Daisy must have drifted off to sleep because the main door opening caused her to start. She blinked and looked about. Though she'd left the desk lamp alight, it still took her a full moment to remember where she was and why she was there. Gavin's study . . . They argued and then he walked out. He was hardly the first man to have done so and yet in his case she'd known he would come back eventually and not only because he lived there. It simply wasn't in his nature to walk away, and yet years before hadn't he done just that?

He was a boy, Daisy, a child the same as you. For-
give him and get on with your life. Her adoptive mother's
words came back to her, their commonsense wisdom a
balm to her bruised heart.

It had gotten chilly in the study. The blanket wrapped about her, she rose to stand on stiff legs. "Gavin,"
she called out in a carrying whisper, loud enough for him
to hear and yet not so loud as to wake the household,
or rather Jamison, whose snores sounded from the far
end of the hall. When no reply was forthcoming, she
wondered if he might be deliberately ignoring her. She
walked over to the door and poked her head out into the
hallway. "Gavin, is that you?"

"It's Rourke, but I've Gavin with me." The Scot, not
Gavin, called back to her from the outer room. "The
surgeon's seen to him and he'll be fine."

Surgeon! Daisy threw aside the blanket and hurried
into the parlor.

Rourke had Gavin propped against the door. Leaning heavily on their friend's arm, Gavin looked up at her
and tried for a smile. "Daisy, you're still here?" followed
by "Sorry . . . didn't mean to wake you." Instead of the
intermittent stammer, a slur thickened his speech.

She looked to Rourke. "Dear God, what's happened
to him? Is he drunk? Was there a fight?"

He'd left the flat in a temper, but Gavin still wasn't
the type to brawl. In the year they spent together at Rox-

bury House, she'd never known him to get into a single scrape whereas Rourke and Harry were always coming to her with blooded noses and blackened eyes.

"In a manner of speaking. Help me get him to bed, will you?"

"Of course. Follow me."

She led them down the hallway to Gavin's bed-chamber, the room in which they'd made a lifetime of memories in such a very short span. It was difficult to believe that just the night before he'd been glowing with health.

She turned up the bedside lamp and threw back the bedcovers. Together they eased Gavin onto the bed. Daisy was shocked to find he was as good as dead weight. His arm floundered when Rourke released them as though he had no more muscle mass than air.

As if reading her mind, Rourke said, "It's the laudanum. The club surgeon dosed him with it before beginning the stitching. Me, I would have called for whiskey instead. I only hope the wee quack dinna give him overmuch."

So that explained the slurred speech and limp muscles. "I want to hear everything from start to finish, and see you leave nothing out." She started on the buttons fronting Gavin's damp jacket.

"The doctor, Pritchard, says he'll call tomorrow morning. I gave him your direction. I hope that's all right."

"Of course." It struck her that even their friends

had begun treating her as though she were Gavin's wife rather than his lover. She ought to feel, if not annoyed, then trapped, only she felt neither. At what point had her gilded cage begun to feel like a happy home?

Gavin's jacket unbuttoned, she set to work on the shirt. She was easing it off his shoulders when he groaned. Looking down, Daisy saw the blood-soaked bandage covering a goodly portion of his left shoulder and felt her own blood turn to ice water.

She jerked her head to Rourke. "Dear God, what happened to him?"

Standing sheepishly by the bed, he could barely meet her gaze, putting her in mind of the boy from all those years ago. "We were fencing, just a friendly match, when the foil slipped off my sword just as I lunged forward and, well . . . I mean to stick with boxing from here on."

She nodded. Men could be such ridiculous creatures. "I don't suppose this doctor of yours left any instructions for his care?"

Her question apparently jiggled Rourke's memory. "Oh, aye, I'd as good as forgotten." He reached into his coat pocket and produced a small, brown glass vial. "It's laudanum. Should he wake up toward morning in pain, you're to give him one drop, no more and no less." Handing her the medicine, he turned to go.

She nodded. "Thank you for bringing him home." As soon as the words were out, it occurred to her how very much like a wife she must sound. *Bad, Daisy, bad.*

On the threshold, he turned back. "Daisy?"

She looked up from Gavin's sweat pearled face. "Yes, Patrick."

"His first words after being struck were for me to be sure to bring him back home."

Wondering where he was headed, she answered with a nod. "I'm sure he'll rest best in his own bed."

Rourke hesitated as if weighing whether or not to say more. "If you'll pardon my saying so, it wasna his bed he was missing. It was you."

❦

As much as Gavin appreciated Rourke bringing him home, now that he was tucked into bed that the night before he shared with Daisy, he couldn't wait for the Scot to leave so he might have her to himself. He knew he was supposed to be angry with her, he remembered that much, but for the life of him he couldn't remember why. Rourke had plied him with whiskey in preparation for the surgeon stitching up his shoulder and the subsequent dosing with laudanum had sent him over the edge of sobriety.

Hearing the outer door close, he let out a relieved sigh and looked up into the beautiful if strained face of his nurse. "Do you realize how close to the heart that blade struck?" she demanded, tone admonishing. "You might have been killed."

She bent over him to arrange his pillows, and he caught a glimpse of her breasts spilling out the top of her black silk wrapper. Remembering how perfectly they fitted his palms, how the hardened nipples felt against his fingers and lips and tongue, he realized he was randy as a game cock.

Straightening, she looked down on him, her lovely face serious. "Mind, you're not to stir from that bed, do you hear me? If you need anything in the middle of the night, I'll get it for you."

"How will you know what I need?" *You, I need you.*

She hesitated. "I'll know because I'll be right here beside you."

Things were definitely looking up. "In the bed?"

Even in his stupefied state, he marked how her gaze slid away. "No, I'll sleep in the chair. I wouldn't want to risk bumping your shoulder."

He'd be only too happy to have her bump into him though he wasn't thinking of his shoulder. "I'll have to bathe. You'll have to help me with that."

Turning back to him, she arched a brow. "It won't hurt you to go to bed dirty for one night."

"Now which of us is being a spoil sport?" Not giving her time to answer, he said, "You look fetching, by the way." He sent her a lopsided grin and reached for her hand.

She let him take it, and he realized it was cold as well as trembling. "Thank you."

"You're welcome." He rubbed his thumb along the seam of her palm, making sure to hit the sensitive spot he knew she liked. "Won't you rest beside me . . . in the bed, I mean?"

She shook her head, apparently adamant. "No."

"How about a goodnight kiss, then?"

She hesitated. "Are you certain you're up to it?"

Glancing down at the erection tenting his trousers, he said, "Yes."

"Very well." Bracing her hands on the mattress on either side of him, she leaned forward and kissed him, a soft, sweet brushing of her mouth over his. Pulling back to look down at him, she asked, "There, better now?"

He nodded and reached up to cup the back of her head. Threading his fingers through her loosened hair, he was aware that his eyelids felt suddenly very heavy as though weighted with sandbags. *The sand man's coming, Daisy. Best close your eyes or you might miss him,* he'd said to her on those nights at Roxbury House when she couldn't seem to settle. So many years spent, so much innocence lost. His eyes drifted shut. Holding **up** his arm suddenly took tremendous effort as though it were made of lead rather than flesh and bone. He dropped it, and it landed bouncing on the mattress like India rubber.

Daisy's hand, cool but no longer cold, descended on his brow, brushing back his hair. As if from the opposite end of a tunnel, he heard her say, "Good night, Gav."

Straightening, Daisy looked down. Gavin was

asleep, which was all to the good. Now that the drama of the moment was past, she realized she could do with a rest herself. Hearing he was hurt had affected her more than she would have thought. Though the wound was a nasty-looking gash, judging from the extent of the dressing, it could have been so very much worse. She hadn't exaggerated when she said he might have been killed. A world without Gavin Carmichael was a world she didn't care to imagine. Even though she meant for them to part ways at the month's end, it was important to her that she leave him alive and well. She pulled the covers up over him and turned down the lamp.

She bent and brushed a kiss across his brow. "Sleep well, Gav. Like as not you'll forget all this by morning, but I'll remember every bloody word you said as well as all the ones you thought to but didn't say."

She pulled the chair up to the bed and settled in to watch and wait.

The club physician, Dr. Pritchard, came the next morning to check on Gavin's progress. Jamison led him into the bedroom where Daisy sat beside the bed memorizing her lines from *As You Like It*. A sickroom might not be the ideal rehearsal hall but Gavin had insisted he didn't want to stall her progress and she was glad enough for the distraction. Neither of them made mention of the found letter, the ensuing argument, or the fact she still meant to leave in another week. Matters between them went back to more or less normal—on the surface anyway.

Small and squat, the doctor reminded Daisy of some species of plump game bird—a squab or perhaps a pigeon. She stood at the bedchamber door while he examined Gavin's wound and came forward when called to assist in changing the bloodied dressing for clean.

After they finished, Pritchard beckoned her out into the hallway. "Am I safe in assuming you are taking primary responsibility for his care?"

"Yes, that's so." If she had to stay past her final week to nurse him, she was prepared to do so.

Beyond a faint lifting of the brow, he gave no indication he found their situation scandalous or even untoward, but then in his profession, he must hear and see a great many situations that skirted the bounds of propriety. "In that case, see the wound is bathed and the dressing changed at least once a day. The salve I'm leaving you should ward off any infection, but if the site turns flush or putrid, send for me at once."

"I will, doctor. Thank you."

Gavin was lying propped up on a pillow, shirt off, the left side of his chest swathed in fresh bandages, when she reentered the room.

"What's that you've got there in your hand?"

She glanced down the brown glass vial. "Laudanum. I'm to give you some just before bed to help you sleep."

"I don't want it," he said, face fierce, and she suspected he must be recalling snippets of the previous night when his drugged state had loosened his tongue and his inhibitions. "You can toss it out for all I care."

Rather than argue with him, Daisy shrugged. "As you wish, but I'd just as soon keep it on hand."

She settled into the chair beside him and picked up the play script. She was searching the page for the place she'd left off when Gavin reached out, his hand going about her wrist. "Daisy, about the other night . . .?" Gaze locking on her face, he let the sentence fall off unfinished.

It had to happen sooner or later. The elephant in the room could not be ignored indefinitely. Stiffening, she looked up from the printed page. "Yes, Gavin?"

"I was heavily drugged before I ever left the club. I might as well have drunk a pint of scotch whiskey. On second thought, I may have done that, too." He sent her the lopsided grin of which she was growing entirely too fond.

She assumed he meant to revisit their argument over the letter. Tensing, she said, "You would have been in a great deal of pain otherwise."

He didn't debate the point. Instead, he said, "You're a very good nurse. I'm sure Dr. Pritchard couldn't have had a better helper had he called in a professional."

"Thank you." Seeing he wanted to talk, she set the script aside. "In theater companies this sort of accident happens more often than you might think."

"Really? I suppose I always assumed sword play was

just that, play."

He'd been making a great many assumptions lately, including that the passion and tenderness Daisy had shown him must mean she was as head-over-heels in love as he was. Clearly, that wasn't the case. And yet visceral instinct told him what they shared was real, that she cared for him even if that caring fell short of love. Should he cast that gift away because it didn't come with the fairytale ending he expected?

She shook her head. "Safeties come off sword tips all the time and even when one fights with prop weapons made of wood, much damage can be done if one isn't careful."

Looking into her lovely, fine-boned face, Gavin realized he wasn't ready to give up on her, not quite yet. He had another full week to change her mind and much might yet happen in that time. This Freddie of hers must be in Paris still. Why else would she bother with sending him a letter? Gavin reasoned he had two powerful advantages over his rival, proximity and history. He was here with Daisy in his London flat and though he certainly hadn't planned it thus, he suspected his injury meant they'd be spending even more time together. They spent a full year of their respective childhoods living in each other's pockets at Roxbury House, spending nearly every waking moment together. If that experience didn't serve as a foundation for a future, he couldn't say what would.

He shifted position to reach for the glass of water on the table beside his bed, wincing when the pain in his shoulder flared to life. All concern, Daisy shot up from her chair. Handing him the glass, she said, "Whatever needs fetching, I can do for you. Does your shoulder hurt you very badly?"

He shook his head. "Pain takes many forms. A nick in the shoulder is in no way the worst sort."

Leaning across the bed, she took his hand in hers. "Oh, Gavin, the very last thing I ever wanted to do is hurt you. Perhaps I shouldn't stay out the month. According to Dr. Pritchard, you'll be up and about in another day or so."

Touched by her tenderness, Gavin lifted her chin on the edge of his other hand, bringing her face up so their gazes met. "I want you to stay. We've another week by my reckoning, and I don't want to waste another single second of it."

Emerald eyes peered into his. "Are you sure?"

He nodded his head. "Yes." He hesitated and then added, "There's something else I'm quite sure of, too."

"What is that?"

"I very much want to make love to you."

She regarded him with shocked eyes. "But, Gavin, you're ill."

"And filthy, I know. You could bathe me first." He shot her a wink.

She hesitated. Eyes going from emerald to smoky

green, she shook her head. "Later, not just yet. I think I fancy you a bit dirty for a change. When Rourke brought you in last night, your shirt was soaked through with sweat and fragrant with musk." She leaned in and slid her tongue down the side of his neck. "Hmm, salty."

He was coming to appreciate her sensual nature. He smiled back at her. "In that case, climb atop and make love with me, Daisy. Lift up your skirts and take me inside you and ride me as though it was the very last time, and the very last day on earth, for both of us."

CHAPTER FOURTEEN

"Love is merely a madness, and, I tell you,
deserves as well a dark house and
a whip as madmen do . . ."
WILLIAM SHAKESPEARE, Rosalind,
As You Like It

Week Four:

They spent their final week more in bed than out of it and not because Gavin was ill. Dr. Pritchard's prognosis of a speedy recovery was borne out. The next day Gavin was up and about and the day after that he insisted on going into the office for part of the day. Though the wound still pained him, the discomfort wasn't great enough to warrant touching the laudanum the doctor had left behind. Making love to Daisy and then falling asleep in her arms was a far better tonic than any drug. She was the consummate lover, the ultimate fantasy woman. She had no inhibitions, or so it seemed to Gavin, and within the rich inner world into which his common sense had retreated he told himself her lack of reserve must be a measure of how deeply she cared for him.

And she must care for him, otherwise how could she respond to him with such . . . exuberance? The little moans and sighs might be manufactured, but he doubted even an actress as talented as Daisy could produce at will the warm stickiness he felt on his fingers and on his member when he entered her or the sudden shiver of inner muscles when she climaxed around him.

But as the days slipped away, doubts began to chip away at his bliss. In his weaker moments, he knew a keen and poisonous jealousy, an irrational hatred of everyone and anyone she'd been with before him, Freddie especially. When one evening he came home from the Garrick to find her waiting for him dressed only in black stockings, garters, and one of his silk cravats loosely knotted about her bare throat, his first thought was, "She's done this before for someone else." When she slid down the length of him and took him inside her mouth and deep into her throat, bringing him to the brink of climax and then back again, prolonging his pleasure until he thought he'd either explode or pass out, later he couldn't turn off his thoughts from wondering how many times she must have used that very same trick to pleasure other men. How else could she get it so completely, perfectly right?

For him nearly everything they did together was a marvel, a first, a minor miracle of sorts.

"I don't deserve you," she said one evening when they were alone in her room. She sat at her dressing table, brushing out her hair. "I'm not half good enough for you."

His eyes met hers in the mirror. "That's rubbish and you know it."

"Do I?" She set the brush down and turned to look at him. "I've been with a lot of men, you know. Not legion but a good many. I suppose you would say a lot."

There it was, out at last, the elephant in the room, the heretofore unspoken and unacknowledged barrier between them. "Why are you bringing this up now?" *Hypocrite!* As if her sexual history wasn't the instrument of his self-torture, the uppermost topic in his mind.

She shrugged. "One of us needs to. You've been punishing me for weeks now. Why not make it official?" She held up a palm, cutting off his protest. "Don't put yourself to the trouble of denying it. I've seen it in your eyes, a coldness that creeps in when you look at me after . . . after we've made love."

He blew out a breath. It was late, coming on eleven o'clock. The weekly dinner with his grandfather had been the usual tense inquisition. He was in no mood. "I know what this is about. You're worrying over your open-ing and now you're overwrought, imagining things." He didn't know who he was working hardest to convince, her or himself.

She rose from the cushioned bench. "Am I, Gavin? You take me to your bed, you enjoy the things we do there, you enjoy them very much, but afterward you can't keep from asking yourself how it is I came to be so bloody good at it. 'She's like a whore, my private whore,' you think to yourself, and then you hate yourself for thinking that, but you hate me more because you know it's more than half true."

He shook his head, feeling drained. "What . . . what is it you want me to say?"

"Why not the truth? Yes, let's have a good dose of that precious honesty you hold so dear."

"Very well, I hate it that you've been with other men, be it one other man or legion. There, happy now?"

She folded her arms over her breasts. "And?"

She was goading him but suddenly Gavin was past caring. He stalked over to her. "Sometimes I lie awake at night and play a game with myself, do a reckoning in my mind. 'She admits she's been with *a lot* of men. What does she mean by a lot?' I ask myself. Five? Ten? Dozens? I imagine you doing the same things you do with me to them. But by far the worst is when I imagine them touching you, making you moan and shift your hips and come just as you do for me, and it's then that I think perhaps, just perhaps, I'll go raving. Satisfied now you've made me say what you set out to hear?"

She shook her head. "No, Gavin, not satisfied. Relieved, perhaps. I'll leave now, of course."

He put his hands on her shoulders and hauled her up against his chest. "No, I don't want you to go."

"I'm not your prisoner, Gavin. You can't keep me here against my will. If I stay, the anger and resentment will only fester and grow into something worse. You'll end in hating me, hating us, and I don't think I could bear that. Better I go while there's still some beauty left to hold on to."

"I don't want memories, I want you."

She settled her gaze on his. "Punish me then."

"Sorry?"

"I said I want you to punish me. That way it will be over, done with, and we can both move on."

He dropped his hands to his sides. The very thought of hitting her made him feel sick. "I would never strike you. I would never strike any woman, but least of all you." He almost said "the woman I love" but stopped himself in time.

"For God's sake, Gavin, I'm not asking you to bloody my nose. Only take me across your lap and . . . spank me."

"And if I don't want to?"

"Trust me, Gavin, you want to. Afterward we'll both feel the better for it."

"Somehow I doubt that very much."

She turned, and after a moment's pause he followed

her to the bed. "Shall I sit on the edge, then? You've obviously more experience at this sort of thing than I, but then that's hardly news." The sharpness in his voice surprised him.

She winced, and it occurred to him that perhaps she was right. He'd been lashing out at her, punishing her with his words and his coldness for weeks now. Even when they made love, he was careful to hold a part of himself back. At least this, distasteful as it was to him, would be honest.

"You should sit wherever you like, if you like. If you'd prefer it, I could just bend over."

"No, no, if we're to do it, then let's do it properly. I'll sit," he answered, telling himself he was only humoring her.

He sat on the side of the bed and waited, his gaze following her as she moved about the room. She had been undressing when he'd come in earlier. She wore her black silk robe and her corset beneath. It occurred to him she'd probably already slipped off her knickers, and he felt himself harden.

"We were rehearsing earlier," she called over her shoulder in the process of checking the contents of a dresser drawer. "One of the props is a paddle. That should serve nicely, I think."

He looked at her, horrified. How desperate she must be for forgiveness, absolution, peace. "The flat of my hand is as far as I'm willing to go. Take it or leave it."

Without speaking, she walked over to him and climbed onto his lap, then arranged herself so she was stretched out face down across his thighs, and against his will he felt his cock coming to life. "You wanted to know how many men I've been with before you. Ask me now."

Distracted, he drew his gaze away from her buttocks pointing upward. "Sorry?"

She turned her head to the side and looked back at him. "If you ask me now, I'll have to tell you, won't I?"

Ah, now he saw how this game was to be played—one strike meted out for each transgression, measured violence to erase salacious sin, forgiveness purchased with pain.

"Very well, how many?"

Silence. Was she goading him?

"Five?" he suggested, aware his heartbeats had quickened.

"No, not five." Her coy tone grated on him. She might be lying prone beneath him and yet, once again, she was the one in control.

"Very well, then, more?"

He landed his hand on her bottom, a carefully controlled smack. She wasn't wearing panties, which of course meant she had staged this in advance just as she staged each and every intimate moment between them. She was playing another of her damned roles, playing him, and he felt a surge of raw anger even as she must feel his penis hardening beneath her.

"Is it ten, then?" His hand came down, this time hard enough for the sting to penetrate the silk of her robe. It felt good, he realized, but not quite good enough.

He threw up the robe, bunching the back of it in his hand. Firm, moon-pale buttocks stared back at him as if begging to be on the receiving end of his hand.

She flinched. "No."

"No more or no fewer?" He waited, hand raised.

"Fewer . . . I think."

"You *think*?" Could it be that taking a man into her body was of such little consequence she hadn't bothered to keep count? If so, then damn her, damn them both.

And then Gavin did what before he'd done only in his deepest, darkest fantasies. He cracked his palm down onto her left buttock and the aftershock quivered up to his elbow.

"Ouch!" She squirmed in his lap. Hands on the mattress, she tried to push herself up and off, but he would have none of it. The friction, along with the sounds of her quickened breathing and the rosy bloom of his hand-print were having an unexpected, powerful effect. Later he would feel guilt if not outright self-loathing, but what he felt at the moment was fully, powerfully aroused.

He brought his hand down once, twice, thrice in rapid succession, savoring the sound of flesh slapping, the residual sting singing across his palm.

"Eight," she gasped, bracing herself on her elbows and arching her back. "It was eight. Nine, counting you."

He heard the catch in her voice and this time when he brought his hand down, it landed lightly, almost a pat. "So I count, do I?"

She twisted her head around to look at him, eyes tear-bright. "You know you do."

"Then tell me so. Tell me I count, that I matter, and say it as though you mean it."

"I do . . . I do mean it. You've always mattered to me, Gavin, and you always will. You're my best friend in the world and . . . and so much more."

At her admission, Gavin felt his own breathing calming, his heart settling to a more placid rhythm. He smoothed a palm over her bottom, rosy red and hot with his handprints. He'd marked her, but it was he who was marked, branded, forever changed.

He pulled down her robe and lifted her to sit upright in his lap. Cradling her in the crook of his arm, he pressed his lips to her damp forehead. "Say it again, once more, so I can look into your eyes and know you mean it."

She reached for him, trembling fingers trailing the side of his face. "I've never had a lover who's meant half as much to me as you do."

"You might have just told me rather than put us both through . . . *this*."

She cast him a skeptical look. "Would you have believed me?"

He hesitated and then shook his head. Against all

odds, he found himself smiling. "No, I suppose not. In that case, stay with me, not only to see the week out but for always."

"I can't." She looked up at him, tears clumping her lashes.

Gavin swallowed hard. How he would bear letting her go again he couldn't begin to say. "Then be with me now." Gently, very gently, he lifted her off his lap and laid her down upon the bed.

Daisy had contrived the spanking scenario not because she was fond of pain but because she'd seen enough of the shadow side of human nature to know a physical remedy was the surest way to force Gavin to confront his conflicted feelings. What she hadn't counted on was her own powerful reaction. The episode had released something deep inside her, freeing her from guilt, freeing her to feel, really *feel,* for the first time in years. After years of living in a state of self-imposed numbness, the rush of emotion was a heady release.

"Let me love you, Daisy." Straddling her, Gavin looked up from kissing her between her tented legs.

She shifted her hips, the sheets a cool balm to her stinging bottom, the contrast between it and the wet silk of his tongue laving her labia almost more pleasure than she could bear. And then he surprised her with a light, purposive flick over just the right spot, sending her spiraling over the edge. She cried out her pleasure and instead of stopping he tongued her more.

She raised herself up on her elbows, her higher purpose drowned by the rush of physical sensation. "Gavin, please, no more. I can't bear it."

He stared up at her, eyes unrelenting, jaw set. "Oh, there's going to be more, Daisy, a great deal more whether you want it or not."

He flipped her over onto her stomach. There were no welts as there would have been had he used a cane or birch rod, just a great deal of warm, pink flesh.

"How pretty you are there," he said, and before she could answer he bent down and soothed the sensitized flesh with his lips, small soft kisses that raised gooseflesh and brought her clitoris to new swelling.

On her knees, she looked back at him over one creamy shoulder, her face the same pink flush as her bottom. "Gavin?"

He slid a hand to the front of her. Leaning in, he whispered, "I'm going to make you come again, Daisy. I'm going to make you come again and again, and no matter how you beg me, I'm not going to stop until you've given in."

The next morning Daisy sat alone at the breakfast table.

Shifting on her tender bottom, she pretended to rehearse her lines, but it was no use. Pushing the dog-eared script aside along with her plate of cold buttered toast, she admitted she couldn't get Gavin out of her mind. She thought if they made love enough, sooner or later she'd be sated and ready to move on. Unfortunately, the very opposite was proving to be true. She couldn't seem to get enough of him and she was beginning to worry that if she stayed with him much longer, she might not find the will to leave when the week was out.

Jamison interrupted her musings, carrying in the post. "A telegram came for you, miss."

"Thank you." Heart pounding, Daisy took the telegram and read,

Arrived Victoria Station. Stop. Can't wait to see you. Stop. Lake in St. James's Park today at noon? Stop. Freddie sends love. Stop. FL. Stop.

FL—Flora Lake. Her dear ones had arrived a week earlier than expected. Daisy held in a sigh, torn between happiness that she would see her parents and Freddie in a few short hours and sadness that their coming meant she would be saying goodbye to Gavin sooner than she planned. Ah, well, all things good and bad must end sooner or later, or so the old adage went. Rising, she shoved the telegram into her robe pocket and got up to dress, never realizing she missed her pocket, the paper hitting the floor instead.

Gavin was halfway to the office when he realized he left his legal brief lying on the breakfast table. Circling back home, he found it on his chair. He was on his way out when he caught sight of Mia batting something small and round about the floor.

"Let's see what you've brought me, you little huntress." He bent to take the dead mouse away from her and discovered it wasn't a mouse at all but a balled up piece of paper.

Straightening, he set the brief down and unfurled the telegram. He came to the name, Freddie, and a cold, glacial rage took possession of him. He shoved the message in his pocket and headed for Daisy's room. They met in the hallway.

Stepping back, she said, "Gavin, this is a surprise."

"Indeed." He ran his gaze over her. She looked very stylish in a canary yellow carriage dress with leg-o'mutton sleeves and a felt hat trimmed with just the right number of ostrich feathers.

"I was just going out for a bit," she said and he noted how her guilty gaze slid away.

"Fancy some company?" he asked, knowing already what her answer would be.

She hesitated. "I have a bit of shopping to do and then I've promised to have lunch with an old friend."

He stared at her, marveling at how glibly the lies

rolled off her tongue. "I didn't know you had any old friends here in London beyond Rourke and Hadrian and surely you don't mean them?"

"Did I say an old friend? Rather I meant to say a new friend, one of the actresses from the company. We thought it might be fun to have a bite and a chat outside the theater. It's always so hectic once we're there."

"Ah, I see." The hell of it was he truly did. "In that case, have a good day. I'll see you tonight?"

Again she gave a hint of hesitation that had his heart lurching. "Yes, tonight."

Heart drumming, he silently counted to ten and then followed her out onto the busy street.

Keeping his distance, Gavin followed Daisy to a confectionary in Piccadilly, a linen draper's in Pall Mall, and finally to St. James's Park. Ordinarily he wouldn't have minded. It was a perfect spring day, the sky a near cloudless canopy the color of cornflowers, the air a perfume of blooming shrubs and freshly mown grass, the sunshine of such a pure golden light you might be tempted to take off your clothes and bask in it. Hiding behind bushes and ducking behind buildings, Gavin felt as if the fine weather were mocking him. Instead of blue skies and golden sunlight, it should be dark, gray-clouded, and better yet, stormy—a mirror for his mood. Who would have ever thought Gavin Carmichael, top barrister and stellar citizen, would sink so low as stalking?

Daisy came to a bench within eyeshot of the Ornithological Society lodge overlooking the eastern portion of the lake. She looked from the left to the right and then sat down to wait. Toes tapping, she was either very impatient or very nervous or both, Gavin suspected. Suddenly she popped up from the bench seat, arm swinging back and forth in a wild wave as though hailing someone from the other side of the water. The lover, Freddie, must have arrived. Holding up a hand to shield his eyes from the sun, Gavin strained to get a good look at the cad.

The couple waving back and walking toward her looked to be in their sixties, perhaps older. A little dark-haired girl of seven or perhaps eight skipped along. Skirting the embankment, they each held one of her small hands though it was obvious she was impatient with their pace. The man walked stiffly, and then stopped as if to catch his breath. The woman broke hands with the little girl to wrap her arm about his thin shoulders. He pulled a handkerchief from his pocket and used it to cover his mouth. All at once, the little girl let out a squeal and sped forward.

"*Maman. Maman!*"

"Freddie!"

Freddie? Gavin swung his head back to Daisy. Skirts hiked high, she ran toward the child. Reaching her, she dropped to her knees on the path, and the little girl flew into her open arms.

"Oh, Freddie, darling, it's been an eternity. Have you been a good girl?" Not waiting for an answer, she rained kisses on the child's rosy cheeks and ran loving fingers through her head of shining dark curls.

Gavin stepped out into the open and walked toward them, his shadow falling over them. The last time he looked down on Daisy kneeling at his feet, she'd been pleasuring him with her mouth. That he should recall such a thing in the midst of the present tender moment struck him as a symptom of just how very low he'd sunk.

Daisy looked up and let out a start. Her smile slipped and the light left her eyes. If anything, he fancied she looked a little afraid. "Gavin, what are you doing here?"

"I hardly think I'm the one who need explain."

The little girl eased out of Daisy's arms and looked up at him with curious blue eyes. "Bonjour, monsieur."

"Bonjour, mademoiselle." Gavin knew a little French from his school days, enough to known *maman* was the word for mother.

Rising, Daisy said, "This is my daughter, Fredericka."

For an awkward several seconds, Gavin could do little more than stare from mother to child. The little girl was dark where Daisy was fair and yet she had Daisy's almond-shaped eyes, albeit blue rather than green, upturned nose, and distinctive upside down mouth.

Finding his voice, he said, "Hello, Fredericka. I am pleased to make your acquaintance."

She offered him her small hand and Gavin made a show of shaking it. Watching it disappear in his broad one, he felt a funny pull in the vicinity of his heart. "My mummy calls me by my grownup name, but everyone else calls me Freddie." Taking back her hand, she cocked her small face to the side and looked up at him as if he were a previously unknown insect or flower she was studying. "Are you my uncle, too?"

Unsure of how to answer that, Gavin turned to Daisy. Cheeks flushed, she gazed down at her daughter, trying for a smile. "This is Mr. Carmichael, darling. He and mummy have been friends since I was scarcely older than you are."

Now that the initial shock was fading, Gavin felt a rush of relief. If this charming child was Daisy's "dearest, darling Freddie," that must mean there was no lover, no serious attachment on either side of the Channel. And yet, if it were the case, why had Daisy taken such pains to lead him to believe there was?

A tug on his coat sleeve had him looking down. "I'll be eight years old next month." Beaming, the child— Freddie—held up the requisite number of fingers.

Daisy cast him a nervous smile. "Turning eight is quite an accomplishment."

"Indeed." Hurt seeped in to fill the void where shock had resided. To have kept up such a ruse, Daisy must have been desperate to rid herself of him.

The older couple reached them, the man leaning heavily on his wife's arm. From his grayish complexion and wheezing breaths, Gavin saw he wasn't well. Daisy stepped back to make the introductions. "These are my adoptive parents, Bob and Flora Lake. Mum, Dad, this is my . . . friend, Gavin Carmichael."

The widening of the older woman's eyes behind the wire-framed spectacles must mean his name was known to her. Wondering what Daisy might have said about him, he stepped forward and shook hands. Turning back to Daisy, he said through set teeth, "A word with you, if you please, before I leave you to your family."

Letting go of her husband's arm, Flora came forward. "Oh, pray don't rush off on our account, Mr. Carmichael. We were just about to search out a teashop and have a cup. Won't you join us?"

Daisy shot her adoptive mother a warning look, and catching it out of the corner of his eye, Gavin said, "I don't think so, but I thank you for your kind invitation."

He turned to Daisy and offered his arm. Unless she wanted to make a scene in front of her family, she would have no choice but to take it. Not giving her the chance to say no, he steered her off the path. Turning his back to screen the staring eyes monitoring their every move, he dropped his voice and demanded, "Why did you let me go on believing Freddie was your lover? Why didn't you tell me the bloody truth for once?"

She lifted her chin. "Why should I? It's not as if I have to apologize for my life to anyone—and certainly not to you, of all people." He opened his mouth to demand just what she meant by that when she cut him off. "Besides, you've been willing enough to believe the worst of me ever since you saw me in that club."

"Perhaps it has something to do with the fact you were parading about onstage more than half-naked before a hundred-odd men like a . . . " He stopped himself.

"Like a whore?" Daisy hauled back her hand and brought it hard across his cheek.

From behind them, a woman, Flora, shouted, "Daisy!" but neither of them paid her any heed.

Rubbing his smarting jaw, Gavin looked down at her and said, "Feel better?"

She shook her head, eyes bright with tears she was too stubborn to shed. "Why did you have to follow me? Why couldn't you just leave me bloody well alone? We're not good for each other, Gavin, not anymore. Can't you see that?"

They had been good for each other, or at least they might have been if Daisy would have only given him a chance to love her. As it was, there was no more left to be said between them—beyond goodbye. Reaching down, he took hold of her shoulders and hauled her up against him, crushing her mouth to his in a bruising, breath-stealing kiss. Setting her from him, he looked down at her startled eyes and flushed cheeks and swollen mouth and wished to God that someday he might know the peace of truly hating her.

"Have no worries, Miss Lake. From here on, you shall receive no more unwanted attention from me."

He turned on his heel and started toward the park gate. For an absurd few seconds, Daisy had to hold herself from running after him. But she was right. There was too much unhealed hurt between them. Even if it might be healed, they were too different, their lives were too set to ever come together as more than casual lovers, and in the end even that had proven too difficult to carry out.

Flora came up beside her. "What was that all about?"

Daisy shook her head and looked away, willing the tears in her eyes to dry. "Not now, Mum."

Flora arched a dark brow and regarded her adopted daughter. She loved Daisy as dearly as if she were her own flesh and blood, but she'd long ago given up on try-ing to shape her into the image of the little girl she and Bob had lost. Daisy was like a strong wind whipping through a stand of trees or a ship's sail. You couldn't control it. You simply had to accept it for what it was and hope that in the end it landed you in a good place.

Daisy would confide in her own time and not a mo-ment sooner. She wrapped her arm about her daughter's slender waist and led her back toward Bob and Freddie, the latter bursting with energy and eager to get on with the day. "In that case, let's see about that tea."

CHAPTER FIFTEEN

"The fool doth think he is wise,
but the wise man knows himself to be a fool."
—WILLIAM SHAKESPEARE, Touchstone in
As You Like It

Daisy was devastated by Gavin's walking away, more devastated than she imagined she might be ever again. Not even Freddie's father taking off upon learning she was pregnant came close to hurting this much. When her other liaisons ended, it was usually with a minimum of bother and a suitably expensive parting gift. No lover from her past had managed to make her feel so wholly miserable, so entirely lost.

Never had she imagined Gavin following her to the park and confronting her in front of her family. That he staged a scene in front of an impressionable child seemed an almost unpardonable sin. She hadn't felt such cutting betrayal since she'd finally given up on him answering any of her letters. The irony was that just when she'd begun to drop her guard, to consider he might really be different from other men she knew, he'd shown himself to be cut from the same cloth. Like them, he didn't care to be saddled with another man's bastard—even if Freddie happened to be the most beautiful, wonderful little girl on the earth.

For Freddie's sake, she kept her emotions in check for the next few hours, through the romp in the park, the outing to the teashop for a cup and a sweet, and finally the stop-over to pick up her things from Gavin's. More than once throughout the day she caught Flora's eye on her, but fortunately Freddie kept up such a stream of chatter she was spared having to answer any questions, at least of the probing, grown-up sort. Once she settled them all into the Whitechapel flat, however, she couldn't hold her feelings in any longer. She hurled a teapot and several vases, all gifts from former lovers, to the far side of the room. Afterward she fled to her bedroom and let the tears flow.

She wasn't really surprised when the soft knock sounded outside her door. Lifting her head from the sopping pillow, she called out, "I'm having a rest. I'll . . . I'll be out in a bit."

"In that case, I'll come in." It was Flora, of course.

She took one look at Daisy and settled her plump form on the side of the bed. "There, there, my dear, no more tears. You'll be puffy-eyed for your rehearsal." Over tea, Daisy had told them all about her winning the part of Rosalind in *As You Like It*.

"I don't care how I look," Daisy said and though a certain degree of vanity was part of her nature, it was more or less the truth. Gavin wouldn't be there to see her and there was no one else for whom she cared to look pretty. After that day, he'd likely not want to lay eyes on her ever again.

"You've had a row with your young man is all. You'll patch things up."

Daisy shook her head. "Not this time. I have a child, an illegitimate child, something someone like Gavin can't begin to accept or understand. He's washed his hands of me. I disgust him as though I was the lowest of whores."

Smoothing back the hair from Daisy's damp brow, Flora shook her head. "I have an inkling your Mr. Carmichael is made of sterner stuff than that."

"He's not my Mr. Carmichael, at least not any more. Oh, Mum, it's all such a mess."

"In that case, begin at the beginning, and we'll sort it out from there."

So much had happened over the past weeks Daisy scarcely knew where to begin. "We quarreled."

"I saw as much. What over?"

"He thought . . . that is to say, he got it into his head I'd a lover coming over from France."

"What rubbish. You most certainly don't—do you?"

Daisy shook her head. "No, of course not."

"Then why ever should he think that?" Flora asked in the same tone she used when as a child Daisy had been hiding some mischief.

"Because . . . well, he came across a letter I was writing to Freddie and assumed she was a 'he.'"

"I see. Well, small wonder he was upset at first but naturally you set him straight . . . didn't you?"

Daisy hesitated and then answered with a miserable shake of her head. "Since he seemed so hell bent on believing me no better than I should be, I let him go on thinking what he would."

Flora's eyes flew open. "Oh, Daisy, why ever didn't you simply tell him the truth?"

"Once he learned I had a daughter, a *bastard* daughter, he was bound to leave anyway. I thought if I let him go on believing there was someone else, someone coming over from France to meet me, we'd end the affair before anyone got hurt."

Flora arched a salt-and-pepper brow. "Is it him you were afraid might be hurt . . . or you?"

"Both, I suppose. Oh, why couldn't matters between us run their natural course and fizzle before you all arrived?"

"Perhaps the natural course for the pair of you isn't

for things to fizzle at all but for the bond to grow stronger with time—if only you'll put aside your pride and fears and let someone love you."

Gavin's words came back to her. *What are you so afraid of? That we might be happy? That I might actually love you?*

"My dear, the plain truth is you've been pushing people away all your young life and while I, of all people, can't fault you for it given the sad start you had, it's time to turn over a new leaf."

Raising herself up on her elbows, Daisy asked, "I don't really push people away . . . do I?"

"Daisy, dear, surely you already know the answer to that? Why, when Papa and I first glimpsed you, we fell in love with you straightaway, but you were considerably less charmed by us. If I had a penny for every time you swore you hated us for taking you away from your friends, I'd be a wealthy enough woman to keep us all. You ran off a score of times that first year, once after we'd crossed the Channel to France."

Too weary to argue, Daisy dropped back down on the mattress. "What does it all matter now? What's past is past and Gavin is gone."

"I'd say it must matter a great deal or else you wouldn't be closeted in your bedroom crying buckets onto your pillow."

Daisy fitted a hand over her pounding forehead. If anyone had told her being a grown woman would be so complicated, she would have gladly stayed a little girl for-ever. "Letting him think I had a lover back in France seemed so much simpler. It's not entirely a lie. There've been men since Freddie's father, as well you know."

Flora stroked a soothing hand over her brow, mak-ing her feel like a beloved child again, comforted and cherished. "My dear, I love you to bits, you know I do, but this shading of the truth simply must stop. If you keep on this path, you'll only make yourself miserable and everyone who loves you miserable into the bargain, including Mr. Carmichael."

"I only did so to keep him at arm's length."

"At arm's length, why, my dear, you've pushed him a great deal farther away than that. At this rate, there'll be the great sea to separate the two of you once again—that and your foolish pride. Had you been honest about Fred-die when he first came upon the letter, he might have had some time to warm up to the idea."

"It's too late now. He loathes me."

Flora shook her head. "Though I only met the man for a few moments and under the worst of circumstances, I'm sure you couldn't be more wrong. What you saw in his face wasn't loathing but a feeling of betrayal, the keenest sort of pain, as well you know. Mr. Carmichael loves you, Daisy. A man doesn't turn his life inside out for a woman he cares for only mildly or not at all. To wound him as you have, he must love you very much."

Gavin hadn't felt so betrayed since the headmaster at Roxbury House turned him over to his grandfather fifteen years before. Looking back on that experience through adult eyes, he saw the man hadn't had a choice. Daisy, on the other hand, had a plethora of choices—and at every turn or so it seemed she'd chosen to deceive him.

It had been a shock to discover she had a love child, but what hurt him most was that she kept such a profound part of herself as motherhood secret from him. No, not a secret—a lie. It was clear she didn't trust him enough, let alone love him enough, to share her life with him. Feeling as though his heart was being wrenched from his chest, he did what he hadn't done since his university years. He went out to a pub and got rip roaring drunk.

Hours later, the barkeep leaned over the scarred wood of the bar and said, "It's coming on closing time, mate."

"I wanna another drink." Gavin clanked his almost empty mug, adding to the spillage.

The barkeep shook his bullet-shaped head. "'Ave it somewhere else. We're closing, so shove off."

Gavin slid off the stool. His weaving feet took him through the smoky taproom to the outside. Once on the street, he started walking and ended up on Rourke's doorstep. As part of his search for a society bride, Rourke had been assembling the gentlemanly trappings money could buy, including a smart townhouse in Hanover Square, one of Mayfair's more fashionable neighborhoods. Eschewing the brass door knocker, Gavin banged his fists upon the lacquered wood.

A butler in nightcap and robe finally answered. "I'm sorry but Mr. O'Rourke is not receiving callers."

Rourke's mussed ginger-colored head and broad shoulders appeared in the doorframe. "That's all right, Sylvester. Mr. Carmichael is a mate of mine."

Gavin staggered inside. Gripping the carved stair banister to steady himself, he gathered a vague impression of walls bedecked in tooled leather, gas lit sconces, and plush Persian carpets. He tried whistling only to find he'd forgotten how.

Rourke closed the door and regarded him with astonished eyes. "Gav, you're drunk."

"Correction, I'm *very* drunk." He bobbed his head and nearly fell forward.

Rourke grabbed him. Draping a steadying arm about his shoulders, he guided him through the hallway. Shooting a look over his shoulder, he called back, "Sylvester, send us up a pot of coffee as strong and black as you can find."

"Right, sir," the butler said and disappeared in the direction of what must be the kitchen.

Gavin shook his spinning head. The evening, like the rest of his life, wasn't going at all as he'd planned. "Don't want coffee, want another drink. Got any . . . got any scotch?"

Rourke steered them inside his study. "None for you, I'm afraid."

"A Scot without any Scotch." For whatever reason, that struck Gavin as exceedingly droll. He collapsed into a leather-covered wing chair, roaring with laughter.

He opened his parched mouth to demand a drink a second time when nausea hit him like a fist in the gut. "Water . . ."

Rourke slipped off the edge of the desk and stood. "You want a glass of water?"

Gavin shook his head, the study seesawing. "Water . . . closet."

"You need to use the WC, man?" Rourke's eyes grew big at the same time another wave of sickness broke over Gavin. "Sylvester!"

"I knew I shouldn't have spent a wee fortune on carpeting," Rourke remarked some time later. He handed over the bucket and sponge to Sylvester and rose from his knees.

Sober, albeit with a thrumming head, Gavin reached a shaking hand for the coffee cup from the tray Sylvester had just carried in. He took a scalding swallow and said, "I'll replace it. You've only to tell me where you purchased it."

Sitting back against the desk, Rourke shrugged.

"Dinna fash yourself. By the looks of it, your belly was empty save for ale and gin. If anything, I think that spot's the cleanest of them all." Turning back to Gavin, he added, "So, are you going to tell me why someone who's always sober as a judge—or a top notch barrister of Her Majesty's Queen's Court, I should say—suddenly decided to get stinking drunk, or am I to play guessing games into the wee hours? Come to think of it, it *is* the wee hours." He lifted a broad-backed hand to his mouth and yawned behind it.

"It's Daisy."

"Now, there's a shock."

Gavin whipped his head about. "What is that supposed to mean?"

Rourke looked up from pouring a dram of whiskey into his coffee cup. "Only that everything's been about Daisy since she turned up again. It's amazing to me that one wee woman can be the cause for so much mischief."

Gavin swallowed more coffee, the scalding chicory blending with the bile scoring his throat. "Mark my words, your day will come."

Rourke took a long swig of the whiskey-laced coffee. "Maybe, maybe not. I'm betting on the latter but, for the present moment, the subject of this conversation is you. What's the trouble, man?"

"She's lied to me—again. Last week I found a letter she was writing to someone named Freddie. Naturally, I assumed Freddie was a man, her lover."

"Naturally."

"As it turns out, Freddie is Fredericka, Daisy's daughter."

"Bonny name." Rourke didn't look nearly as shocked as Gavin thought he should.

"The very worst part is that when I confronted Daisy with the letter, she let me go on thinking Freddie was a man, a lover."

"Did she? Sounds to me like maybe she was scared to come to you with the truth. I wonder why that might be, hmm?"

Gavin didn't much care for the Scot's tone of voice. He'd come in search of a friendly ear to bend, a sympathetic shoulder, and instead he'd gotten what must be the world's worst coffee—and what was beginning to feel suspiciously like a lecture.

"Suffice it to say she's not the same sweet girl we knew in Roxbury House."

Rourke shrugged. "I wouldn't expect her to be. For one thing, she's a grown woman, not a girl. For another, life has a way of marking us all. Daisy's spent the past fifteen or so years in and out of Paris playhouses, not convents in the country. Anyone who takes the name Delilah can be counted on to have had . . . *experiences*, shall we say. Mind, you knew the rumors before she ever stepped out on that stage."

"That was before I knew Delilah was Daisy or rather vice versa."

"Must be a family trait?" Rourke murmured beneath his breath.

The remark hit Gavin squarely on his softest, weakest spot. "What is that supposed to mean?"

"Oh, I was only wondering aloud whether you and your grandsire are so verra different after all. I mean, it looks to me as if the both of you have verra high, some might say *lofty* expectations for the loved ones in your lives. Daisy's disappointed you, but is it her current actions you canna abide or the parts of her past she canna change?"

"She lied to me."

"Daisy's disappointed you, fair enough. You canna change what's past, but you can decide where you go from here. Do you turn your back on her and walk away, cut her out of your life as your grandsire did your mum? Or do you go back and fight for her? Were I you, I'd tie her up, sit on her if need be until she tells you why she's acted as she has."

"What possible excuse can there be?"

Rourke shrugged. "Who knows why any of us do what we do? Maybe she was afraid of getting hurt? Maybe the other men she's known have turned tail once they found out about the wee lassie and she feared you'd do the same? People are no perfect, Gavin, not Daisy and not even you. Sure you'll never find out the answer unless you ask her."

Gavin rose to leave, the ache in his head second to

the ache in his heart. Rourke called him back. "Gav?"

Gavin turned about. "Yes?"

"One more thing occurs to me."

Gavin groaned. "I'm not sure I can absorb much more self-reflection at the moment."

"Nothing profound, just a wee afterthought. Daisy let you believe Freddie was her lover, aye?" Gavin nodded. "If she had to invent a lover, that must mean she doesna have a lover . . . other than you?"

When Gavin walked out of Rourke's, the first streaks of daylight were slicing through the fog. On the hansom ride home, he allowed Rourke might have a point. He had always detested his grandfather's rigidity, his absolute belief that he and he alone knew what was best. But isn't that how he behaved toward Daisy? He discouraged her from trying out for the latest Gilbert & Sullivan production because, in his estimation, operetta wasn't proper theater. When she finally came up with something, in this case, an illegitimate daughter, that he could neither manage nor wish away, he'd as good as walked out of her life.

He had to see her. But when he reached his flat, a grim-faced Jamison met him at the door. "Where is Daisy . . . Miss Lake, I mean?"

The butler shook his head. "Gone, sir."

"What do you mean gone?" It was all Gavin could do to keep himself from shaking the information out of the older man.

"She packed her bags and left while you were out the other day."

Pushing past the butler, Gavin raced to Daisy's room. It was empty and depressingly neat except for Mia who lay stretched out across the foot of the bed. In her short time there, Daisy had even managed to win over his cat.

Sitting on the edge of the bed stroking Mia's fur, the unnatural quiet churning about him, Gavin forced himself to consider what Rourke had said. Was he more like his grandfather than he might care to admit? Like the old man, was he rigid and unforgiving? Did he hold people to an impossible standard, starting with himself, and then punish them when they invariably failed? He'd faulted Daisy for not coming to him with the truth but if she had, how accepting would he have been?

Jamison stuck his head in the doorway. "If you'll pardon my intrusion, sir, I thought you might wish to have this."

Lifting his head from his hands, Gavin regarded the folded paper Jamison held out. "What is it? Never say it's another letter."

"It's Miss Lake's direction. I, er . . . overheard her mention it to her parents when she was packing and took the liberty of writing it down."

For the first time that morning, Gavin smiled. Taking the folded paper, he said, "Jamison, you are worth your weight in gold. However much it is I pay you in salary, consider it doubled."

The butler blushed but he looked well-pleased. "Bring Miss Lake home, sir. I shall consider that reward enough."

CHAPTER SIXTEEN

"Speak you so gently?
Pardon me, I pray you:
I thought that all things had been savage here,
And therefore put I on the countenance of
stern commandment."
—WILLIAM SHAKESPEARE, Orlando,
As You Like It

The rooms Daisy had let were off of Mitre Square in Aldergate, the scene of one of the Ripper's more grisly murders a mere two years before. Once his hired hansom turned off the heavily trafficked Whitechapel High Street and deposited him in St. James's Place, Gavin found himself stepping over drunkards and digging into his pockets for spare coins to give the beggars who approached. Taking in the tempo of the neighborhood, he worried about her coming home from the theater at night by herself. Surely this was no place to bring up a child.

The flat she rented set atop a bakery. He walked up the ladder steps, the wholesome aroma of oven-fresh bread at odds with the foulness of rotting garbage and piss. In the absence of a door knocker, he rapped his gloved knuckles upon the peeling paint.

Daisy answered the door, a look of surprise on her face. Hair pinned into a haphazard knot and lovely, long-limbed body ensconced in a loosely belted black silk dressing gown, she looked as though she'd just risen though it was nearing noon. Following closely on the heels of that observation was the worry she might not be alone, that he might have interrupted . . . *something* . . . but the misery reflected in the hollow-eyed gaze meeting his put that fear at least to rest.

"Gavin, what the devil are you doing here?" Not the most promising of greetings, but at least she wasn't slamming the door in his face, not yet at any rate.

From within, an older woman's voice called out, "Daisy, dear, aren't you going to invite your gentleman caller inside?"

Saved from floundering, Gavin looked beyond Daisy's slender shoulder and saw the pleasant-faced matriarch he remembered from the park. "Good day, madam."

"Best call me Flora." She nudged Daisy to the side and waved him in. "Bob, look who's come to call." She addressed herself to the thin, gray-complexioned man seated on the sofa, a blanket about his knees.

Crossing inside the narrow threshold, Gavin hunkered down to avoid scraping his head on the low hanging lintel. "I am pleased to meet you again, sir." He reached to shake the man's hand, belatedly remembering the slightly wilted bouquet of field daisies he purchased from a street corner flower seller.

Flora snatched them up. "Oh, why, these are lovely. Aren't they lovely, Daisy?" Flora held them up to be admired as though they were the finest long-stemmed roses. When Daisy didn't answer beyond a nod, she added, "I'll just go and put these in some water and put on my fine new kettle for tea." Gaze shifting to Daisy, she added, "Dearest, why don't you go and put on one of your pretty morning frocks and comb out your hair. Papa and I will keep Mr. Carmichael company whilst he waits."

Daisy hesitated. Tossing her adoptive mother a glare, she exited from the room.

"Won't you take a seat, Mr. Carmichael? I'll be back in two shakes of a lamb's tail with that tea." Round cheeks red as apples, Flora Lake scurried off in the direction of what must serve as the kitchen.

Gavin accepted a seat on the sofa next to Daisy's adoptive father. The peeling plasterwork, bare floors, and threadbare furniture brought to mind the flat his family had let when he was growing up. Holding his hat in his lap, he acknowledged it had been a long time since he'd felt quite this uncomfortable. Though he loved Daisy and had every intention of making her his wife once he got past her stubbornness, the fact remained he'd spent the better part of the past month bedding her. He found it difficult to look Bob Lake in the eye. Conversation between the two men did not come easily.

"Are you a rugby man?" Bob asked at length, tenting his fingers and twiddling his thumbs.

"Pardon?"

"Do you follow the matches?"

Gavin hesitated, wondering where this was leading. "I captained the team when I was at university, but that was quite a while ago."

"I'm a boxer myself though you wouldn't know it to look at me now. The consumption's winnowed me down to skin and bones." Given the wracking cough and un-natural pallor, Gavin suspected that might be the case. He nodded his sympathy. "Bare knuckles boxing was my specialty," Bob continued, eyes shining at the memory of those halcyon days. "I did a stint in Her Majesty's navy when I was a youth. Back then I was known as Blarney Bob, and I won nearly every match I fought."

The emergence of Daisy saved them from further floundering. Living with her, albeit briefly, had afforded him quite an education in cosmetics; otherwise he would never have attributed the slight tint to her cheeks to rouge nor the disappearance of the dark circles beneath her eyes to skillfully applied powder.

She glanced down at her gown, a smart emerald-colored carriage dress trimmed in blond braiding with matching hat he remembered seeing her wear before. "I wasn't certain where we were going. I can change if you prefer."

Gavin hid a smile. She just assumed he'd come to take her out, but that was not the case, not just yet. "Actually it was Freddie I came to see. It occurred to me she might fancy the Zoological Gardens at Regent's Park."

Freddie must have been nearby because at the mention of her name, she flew into the room. *"Maman, Maman, may I go? I want to go, s'il vous plaît?"*

Feeling as though the tide had begun to turn in his favor, Gavin shot Daisy a wink. "Indeed, I'm told the elephants are very popular with children."

From the back of the flat, Flora called for her husband to join her in the kitchen.

Expression rueful, Bob got up to go. "If you'll excuse me, I mean, us." The closing of a door confirmed they'd gone into another room, though Gavin had a strong suspicion there were two ears pressed against the wood panel.

"Maman, Maman, s'il vous plaît."

Looking up from her daughter's small hand tugging at her sleeve, Daisy sent Gavin a dagger glare. Turning back to her daughter, there was a rapid fire exchange spoken in French and then the child seemed to settle.

"Go to your room and find a jacket to carry with you. It gets chilly in London in the evenings once the fog sets in."

Freddie's tense little face dissolved into delight.

"*Merci beaucoup, Maman, merci.*" She let out a delighted squeal and sped off.

Daisy's gaze stabbed into Gavin's. "I know what you're about, Gavin Carmichael, and I'm warning you, don't you so much as try it."

He contrived to look innocent. "You act as though I'm out to abduct her."

She wagged a finger at him, looking very maternal. "Freddie may be not yet eight, but she's cannier than a great many adults."

"That doesn't surprise me. She's your daughter, after all."

Ignoring the compliment, she continued, "You can't pull the wool over her eyes and you can't buy her, either, so don't even try."

"I'll remember that."

"And mind you don't go feeding her a great deal of romantic rot about us getting married because we're not."

To avoid further argument, he declined to disagree. "Will that be all?"

She hesitated. "I suppose so . . . for now."

"Fine, then. I'll have her back by suppertime."

"See that you do."

Freddie exploded back into the room, wearing a charming blue felt bonnet with a wide black velvet band and carrying her coat. Gaze softening, Daisy lifted Freddie's small chin in her hand. "Mind your manners, Freddie, and promise me you'll stay close to Mr. Carmichael."

"*Oui, Maman.* I promise."

Spearing Gavin's gaze over Freddie's ebony curls, Daisy whispered the words weighing most on her mind. "Take care of her. She's my whole life."

"Don't worry," he spoke aloud. "I'll guard her as if she were my own."

I'll guard her as if she were my own.

Watching Gavin walk off with her daughter's small hand wrapped about his was almost more than Daisy could bear. Tears building, she closed the door to the flat and turned back inside. Sinking into a moth-eaten armchair, she fitted a hand over her forehead. The pattering of approaching feet had her looking up.

Flora entered the room carrying the tea tray. "You let her go off with him after all?"

Biting back tears, Daisy nodded. "Yes."

She set the tray between them. "You must trust him very much."

Daisy nodded. "I do . . . with some things."

When it came to Freddie's safety, Daisy had no doubt Gavin would guard her with his life. It was her heart she didn't trust to place in his keeping, not now at any rate. Fifteen years ago, it had been a very different story. She had trusted him completely, believed every word that had come out of his mouth, and ended up deeply hurt.

She buried her head in her hands. "She was supposed to have been his, you know."

There was a pause followed by the sound of liquid—tea—splashing against the bottom of a cup. "Life doesn't always work out according to plan, ours at least, but sometimes The Powers That Be grant us a second chance to set matters to rights. This may well be that second chance you've been dreaming of."

Looking up through her spread fingers, she asked, "How can you be so sure?"

Flora handed her a cup and saucer, but she shook her head. She'd lived abroad too long to think of tea as the antidote to all ills.

Stirring cream and two sugar lumps into her tea, Flora thought for a moment. "When you were separated before, it was beyond either of your controls, but this time if you separate, it will be by choice."

"In coming here today, Mr. Carmichael—Gavin— has made his intentions perfectly clear. He's taking an interest in Freddie because he's interested in you. More than interested, the man's in love with you, Daisy. He means to do right by the pair of you. I can feel it in my bones."

Over the years, Flora's bones had proven a cannily accurate barometer for gauging whether a play's opening night would go off without a hitch or be plagued with problems, or whether the critiques would print a glowing review or a gloomy one. While Daisy had a great respect for her adoptive mother's skeletally inclined intuition, she feared this once Flora might have overstepped her bounds.

"Gentlemen like Gavin don't marry actresses, Mum—especially actresses with readymade families."

There had been far too many men as it was walk into her life only to promptly walk out again once they discovered she had a child. One or two of them had even made a show of playing the father to Freddie—but only as long as it took to win their way into Daisy's bed. She'd never forget the night she'd come to Freddie's door and overheard her daughter asking God to please send her a papa. The memory brought a telltale tightening to her throat—and a fresh ferocity to her heart. She absolutely refused to stand by and allow her precious child to have her hopes dashed yet again.

And yet in letting Freddie go off with Gavin, wasn't that precisely what she was doing? Even if the outing was perfectly innocent on Gavin's part, and she very much doubted it was, she hadn't been prepared for the heart-wrenching feeling of watching her little girl walk off hand in hand with the man who, by rights, should have been her father.

Leaning forward in her seat, Flora wagged a stubby finger in the air. "Rubbish. Mr. Carmichael strikes me as a man who does exactly as he pleases and the consequences be damned. Mind, if you turn your back on this chance for happiness, if you turn your back on him, you've only yourself to fault for it."

Staring into her untouched tea, Daisy admitted to herself she was spoiling for a fight. Irrational though it might be for her to continue to fault a fourteen-year-old boy for breaking his promise, all those years of pent-up pain had to spill over sometime. It might as well be that night. When he brought Freddie back, she fully meant for all hell to break loose.

You swore, Gavin. You bloody well swore.

The Zoological Gardens at Regent's Park were among Gavin's favorite London outdoor spots. The zoo's collection included Indian an elephant, an alligator, a boa, an anaconda, and an Australian koala bear. The grounds boasted the world's first reptile house, first aquarium, and first insect house. With Freddie's small hand wrapped trustingly about his little finger, he paid their admission and they walked through the main entrance gate.

Gavin was fond of children, but beyond the rare occasion when a client carted his or her brood to his office from necessity, he hadn't much experience around them. Having Daisy's daughter entrusted to his care, even for a few hours, struck him as an enormous responsibility. Small wonder Daisy watched over her daughter with a fierce vigilance not unlike the mother mountain lion and cub they observed from the other side of the caged enclosure. That Daisy, his Daisy, had shouldered the burden of motherhood at such a tender age, and without a husband's help, filled him with awe and admiration. For the first time since stumbling upon the truth of Freddie's existence, he considered what it must have been like for her all these years. She hadn't been more than a child herself when Freddie was born and yet she had to be both mother and father to her small daughter while serving as the main wage earner for her aging adoptive parents. Had he been thrust into such an adult position at such a young age, Gavin wasn't sure he could have managed half so well, but judging from Freddie, Daisy had done a great deal better than manage. She'd done a marvelous job.

Precocious and high-spirited yet surprisingly well-behaved for one her age, Freddie was just the sort of little girl he would have been delighted to call his own. When a passing matron remarked on what a "pert and pretty little daughter" he had, and added he must be a proud papa indeed, he hadn't the heart to correct the error.

Freddie dragged her attention from the caged mountain lions and turned her cornflower blue eyes up to his face. "That lady thinks you're my papa. *Are* you?"

If only it might be so. Not only did he want to marry Daisy but he wanted to be a family with her and her daughter. The realization rocked him to his very core. Stepping in to parent another man's offspring didn't at all fit the way he envisioned his life, but as the afternoon wore on, he found that the identity of Freddie's father didn't matter half so much as it had a mere day before.

Freddie was Daisy's child and that sufficed to make her the most wonderful little girl in the world, his world at least.

He shook his head, feeling genuine regret. "No, Freddie, I'm afraid I'm not. I'd very much like to be your friend, though. Would that be all right?"

She hesitated and then, as if coming to a decision, answered with a definitive shake of her glossy black curls. "A papa would be better but a friend will be all right, too, I suppose."

"Thank you."

Freddie's expression turned worldly. "*Maman* fancies you—a jolly lot." In the course of the afternoon, he'd found her French phrases interspersed with vernacular English to be charming.

"Really? What makes you think so?" he asked, knowing he was fishing, hoping he didn't sound overly eager, overly . . . desperate.

Freddie gave a shrug of her small shoulders. A maddening silence ensued during which she occupied herself with sucking the melted candy from her thumb. Drawing the digit from her mouth, she finally answered, "After you left the other day, she smashed two vases and then the china tea urn—the *good* one, from Sevres. Grandmama Lake said she was to stop right there, that we'd be taking our tea out of crockery and putting our flowers to water in jelly jars if she kept on so. Afterward, she said she'd never seen *Maman* in such a state, not even after the Duke."

"The Duke?"

"Uh-oh." She cast him a guilty glance and clamped a sticky fingered hand over her mouth, a child once more. "I expect I wasn't to say anything about him."

"I expect not," he allowed, feeling his gut tighten. "But since the proverbial cat is out of the bag, why don't I buy you an ice and you can tell me the whole of it?"

CHAPTER SEVENTEEN

"You touch'd my vein at first: the thorny point
Of bare distress hath ta'en from me the show
Of smooth civility . . . "
—WILLIAM SHAKESPEARE, Orlando,
As You Like It

Pleading a cold, Daisy begged off rehearsal and instead waited for Gavin to bring home her daughter. In preparation for bed, she combed her hair and washed the paint from her face and changed back into her wrapper although it was scarcely past six. Ordinarily she would be thinking about beginning her day starting about now but the earlier argument and bout of crying had drained her. One eye fixed upon the closed door, she sat in the worn armchair twisting a daisy stem around and around her finger and allowed she'd let

Gavin do the one thing she vowed never to let a grownup man do.

He'd hurt her. Hurt her these past weeks with his arm's-length civility and his perfect manners and his frozen smiles and his absolute refusal to let her close enough to touch any part of him that might mean something, that might matter. He'd hurt her, he was hurting her still, deeply and lastingly, sharply and truly, and the warm trickle tracking her cheek might as well have been blood.

At the sound of the door knob turning, she jerked up her head and dashed a hand across her eyes. The door opened and Freddie rushed inside. Clutching a cloth-covered doll with black button eyes in one hand and a large, sticky lollipop in the other, she'd obviously had quite a day. Gavin came up behind, his tall, broad-shouldered frame filling the doorway, the sight of him stealing her breath and setting her poor, sad heart aflutter. *God, must he always have this effect on me?*

Hoping he wouldn't see how flustered she was, she rose and shifted her gaze to Freddie who was all but dancing on the balls of her feet. "Did you have a good time, poppet?" Her daughter's mouth wore several layers of sweets, answering the question already, but talking served to fill up the silence as well as to distract her from Gavin's quietly studying gaze.

"*Oui, Maman*, jolly good." Freddie's intermingling of French words with the English vernacular, the latter picked up from the Lakes, could always bring out Daisy's smile. "*Monsieur* Carmichael took me to the zoo. We saw an elephant as big, no bigger, than this house, and a giraffe, too. He was so tall he could see straight down to the trees."

Freddie looked back over her shoulder at Gavin, and the beaming smile she sent him slashed at Daisy's heart like a razor. *She should have been his. She bloody well should have been his.* Careful to smooth out any rancor from her voice, she smiled and said, "That sounds splendid, darling. Now run along and have Grandmamma help you wash your face."

Turning back to her, Freddie's expression turned fretful. "But *Maman*."

Determined to circumvent any whining, Daisy gave a firm shake of her head. "*Vite, vite!*"

"*D'accord*." Freddie shuffled toward the back of the flat.

Daisy called her back. "Fredericka, don't you have something you wish to say to Mr. Carmichael before you take your leave?"

The child turned about and bolted to Gavin. Throwing herself at his knees, she looked up and said, "*Merci beaucoup, monsieur*."

He knelt down so they were closer to eye level. "You are most welcome, Freddie. I hope you will accompany me soon again."

She cast a look back to her mother. "I hope so, too."

"Freddie, love, come to Grandmamma." Flora's voice coming from the other room had Freddie scampering away.

Daisy lifted her gaze to Gavin, a slow, simmering anger taking possession of her. "It sounds as though you two had quite a day."

"We did." He let the door drop closed and came toward her. "She's a remarkable child. You must be very proud."

Daisy lifted her chin. "I am."

They stared at one another for a long moment, and Daisy counted out the seconds by each pound of her heart. "It's the oddest thing," Gavin said at last. "We were standing outside the lion pen and a woman came up to us and complimented me on what a charming little daughter I had."

Arms crossed over her breasts, Daisy regarded him, feeling the heat of tears and fifteen years of lost dreams welling up inside her. "You both have dark hair and blue eyes. It was a natural mistake."

Gavin hesitated. "I suppose so only it didn't feel like a mistake. It felt, well . . . right somehow."

Flora's voice calling out to them saved her from answering. "Mr. Carmichael, I was afraid I might have missed you." She waddled inside the room, a damp apron thrown over her forest green plaid skirts. I just wanted to thank you for taking Freddie on such a grand outing. I expect she'll speak of little else for the rest of the week."

Gavin transferred his gaze to Daisy's adoptive mother. "As I was just telling your daughter, it was my pleasure, but I wonder if I might ask a favor of you and your husband."

Daisy tensed, wondering what he might be up to now.

"Oh, anything, Mr. Carmichael," Flora gushed. The way she fawned over Gavin set Daisy's teeth on edge. "You've only to ask."

"I wonder if you and your husband would be so kind as to take Freddie out to supper. You'd all be my guests, of course."

Two hot spots appeared on either of Flora's apple cheeks. "That won't be necessary, sir."

Daisy's father must have been listening close by for he popped his head through the alcove as if responding to a stage cue. "Aye, we'll be happy to take the little one for a stroll and a bite. Come on with you, Freddie. I spotted a sandwich shop around the corner."

"There's a pub not far from here called the Hart and Dove. The whitebait is the specialty of the house. I trust you'll find it to your liking. You've only to tell the proprietor you're my guests, and he'll see you accommodated."

Bob shook his graying head. "That's very kind of you, sir, but it sounds a bit rich for our blood."

"Bob!" His wife reached out and swatted his arm.

Rubbing the spot, Bob turned to his wife. "There's

no point in putting on airs, Flora. A canny chap like Mr. Carmichael can see we've scarcely one penny to rub against the next. This isn't the Claridge, after all, though it suits me well enough, m'dear." He cast an apologetic glance at Daisy.

"Will there be fish and chips?" Freddie stood in the alcove, a soapy face cloth pressed to one partially scrubbed cheek. "*Maman* says the fish and chips are one of the things she missed most about England. What are chips?"

Bypassing Daisy, Gavin crossed the room and bent down to rub his nose against Freddie's soapy one, drawing her giggle. "Why, Freddie, I can't say for certain that fish and chips will appear on the menu, but if you tell the waiter that's what you fancy, I've no doubt he'll find a way to accommodate you, and then you can taste for yourself how delicious chips are. For now, though, finish washing your face."

Freddie giggled and scampered from the room. Gavin straightened and turned back to the adults.

Flora beamed at him. "You're so good with her, Mr. Carmichael. He's what I call a natural father, isn't he, Bob?"

Daisy cringed and Bob cast his wife a warning look. "Now, Flora, mind that chat we had about meddling in other people's lives."

The comment earned him a scowl from his wife. "I'll just go and fetch our things. If my memory serves me, springtime in London can be a chilly affair at night."

It took several minutes for the Lakes to collect bonnets, wrappers and, of course, Freddie, who insisted the new doll from Gavin must come to supper, too.

Daisy had gone from dreading Gavin's arrival to counting out the minutes until she might be alone with him if only to give him his comeuppance. As soon as the door closed behind the happy trio, she rounded on him. "You've no right to use my family against me."

"I wasn't aware I was using them." Determined not to back down, Gavin tossed his hat into the empty chair seat and strode nearer her. "But for argument's sake, I'll point out that you certainly use them well enough when the fancy strikes you—the fancy to hide, that is."

She swung her head from side to side, looking very much like that little girl who'd been caught in the act of pilfering pies from the orphanage kitchen. "That's not true."

"Isn't it? You've had innumerable opportunities to tell me you had a daughter. The night we first made love, you might have told me then. Even when I found your letter to her you let me go on thinking you were another man's mistress. Why, Daisy, why?"

"I have been another man's mistress—several men's mistress, though not at the same time, at least not usually." She smiled what he'd come to think of as her Delilah smile, and the result was so painful he might as well have plunged a knife into his heart and twisted it.

"Stop it."

She quirked a perfect half-moon brow and stared at

him. "Stop what?"

"Stop working so hard at shocking me. After the other day in the park, I think I may be beyond shock or at least halfway to numbness."

"I wouldn't wager on it, Gavin. Besides, I'm only being honest. That's what you wanted, isn't it? Complete honesty, no secrets, your precious truth unmasked in all its ghoulish glory. Do you fancy hearing about Freddie's father? Pierre was a good deal older than I and a bit of a bastard, but he had a look of you about him and, well, I was far from home and lonely. He didn't have to work terribly hard at seducing me beyond telling me I was pretty and brushing up against my breasts a time or two. Oh, and he bought me my first absinthe—did you know that as well as having narcotic properties, the wormwood acts as an aphrodisiac? But more powerful than that, it was the look he had of you that won me to him. When I closed my eyes and spread my legs for him, I could almost believe it was you—almost but not quite."

"Daisy, I—"

She held up a palm to silence him. She'd waited fifteen years for this moment, and she quite simply wasn't finished with hurting him, not yet at any rate.

"There've been a number of men since Pierre, quite a rogue's gallery, all in all. If you must know, I'd be rather hard-put to name them all."

"Stop it." He closed the distance between them in two long strides.

Refusing to back down, she lifted her chin and laughed though she felt as if her heart was breaking. It turned out that hurting Gavin meant hurting herself, too. She hadn't counted on matters working out that way. And yet she couldn't stop or at least she wasn't yet willing to. Surely she'd feel good, or perhaps better, at any moment, if only she stayed the course.

"Shall I start out with the stage manager who shared me with his twin brother, the acrobat, or would you rather hear about the Duke who called in his pretty young housemaid to join us? She was French, too, and a jolly good fuck from the looks of it. He certainly seemed to enjoy her, or maybe it was my watching he enjoyed so much."

"Stop it." He grabbed her by the shoulders and gave her a sharp shake. When that didn't work, he covered her mouth with his in a hard kiss.

Breaking free, she backed away. "See, it's changed already. Yesterday you touched me as though I were made of finest china, something precious and fragile and so dear you couldn't bear to think of it breaking. But now you know better, don't you, Gavin? You know well enough to use me like the whore I am. Don't just stand there. What are you waiting for? You're stronger than I am and you're angry, I can see it in your eyes. Did you know that your top lip all but disappears when you're in a mood? It has ever since you were a boy."

"Stop it."

But the wildness was upon her and there would be

no turning back. "Stop what, being so bloody honest? Very well then, we'll call it your turn, shall we? Why don't you be honest and confess what you're really thinking? Say it, Gavin. Admit that despite everything you want me now. You want me more than ever, only this time you want me rough."

He shook his head. His eyes were very dark, his face flushed. "I want you, God help me, that much is true."

"Well, then, what's stopping you? Pull up my skirts and have me. That table over there should suit me well enough. Softness is wasted on a woman such as me."

"Stop this, Daisy. I want you, but not like this."

"The name's Delilah, sport. Look, I'll even make it easy for you." She opened her dressing robe and gave him an eyeful. "What's the matter, Gavin? Yesterday you couldn't get enough of me. Now you can barely bring yourself to look at me. Don't you want me? Shall I start without you?" She lifted her breasts, a silent offering.

"Of course I want you, but not like this."

"Sorry, love, but this is the only way that'll serve. Take it or leave it, what shall it be?"

"God help me, yes."

She fell upon her knees. There would be bruises tomorrow but for tonight it felt right, it felt good. With so much pain to be reckoned between them, a feather soft mattress or even her present lumpy one would never do. "Good call, love. In a bit I'll give you the ride of your life, but first I'll give you this."

She anchored her hands to his waist and pressed an open mouth kiss to his erection, tongue circling the bulge, dampening the wool.

"God, Daisy." He speared hard hands through her hair, anchoring her to him.

Now they were getting somewhere though he needn't have bothered. The bald truth was there was nowhere else she'd rather be. She turned her head to the side and stroked him with her cheek.

Gavin's desire was a traitor to his higher purpose. Even as his mind and heart recoiled from what they were about to do—soulless sex, bodies for barter—his manhood shot to life, penis hard and thick, balls heavy and aching.

"God, Daisy." He laid a hand on either side of her jaw and turned her back to face him.

Looking up at him with triumphant eyes, she rested her chin on his crotch. "Yes, Gavin?"

"You're right. I do want this—you."

"I thought as much." She unbuttoned the front of his trousers and took him between her hands.

She brought his trousers down to the floor with her. Standing with them in a puddle about his ankles, he suddenly felt ridiculous, like a circus clown.

As if reading his thoughts, she pushed him back into the chair seat. Kneeling between his splayed legs, she busied herself with slipping off his shoes and stockings. *Ah, better.* He dropped back his head and closed his eyes, aware of everything she did, every move she made, every breath she exhaled. He'd been hard already and when her fingers closed about his cock, he thought he might flare into flame and be devoured into smoldering ash not unlike the house fire that had destroyed his family. She took her time with him, toying with his testicles, lifting each one in turn, fondling and suckling as though they were firm fruit. By the time she drew him inside her mouth, he was already on fire for her, entirely her slave.

Pulling back, she looked up at him with dark, intense eyes. "Pretend you're inside me. I want you to fuck me in my mouth, Gavin, hard and deep, and after you're done fucking me, I want you to stay inside my mouth and come."

He opened his eyes and looked down at her. "Why are you doing this?"

"Because I can, because you're letting me, because as much as you want to appear civilized and honorable and proper to the outside world, you're still a man and having me go down on my knees for you, on my knees like a slave, excites you whether you admit it or not."

"Have it your way." He slid a hand into the fall of her hair and pulled her down to his groin. She didn't fight him but went willingly, her nipples standing out hard as berries, her breasts rising and falling in time with each jagged, rushed breath. Parting her lips, she sucked him into her mouth, lapping at him with her tongue and then taking him all the way inside and milking him with the muscles of her throat. He thrust back and forth, inside and out, imagining her lips were her nether lips, that the warm wetness sheathing him was her pulsing vulva.

She pulled back to lick him, stroking the length of his shaft from base to tip and then back again. She nipped him. She sucked him. She teased and tortured him. Each time he thought he'd climbed pleasure's pinnacle, that surely this time sweet release would be his, she coaxed him back to start the climb anew.

"Not yet, love, almost but not quite." Her breath was a warm breeze against his shaft, her eyelashes the sweep of butterfly wings.

He sank hard fingers into her hair, loving her and hating her in equal measure. "What the devil are you doing to me? Who the hell do you think you are?"

She tilted her face up and smiled at him with lips that were wet and rosy. "Why, I told you, I'm Delilah."

"You're Daisy. You're my Daisy." He rose, caught her by the elbows, and brought her to her feet, erection spearing the distance between them.

She shook her head. "No, I'm not. That girl you knew is dead, long dead."

"No, she's not. She's standing right her before me."

"Why can't you see it's too late?" Her face crumpled and all at once tears spilled down her cheeks.

His balls ached, his cock ached, and as for his heart, it ached with an empty longing the likes of which he'd never known. "No, it's not. Why can't you see this isn't the end? It's only the beginning."

His arms went about her, and he lifted her against his chest. One arm about her shoulders and the other braced beneath her knees, he said, "Where is your bedroom?"

He carried her through the flat to the very back. Daisy's bedroom was scarcely larger than a closet and yet in his present state a suite at The Claridge couldn't have suited him better. He laid her in the center of the narrow bed and came down atop her.

"For the rest of the night, we make love my way. Think of me as your master, if that helps you."

She wrapped her hands about the headboard's rusted metal bars and opened her legs around him. "I'll be your slave, you know. I'll be whatever you want me to be, do whatever you want to please you."

He looked down at her sex, glistening pink and swollen, and sank two fingers inside her. She was slippery wet, and she smelled like heaven. He slowly withdrew and sat back on his heels, watching the shiver ripple through her, smearing his damp fingers across her mouth, getting harder still when she ran her tongue along the seam of her lips, tasting herself.

"You can hurt me if you want. I won't mind."

"I don't ever want to hurt you again." He entered her slowly, not because he didn't think she was ready for him, but because he wanted to show her that despite everything she was still precious to him, still dear. And maybe, just maybe because he wanted to torture her a bit by making her wait, master her and make her his willing slave as the moment before he had been hers.

"More." Shifting her hips, it was her turn to ask, to beg.

Loving it, he gave her another inch and then stopped, forcing himself to hold back, to hold on. "More?"

She bit her bottom lip. The knuckles of her hands gripping the bedposts were very white. "Yes, God, *yes.*"

He gave her another inch and stopped again. "I'll give you more, as much as you want, but you're going to have to ask. In fact, you're going to have to beg for it."

She let go of the headboard and reached for him, fingers clawing his shoulders. "Please, God, please."

She tried thrusting up against him, but he anchored her hips to the mattress with his hands, pinning her so she had no choice but to accept what he was willing to give or beg for more. And Gavin was determined to make her beg for it, every inch of it, until he was fully sheathed with the wet silk of her pulsing around him. Once he was, he stopped, stilled, and made her beg some more.

Arching against him, straining for release, she ground out, "Gavin, please. I'm dying. You're *killing* me."

"Too bloody bad."

He went slowly, a measured glide in and out, reveling in the way her sweat pearled breasts lapped against his chest when their bodies met, the slapping sound putting him in mind of surf washing up against sandy beach. After each stroke he stopped, holding back until she pleaded with him, until the frustrated tears mingled with the perspiration gliding down her cheeks. Then and only then did he reach between them, his thumb going to the spot just above the place where they were joined. He flicked over the sensitive nub once, twice . . .

Daisy cried out, her inner muscles convulsing, her climax milking his member until he could wait no more. He thrust hard and deep, pouring himself into her.

"Oh, God. Oh, Daisy!"

They lay spoon-style on the bed, Gavin's arm wrapped about her waist, Daisy's back fitted against his chest and her buttocks pressed to his thighs. Lifting up on an elbow, he looked over at her and asked the one question whose uncertain answer kept him from complete happiness. "Did you love him?"

Daisy unwound her leg from his and stretched her arms out in front of her though he knew her body well enough by now to sense the tension in the movement. "Who?" That she paused at all confirmed she knew full well whom he meant.

"The father."

He didn't say "Freddie's father" or "the child's father" or even "her father." Somehow it felt easier that way to keep things calm, detached, to steer clear of the terrible pain that stabbed through him every time he let himself think of Daisy bearing a child all alone. A child who wasn't his.

"No," she answered, sounding fully awake. "I never loved Pierre though at the time I tried telling myself I did. It scarcely matters now. He's long gone."

"Dead?" he offered, hoping he didn't sound too bloodthirsty, too eager.

"Hardly, or at least I shouldn't think so. He ran off with the contents of the company till and a curvy blonde from the chorus."

"I see." He tried not to sound too relieved—or too glad.

"Do you?"

He pressed a kiss to her fragrant hair and promised himself to keep her safe from here on as he hadn't been able to do when they were young. "You made a youthful mistake, an indiscretion, if you will."

She turned over to face him. Lifting her head from the pillow, she frowned. "My daughter may not have been conceived in love, but she has brought only love, only joy."

What the Devil was she getting so worked up over? He thought he'd taken the news of the daughter pretty bloody well, all things considered. Most men would have run off like a shot. Instead it was Daisy who looked about to bolt from the bed.

He eased her back down. "I didn't mean it as a reproach. I'm only trying to understand and, well, to make up for lost time."

"Lost time, indeed." She shifted away and gave him her back.

He laid his hand on her shoulder, the skin porcelain smooth and very soft, and asked, "Daisy, are you crying?"

She moved her head back and forth on the pillow, a mute denial that didn't fool him for a minute. He reached down and caught a fat tear on the edge of his thumb. "Oh, Daisy, the very last thing I wanted to do was make you sad."

Turning her head to the side, she said, "Freddie, she was supposed to be . . . that is to say . . . Damn it, Gav, she was supposed to be yours. I'd give anything to be able to go back in time and make her yours." She brought her hands up to her face, the mattress rocking with the force of her sobbing.

Gently, very gently, he carried her hands down. "It's not too late, sweetheart. We may not be able to go back in time but we can look forward to the future. I don't care who Freddie's father was. I only care that she's yours. I want us to be a family."

"Oh, Gav, do you mean it?"

"Must you even ask? You must know by now I'm in love with you. Our arrangement be damned, I don't want to let you go in a month, and I don't want to let Freddie go either. Promise me both of you will stay with me after the month is up?"

"If you're sure that's what you want, then, yes, I promise. We'll stay."

CHAPTER EIGHTEEN

Is't possible that on so little acquaintance you should
like her? That but seeing you should love her? And lov-
ing woo? And, wooing, she should grant?
And will you persevere to enjoy her?
—WILLIAM SHAKESPEARE, Orlando,
As You Like It

One Week Later:

Gavin awoke several days later feeling more re-
freshed and at peace than he could ever remember feeling. He turned over on his side to find
Daisy awake and watching him. Hands tucked beneath
her head, she looked like an angel in repose. His angel.

"It's good between us, isn't it?" she asked though
the contented smile she wore told him she already knew
what his answer would be.

"I'd say it's very good. Better than very good, it's a

miracle, a dream-come-true." He reached for her and laid his lips along her neck.

"That tickles." Giggling, she made a show of pushing him away though she liked it, he could tell. "Besides, you'll make me late for the dress rehearsal." The following night would see the play's debut.

"It might be worth it. I don't have court this morning. I could send word to the office that I'll be in late."

She grinned. "My, my, Gavin, whatever has happened to you? It used to be I couldn't lure you from work and now you want to do nothing but play. I believe I've created a monster."

"You've happened to me. I may not be a monster exactly, but it's fair to say you bring out the beast in me." Rising up on all fours, he let out a mock roar and grabbed for her.

She pretended to fight him but she was all too willing to be subdued. He pinned her arms over her head and suddenly they stopped playing, stopped pretending, and looked deeply into one another's eyes.

"I love you, you know."

"I know." She'd yet to say the words back but the admission was coming soon, he could feel it. Once that final barrier was surmounted, there would be nothing left standing between them.

They made love, a tender coupling that brought them both to a quick, satisfying climax. Lying beneath him, Daisy ran gentle fingers over his shoulders, his buttocks, the backs of his thighs, telling him in every way but words how very much she loved him. A little while later she rolled onto her side, and he slapped her bottom with a light hand. He only meant the touch as a tease, but it put him in mind of that time when she insisted he spank her in earnest. Remembering the sight of her lovely white ass wearing only his handprints, he felt himself growing hard again.

"You'd best go on while I can still muster the will to let you leave."

She hesitated, nibbling at her bottom lip as she always had when she was considering whether or not to tell him something. "Gavin, I'm nervous. I have the most dreadful case of stage fright. Just thinking about tomorrow night, I can feel my hands go clammy and my stomach turn over."

Relieved, he let out the breath he hadn't realized he was holding. Even after the past wonderful week, he still had moments when he feared she might yet walk away from him again, that he might yet lose her.

"Rubbish, you're going to be brilliant. You are brilliant." He pressed a kiss atop her head. "But if you don't get a move on, you're also going to be late for your dress rehearsal. Off with you now."

"Oh, very well." Giggling, she rolled away from him and tossed first one shapely long leg and then the other over the side of the bed. Sitting on the edge of the mattress, she looked back at him over the top of one creamy shoulder and smiled. "Has anyone told you you're a hard taskmaster, Mr. St. Carmichael?"

"You've got half of it right. I am hard—I should say *very* hard—for one very sexy albeit truant actress." He cast a significant glance downward to the erection tenting the sheet.

Wearing a wicked smile, she reached back and settled her palm over the bulge. "Promise you'll save this for later?"

"You have my most solemn word on it. In fact, why don't I call on you in your dressing room later and give you a good luck kiss before the rehearsal?"

"Only a kiss, Mr. Carmichael?" She affected a hurt look.

Suddenly his mood turned serious. Cupping her soft cheek, he said, "I'd give you anything you want, you know that, don't you? You've only to ask."

"I know, but for the time being, duty calls." She made a face, but her eyes were sparkling, her face radiant, her whole self glowing, or so it seemed to him.

❧

Unbeknown to Daisy, Gavin had awakened with the full intention of asking her to marry him. He intended to hold off on proposing until her debut as Rosalind was behind them, but now he found himself wondering why he should. Arguably, there was no cause for rushing to the altar, and yet he couldn't shake an inexplicable sense of urgency. Besides, if he asked Daisy in advance of the performance, there would be reason for a double celebration in the theater's Green Room the following night. Really, could one ever have too much happiness?

The sexual connection they shared had deepened to include intimacy on all planes, not only the physical. These days after they made love, Daisy seemed content to spend long, languorous hours letting him simply hold her. Holding invariably led to more lovemaking, not that he was complaining. Stroking the arch of her elegant spine, brushing kisses over her smooth shoulder, the sensitive spot below her shell-shaped ear, the perfect pink palm of her slender hand was the closest he'd come to touching heaven while still on earth. He couldn't get enough of her and he was coming to suspect he never would. But then satiety was an overrated state. So long as their passions matched, why bother with sleeping?

Over the past few days, she confided her dreams for Freddie. Like most mothers who'd grown up doing without, Daisy was determined her child would never struggle as she had done. For his part, Gavin was growing exceedingly fond of the little girl and not only because she was Daisy's. Inquisitive, energetic, and full of good-natured mischief, Freddie was a picture-perfect little girl. Over the past week, he felt as if the three of them were fast becoming a family. He fancied Freddie was more than ready to accept him as a father.

For his part, he was becoming so attached to her that for long stretches of time he found himself forgetting he wasn't her real father. He was more than prepared to legally adopt Freddie and give her the protection of his name. The latter proposal he meant to hold off on making until after Daisy said yes. He wanted Daisy to marry him for himself, not for the privileges he could shower on her child.

Before he approached her, however, there was someone whom honor mandated he speak to first. Though he and his grandfather had been at odds the whole of his adult life, he didn't want the old man to learn of his plans by reading the wedding announcement. Tyrant though he was, Maximilian St. John deserved the courtesy of a face-to-face appraisal of Gavin's plans. Rather than heading directly to the theater to deliver the promised good luck kiss, he sent a message around to his grandfather asking him to join him for lunch at his club at 12:30.

The dining room of the Garrick was filling up when Gavin entered at precisely 12:15 that afternoon. Even though he was early, he wasn't really surprised to find his grandfather already seated at one of the cloth-covered side tables. Frowning down at his pocket watch, he looked up as Gavin approached.

They shook hands, and Gavin took his seat. "Grandfather, it was good of you to come on such short notice."

Maximilian snapped the engraved casing on the timepiece closed and slipped it back into his vest pocket

303

before answering, "Your invitation came as something of a surprise. What is the trouble?"

Tamping down his annoyance—must something always be the matter?—Gavin signaled the waiter and they ordered sherries. Turning back to the table, he said, "There is no trouble, Grandfather. Quite the contrary, I asked you here to share some happy news. I wanted you to hear it directly from me."

Maximilian's craggy countenance softened. "You landed the Stonebridge account? Good show! I knew you'd bring it in if only you'd stop taking on every milksop charity case and set your mind to it."

Gavin felt his earlier good humor souring. True to form, his grandfather was incapable of thinking of anything but work and, of course, only the profitable clients counted as worthy of his notice. "My news is of a personal nature."

The light in Maximilian's eyes dimmed. "I see."

Gavin rather doubted he did but forged ahead anyway. "I've decided to marry."

"Why, Gavin, that is jolly good news. Isabel will make you an admirable wife. Her father has been a friend of mine since our Harrow days."

The waiter returned with their drinks and two menus. They gave them a perfunctory glance and then ordered the oxtail soup and turbot in brown butter.

Gavin took a sip of sherry and set the glass aside. "I'm not marrying Isabel Duncan."

Good manners precluded his adding he'd sooner spend the rest of his days rotting in a monk's cell than sign up for marriage with a mean-spirited shrew like Isabel. He'd never been fond of her but knowing how she called out the Vigilance Committee on Daisy, he couldn't abide the sight of her.

His grandfather hoisted a heavy brow and regarded him. "If not Isabel, then who?"

Gavin girded himself. He knew full well his grandfather's poor opinion of anyone in the theatrical profession and that Daisy had started her career in music halls would paint a dark portrait of her. Still, she was his choice and his grandfather would simply have to grow accustomed to the idea.

"Miss Daisy Lake."

"The actress you're keeping?" Maximillian's jaw dropped and his gaze widened as if Gavin had just admitted she carried syphilis or the plague."

"She's an actress and she's absolutely brilliant. In fact, she's landed the lead of Rosalind in *As You Like It* at Drury Lane, quite a feat for a newcomer."

"If this is meant to be a joke, Gavin, and I dearly hope it is, then I must say it's in very poor taste."

The waiter returned and set down their soup. When he asked if they wished for rolls with their meal, they both turned to him and barked "no" in unison. Looking between them, he murmured "Very good, then" and hurried away.

They left the soup to grow cold and regarded one another. The thunderous expression on St. John's face had cowed Gavin many times as a boy, but he was a man now and instead of the familiar gut twisting terror, he felt his own answering anger escalating apace. "I assure you it's no joke, Grandfather. I love Daisy and she loves me."

"Keep her as your mistress if you must, but for God's sake, Gavin, don't fling your future away on a dance hall doxy."

Gavin gripped the table's edge. Over the years, he fantasized about hitting his grandfather on more than one occasion, but never before had he come so close to doing so as he was now. "Like my mother flung hers away on an under-gardener, you mean?"

Max St. Claire's rheumy gaze flared. "Mind where you tread, boy."

His jaw clenching, Gavin ground out, "I'm not a boy. I'm a man."

The fish course arrived. The waiter hesitated and then bent to clear away the soup, but Gavin's grandfather waved him off with a rough hand. "Since you have the poor taste to bring up your mother's indiscretion, you should know I'll not sit by and watch history repeat itself. If I must, I'll cut you off without a farthing."

A moment of silence fell as the two men sat back and took each other's measure. Grappling for self-control, Gavin was the first to break the stony silence. "You should know, sir, I invited you here as a courtesy only.

With or without your blessing, I mean to make Daisy my wife. As for your money, both it and you can go directly to the Devil for all I care."

Maximilian's mouth twisted in a snarl. "I wouldn't be so hasty to consign either it or me to Hades, were I you. These days a pretty young actress with half a wit about her might have her pick of any number of wealthy protectors, titled ones even. You may find your Daisy considerably less eager to wed a struggling barrister than the heir to a sizeable fortune. On the other hand, if you paused long enough to employ that famous brain of yours, you'd see you can have your cake and eat it, too. Marry as duty dictates, Gavin, and you can still keep your canary on the side and in high style."

"The crassness of that suggestion, Grandfather, only goes to prove how little you know of Daisy's character— or of mine, for that matter. She's not like that. She's warm and loving and bold and brilliant and a wonderful mother to her daughter, Freddie."

They were drawing stares from the occupants of the adjacent tables. There was really no point in going on. Gavin scraped back his chair and rose.

"If you had managed to put aside your prejudices all those years ago, your daughter and son-in-law and granddaughter would have had no need to live in a fire trap of a tenement house. They would all be alive today. Now, answer me this, Grandfather. Which of us is the greater fool?" Throwing his napkin down, Gavin turned on his heel and strode out of the room.

Sitting alone at the table, Maximilian felt the trembling he struggled to hold in check during the argument take over. He reached out a shaking hand for the glass of water and, with difficulty, brought the rim to his lips. Swallowing, he set it back down but not before spilling a liberal amount on the white table cloth. The waiter came around to clean it up, and feeling feeble and old, Maximilian took the opportunity to leave before he invited further disgrace. In public he might muster the appearance of an avenging Old Testament patriarch, but the truth was he was crushed. If he made good on his threat to disinherit Gavin, both the money and law firm would pass to the son of a cousin. The St. John line would be a good as dead. Beyond that, over the past decade and a half he'd come to love this strange young man whose blue eyes and poet's soul brought back his dear Lucy. The very last thing he wanted was another rift in the family. He'd disowned his daughter and, as a result, his darling girl had lost her life. Though he'd never admit it, he bore the blame for her death and that of her baby daughter and, yes, her Irish husband, as his personal cross every day of his life for the past fifteen years. He was simply too bloody old to weather that cataclysmic a heartache again. Stopping at the coatroom to retrieve his hat and walking stick, he swore to himself he wouldn't lose Gavin, too, and certainly not to some strumpet only after his fortune.

Delilah du Lac or Daisy Lake—whatever you call yourself, you've met your match in me.

"Were it not better,
Because that I am more than common tall,
That I did suit me all points like a man?
A gallant curtle-axe upon my thigh,
A boar-spear in my hand; and—in my heart
Lie there what hidden woman's fear there will . . ."

Reciting her lines later that afternoon, the early pivotal point of the play where Rosalind decides to disguise herself as a boy, Daisy paced the four corners of her dressing room, dog-eared script in hand. She didn't know why she bothered with holding the thing. She knew her lines by heart as well as those of every other cast member. The weight of the play in hand was a comforting feeling, for whatever reason. Theater people were notoriously superstitious and though she was less credulous than many, she was not above observing a small ritual here and there. In her case, she kept a copper penny she always tucked into her left shoe before going on for luck.

The past week with Gavin had been not only the luckiest but the happiest of her life. Before, missing Freddie had blunted her bliss, not to mention the effort she expended on deceiving Gavin into believing she had a lover waiting for her. Looking back from the vantage point of only a week, the ruse seemed silly, certainly self-defeating. Now that she'd sworn off lying to him, the scattered pieces of her life seemed to be finally falling into place. She had the man she loved, the child she adored, and the parents to whom she was devoted, finally all on English soil. Her future was by no means assured, but it was shaping up to look as if she'd be able to provide for them in their old age. Last but surely not least, she had the leading role in a proper play—by Shakespeare, no less. With so many blessings raining down upon her, how could she possibly feel otherwise than blissfully, extravagantly happy?

Impatient rapping outside her dressing room door interrupted her musing. Wondering if it might be Gavin come to deliver that good luck kiss he promised her earlier, she took a moment to check her reflection in the mirror. She might not be the most beautiful woman in the theater—her upside down mouth and turned up nose guaranteed she was not—but she was definitely the happiest. And happiness, she was discovering, lent one a radiance which was impossible to manufacture with powder and paint. Tucking a loose curl behind one ear, she gave the call to enter.

"Gavin, *chéri*, I wasn't really expecting—"

Instead of Gavin, a fierce-faced man of sixty-odd stepped inside the narrow room. "Miss Lake, I presume?"

Daisy backed up a step and nodded. "That is so.

I'm afraid the theater is closed to the public at present. If you've come about tomorrow's performance, you can purchase your ticket when the box office opens at five."

"I'm not here about a play but about my grandson. I'm Maximilian St. John, Gavin's grandfather."

Feeling as if a cold draught had just swept inside the room, she stepped back for him to enter. "Won't you come in?"

He stepped inside, the tip of his cane clacking on the uncarpeted floor. She gestured him to a pair of chairs but he shook his head. Looking her up and down, he said, "I haven't set foot in Paris since my Grand Tour as a young man, but still you don't sound very French to me."

Wishing she might be wearing anything other than her breeches, she answered, "I'm not. I'm English . . . as English as you are," she added on impulse, and regretted it at once.

This sour-faced gentleman was Gavin's grandfather, after all. Determined to demonstrate her manners, if not her pedigree, were those of a lady, she asked, "Would you care for some refreshment? Shall I send out for tea?"

"Don't trouble yourself. This isn't a social call but a business one."

Determined not to let him intimidate her, she lifted her chin and squared her shoulders. "What business could you possibly have with me?"

"I'm here on behalf of my grandson."

Already on alert, his statement sent her spiraling

toward full-blown panic. "Gavin's all right, isn't he? I mean, nothing has happened, has it? I left him just a few hours ago."

She stopped short of saying more, such as the circumstances in which she'd left him—lying naked in her bed. Snuggled next to him so close she could feel his heart beating against her breast, their limbs interleaved as though they were of one body in truth, she'd felt utterly warm and replete, wholly satisfied and content for, quite possibly, the first time in her adult life. Even jittery with nerves about this night's performance and how its success or failure would decide her future, tearing herself away from all that peace and contentment had required considerable willpower.

"His physical condition is sound though his judgment at the moment is fatally flawed."

"I'm afraid I don't understand."

"I've just come from lunching with Gavin at my club. It seems my grandson has his mind set on marrying you."

It took Daisy several heartbeats to absorb the news. As often as Gavin had mentioned their being a family, she hadn't counted on that meaning marriage. To broach the subject with his grandfather, he must be seriously considering it. "I beg your pardon."

"Please don't feel obliged to demonstrate your acting skills on my behalf, Miss Lake. I have no doubt you've been leading Gavin to this point for some time, ever since you arranged to have him see you perform at that . . . that supper club. It wouldn't surprise me to learn his other two chums, the Scot and that photographer chap were in league with you all along."

"I assure you, I arranged nothing. Our meeting again was purely by chance. If you must know, I tried sending him away."

St. John let out a snort. "Which as a woman of the world you well knew would only increase his ardor, but no matter. Be that as it may, you should know I have no intention of allowing you to ruin Gavin's life. If I must, I will cut him off without so much as a penny."

"I wouldn't hurt Gavin for the world. I . . . I love him." She'd yet to say those words to Gavin. Confronted with this cold-eyed man, she worried she might never find the courage—or the chance—to do so.

"I have in my pocket a bank draft for five thousand pounds, enough to keep you in reasonable comfort for the rest of your days, more than modest if you invest it wisely."

"You can't think to bribe me." He tried handing her the note but she backed away, shaking her head.

"Don't be a fool, Miss Lake. Take this and send him away and start a new life for yourself and your family."

"It is you who are the fool, Mr. St. John. Your bribe and your threats are both unnecessary. There is no need to induce me to cry off an engagement to which I never would have consented. As much as I love Gavin, I'm not such a fool to think a marriage between us would ever be acceptable to his family or anyone else in society."

"If that is even half of the truth then you, Miss Lake, are a young woman of rare good sense."

She tore the bank draft in half and handed him back the pieces.

"What's this? I don't understand. I warn you, young woman, if you're angling for more . . . "

Daisy felt tears burning the backs of her eyes, but she'd sooner go blind than give him the satisfaction of shedding them. "I don't care if your offer is five thousand pounds or five hundred thousand. Arguably, I may need it, I most certainly could use it, and yet I won't take it, not so much as a farthing."

For the first time since barging in, the old man looked less than sure of himself. "In that case, I rescind my earlier statement. You, young woman, are a fool, indeed. If you won't look to your own future, then look to your daughter's."

At his contemptuous mention of her child, Daisy felt her tether hold on her temper snap. "My family's well-being is my affair, and I don't welcome your intrusion any more than you would welcome mine. As for the other, when it comes to Gavin, I am a very great fool, a fool for love."

Sweeping past him, she reached for the brass knob and yanked open the door. Standing aside, she sent a pointed look out into the empty corridor.

"Good day to you, sir. Consider whatever business you thought to have with me concluded once and for all."

CHAPTER NINETEEN

"I pray you, do not fall in love with me,
For I am falser than vows made in wine."
—WILLIAM SHAKESPEARE, Rosalind,
As You Like It

The slam of the dressing room door at his back brought Maximilian St. John out of his stupefied state. Never had it occurred to him the chit might turn down his offer—or his check. When she first refused, he supposed her game was to bargain for more money, but now it seemed that wasn't so. Instead of haggling, she turned him down flat and showed him the door, hardly the actions of a scheming adventuress. Might Gavin's actress have more substance to her than met the eye?

When it comes to Gavin, I am a very great fool, a fool for love.

It was a pretty speech, but for any actress worth her salt, such a siloquy must roll off the tongue easily enough. More than the words, it was the earnestness in her eyes and the trembling about her mouth when she'd said them that caught at his curmudgeon's heart. Old age must be softening his brain as well because he could almost believe the gel really loved his grandson.

Her stage name was Delilah du Lac, a tart's moniker, but earlier Gavin had called her by her true name. Daisy Lake, wasn't it? Why that name should ring so familiar he couldn't say. Ah, yes, wasn't that the name of the little orphan girl Gavin had always run on about, that first year especially?

The same little orphan girl whose letters he made very certain Gavin never saw?

All at once he felt as if his cravat was choking him. *Dear God, what have I done?*

Stepping out onto the sunlit street, he set out in the direction of his parked carriage. At his approach, his driver started up from the box but Maximilian shook his head. "I'll walk a bit."

He forged blindly on, for the first time in his sixty-five years not caring where he went or how long it took him to get there. It was one of those rare spring days blessed with a canopy of cornflower blue sky without a rain cloud in sight. There was even a bit of balm to the breeze, and yet Maximilian fancied he felt the draft of Daisy Lake's icy emerald gaze at his back as though it were November instead of May. Before he knew it, he was at the entrance to a small public park. Stopping to catch his breath, he took out his pocket watch, a relic from his own grandfather's day which still managed to keep the time, and realized he'd been walking for nearly an hour.

The park wasn't much of a park at all but rather a gated green space scattered with benches and boasting a small pond in its center that was obviously manmade. Across the green, a trio of boys played ducks and drakes, skipping stones across the still water and taking delight in terrorizing the ornamental fishes. Picnicking on the grassy knoll were a young man and young woman, new-lyweds, he suspected, and seemingly very much in love. Perched on the edge of the blanket with the remains of their feast spread out before them, the woman leaned over the wicker hamper and accepted the slice of cheese the man slid between her parted lips.

The sight made Max feel weary and wistful and irre-deemably old. Turning away, he eyed the nearest bench, the one end occupied by a smartly dressed woman of his age or thereabouts. Though her delicately lined face was shadowed by the brim of her bonnet, something about her struck him as exceedingly familiar. He squinted, blinked, and then looked again before it struck him. The woman sedately knitting and occasionally glancing out onto the green was his old friend, Lottie Rivers. He hadn't seen her since the Stonevale charity ball where her niece-by-marriage, Caledonia, had come in the company of Gavin's photographer friend, whom she married under somewhat sketchy circumstances. Good Lord, had a year really passed by so quickly?

For a fleeting moment, he considered turning away and leaving before she saw him, but all at once she looked up, snagging his gaze. She smiled and raised a glove hand, beckoning him over, and courtesy demanded he pause long enough to at least say hello.

Reaching her, he said, "I thought it might be you, but I wasn't certain at first."

Shielding her eyes from the sun with the edge of one slender hand, she looked up at him and smiled. "I thought it might be you, too, but without my spectacles I couldn't be sure."

"I didn't know you wore spectacles." Staring down at her, he noted how the years had softened her once brilliant violet eyes to an equally lovely shade of gray-blue. Whatever their color, it would be a shame to hide their light behind glass and wire rims.

"I don't. That's my very problem." She tapped him with her closed parasol and let out a little laugh, the sort that brought to mind a hand bell's tinkling or the clinking of champagne flutes joining in a toast, and against all odds Maximilian found himself laughing with her.

"Do have a seat, Max." She patted the vacant space

beside her and shifted over to make room.

He hesitated and then settled beside her, the stiffness in his knees scarcely bothering him at all. "Thank you."

They sat in companionable silence for some time, looking out onto the park, and it occurred to Maximilian it had been a very long time since he'd sat with a woman thus. So long, in point, he'd come close to forgetting what an exceedingly pleasant feeling it was.

At length, Lottie turned to him and said, "If you don't mind my asking, what brings you here, Max?"

Not yet ready to surrender the serenity of the moment, he regarded the knob of his walking stick and shrugged. "Can't a man seek sojourn on a park bench and enjoy a fine spring day if he chooses?"

"Of course he can only I've never before known that man to be you. I come here and sit nearly every day when the weather is fine and today is the first I've ever crossed paths with you."

Giving up the game, he turned to her and admitted, "I've just had an interview with a young woman, an actress, and I'm afraid I muddled things rather badly."

She arched one half-moon brow and regarded him. "An actress, Max, at your age? Why, I'm not certain whether I should offer my congratulations or rap your knuckles and give you a good dressing down."

"Neither will be necessary." He felt his face heat though his hat brim more than shielded him from the sun. "It wasn't . . . that is to say, it wasn't that sort of, er . . . interview."

Looking over at her, he saw she was smiling again, a mischievous and rather sexy smile that shot a funny little fluttering sensation in the vicinity of his heart. Leave it to Lottie to tease him out of his sourness.

"What sort was it, then? I don't mean to pry but you look . . . troubled."

She'd always had a canny knack for reading him. "It's a rather long and involved story, I'm afraid."

Reaching over, she patted the top of his hand. "That's all right, Max. At our age, what have we but time?"

"Very well, but once I've done, don't be surprised if you don't find yourself wanting to poke the point of that knitting needle into my eye."

She cocked her head to the side and regarded him. "That bad, is it?"

"Worse, I'm afraid."

He took a deep breath and recounted the story. Not sparing himself, he started with the day fifteen years before when he swept into the headmaster's office at Roxbury House hell bent on erasing every painful memory in Gavin's past, including his year-long stay in the orphanage, by sheer force of will.

She listened in patient silence. Only when he concluded with the recent disastrous meeting with Daisy did he dare glance her way. He steeled himself to see loathing in her lovely face, but instead he saw only compassion and sadness.

"Oh Lottie, what am I to do? If I've misjudged the gel then I may have lost my grandson his chance at happiness. And yet, even if she does love Gavin as she claims, she's an actress, even worse, a former dance hall girl. I want Gavin to be happy, but how can I possibly give my blessing to such a union?"

"How, indeed?" Regarding the knitting lying neglected in her lap, she took a moment to gather her thoughts. "Let me ask you this: were you happy married to your Rose?"

Even wondering down what path she was leading him, he didn't hesitate. "Yes, I was."

"Rose and I attended the same French finishing school. We were chums, if you recall, or had you forgotten?" When he admitted he had forgotten, she added, "Would it surprise you to learn that Rose was considered quite scandalous in our day? She was always finding ways to sneak out at night and during our last term there was even a flirtation with a French dancing master that very nearly got her expelled. You knew about that, of course."

"I'd heard . . . talk. It all took place so very long ago, I haven't thought about it in years."

"But at the time you knew and yet you married her anyway and, as you've just said, you were happy with her."

Swallowing against the sudden tightness banding his throat, he nodded. "She was the light of my life." He turned away, feeling moisture dampen his eye. "Until

Lucy ran off and eloped, there was never a cross word between us. She never forgave me for not bringing our daughter and her husband home."

"In that case, don't make the same mistake a second time."

"I'm afraid it's too late."

"Poppycock, as long as you're breathing, it's never too late."

"What are you saying?"

"I'm saying it falls to you to find the means to set matters between Gavin and his actress to rights. Do whatever you must, Max, but above all make it right."

❦

For Daisy, the rest of the afternoon slipped by in a sort of semi-recollected haze. She navigated the dress rehearsal without conscious thought or deliberate action much as she imagined a sleepwalker might. Several times the director had to stop to feed her a line she memorized weeks before but only just forgot, or to call out a cue she missed for the very first time. By the end of Act Three, both he and her fellow players were thoroughly exasperated with her, not that she faulted them for it. Rosalind was the pivotal character of the play, after all. The success of the performance rested heavily on her shoulders. If she failed her first night out, the critics would lambaste the performance, and her theatrical career would be finished before it had even begun. And yet more than worrying over forgotten lines or slighting reviews, she couldn't stop thinking about Gavin. It was as if the real play, the real drama, was taking place not onstage but in her head.

Back in her dressing room, she stripped off her costume, slipped on her silk dressing gown, and tied back her hair. She was reaching for her pot of cleansing cream when she heard raised voices in the hallway outside her door. Mr. St. John returned? She certainly hoped not. The visitation by her lover's grandsire was not an experience she cared to repeat this day or any day thereafter. She opened the door and poked her head out. Somehow she wasn't really surprised to see Gavin striding down the barrow hallway, two burly stagehands in tow.

He gained her door along with the stagehands who rushed in behind him, apologies bubbling forth. "Sorry, miss. He slipped straight by us."

"No, really, it's perfectly fine, lads. Mr. Carmichael is a . . . friend."

They bobbed their capped heads and backed out, pulling the door closed. Knowing what she must do, Daisy hated to see them go.

Gavin came toward her, arms open, a bouquet of daisies clenched in one gloved hand. "A friend, am I? I rather hoped at this point I was more to you than that. Serves me right, I suppose. I'm late delivering that good luck kiss I promised you this morning. Better late than never, I hope?" He leaned toward her.

She turned her head so his lips fell upon her cheek. "The rehearsal ended a few minutes ago. I was just about to wash my face. You'll get paint on you."

"It won't be the first time or the last, for that matter. A spot of stage paint here and there is one of the hazards of keeping company with an actress and an altogether trifling price to pay for kissing such sweet lips as yours. I believe I'll risk it." He reached for her again.

"Is that what we're doing? Keeping company?" Such a thoroughly proper phrase made it sound as though she were a debutante at her come-out ball and Gavin her suitor rather than what they were—lovers who could never be more.

Gavin slid a single gloved finger down the line of her throat, drawing a shiver from her. "Among other things."

Even with her heart breaking, she couldn't help wanting to be with him one more time, couldn't help thinking how easy it would be to simply open her robe and her legs and take him inside her.

She saw the flash of desire in his eyes just before he reached for her. Not trusting herself to resist, she held out a hand to stay him. Flattening a palm against his chest, she made herself push him away. "Gavin, I said no."

"I see." Smile slipping, he handed her the bouquet, a far more reputable bunch of daisies than he'd given her the last time. "I take it the rehearsal went poorly?"

She turned away. "It did indeed."

Coming up behind her, he laid warm hands atop

her shoulders. "It's only a rehearsal. Nerves are to be expected, but once the curtain goes up on the real performance, you'll be splendid, you'll see." He pulled her against him and for a brief moment she let herself fall back into all that masculine strength and pretend everything could still be made right.

"I intended to wait until you came home but I couldn't, or at least I didn't want to." He stepped back and turned her in his arms to face him. "This may not be the most opportune time to give you this, but I confess I can't wait any longer." Eyes beaming, he pulled a velvet-covered ring box from his jacket pocket.

"Oh, Gavin." Reaching for him, she slid her hand into his silky hair, wishing they might stay in the moment forever and never move beyond it.

But of course, that was fantasy. She could no more stall time than she could conjure a magic wand and wave it to transform herself into a proper lady instead of what she was, an actress with a scandalous past and an illegitimate child.

"I love that you asked me, but you must know my answer can only be no."

The light went out of his smile and his eyes. "Why is that?"

"Do you even need to ask? Surely you must know I'm no fit mate for you?"

He shook his head. "You're my soul mate, the queen of my heart, the love of my life. What else might possibly matter?"

He was so unspeakably earnest, so impossibly honorable and dear it broke her heart to send him away but send him away she must. "Oh, Gavin, it's a lovely fairytale we've been living these past weeks, but it's coming time for it to end so we can both move forward with our lives. I'm an aspiring actress with a sketchy past and nothing to recommend me beyond a pair of dancer's legs and a trunk full of musty costumes and paste baubles."

"You've a great deal more to recommend you, and we both know it. And I love you. I should like to think that counted for something?"

Fearing she would weaken if he didn't leave, and soon, Daisy reached inside herself for the one thing certain to drive him away forever.

"I had a visit earlier today . . . from your grandfather."

The scowl that admission prompted put her in mind of his grandfather indeed, making her aware of a fleeting family resemblance. "What the devil did he want? Never mind, I'll ask him myself and while I'm at it tell him to mind his own bloody business." He turned as if to go.

"No, wait, don't." She reached out and caught at his coat sleeve. "Your grandfather offered me money, a great deal of money, in exchange for my promise to walk out of your life forever."

He blew out a heavy breath. "The old badger never

ceases trying to run my life. He must have been shocked when you turned him down. I wish I'd been a fly on the wall when you told him to sod off." Unable to meet his gaze, Daisy dropped hers to the floor. He raised a dark brow and regarded her. "You did turn him down . . . didn't you?"

Biting her bottom lip, she shook her head. "No, Gavin, I didn't. I . . . I accepted. I'm . . . I'm sorry but five thousand pounds is a great deal of money for a girl like me, and I've a daughter to think of."

"I would have provided for you and Freddie both, cared for her as though she were my own flesh and blood. Christ, Daisy, I was even thinking to legally adopt her."

"Gavin, I'm . . . sorry."

"Sorry?" He stared at her as though she'd just sprouted a second head—one crowned by devil's horns and a great many hairy moles and hideous warts. "Can it be that's all you have to say for yourself? You're *sorry?*"

She'd done her work well, perhaps too well, because judging from the glacial gleam in his eyes and the cutting coldness of his voice, he well and truly hated her. That was what she wanted, wasn't it? In a span of mere minutes she accomplished precisely what she set out to do. She'd driven him away once and for all. Huzzah for her. Whether she called herself Delilah du Lac or Daisy Lake no longer mattered, not really. Either way, she was a far better actress than anyone, herself included, had supposed.

Every sinew of her being screamed out for her to take back the lie and set things right with him while there was still time. For Gavin's good she tamped down the temptation and forced herself to meet the raw pain in his gaze without flinching. "What else is there to say?"

"What else, indeed?" He threw back his head and let out a crack of laughter sharp as shattered glass.

"I am sorry, Gavin."

"I'm sorry, too, Daisy—royally sorry I ever set eyes on you, sorrier still I let myself fall in love with you all over again. I do love you, you know. Greedy, grasping bitch that you are, God help me, I still want you in my bed and in my life. As it is, I'm not entirely certain how I'm to get you out of my head let alone my heart, or the scattered scraps left of it, and go on again."

Tears sliding down her cheeks, Daisy shook her head. "Oh, Gavin, don't you know Shakespeare had the right of it?" Swallowing hard, she recalled the one line of Rosalind's she managed to miss several times earlier in rehearsal but now recalled with crystalline clarity. "'Men have died from time to time and worms have eaten them, but not for love.'"

Staggering out onto the street, Gavin felt as though the future he built for himself was falling down in flames around him. The ring he left behind on Daisy's dressing table, not because he'd forgotten it but because he never wanted to see it, or her, again.

But there was someone he despised far more than Daisy at the moment and that someone was his grandfather. He stormed into the old man's law office only to have the buttoned-up secretary inform him Mr. St. John had not yet returned from luncheon. According to the ticking grandfather's clock, it was coming on four o' clock. For a man who typically took his meals at his desk, such an extended absence was noteworthy.

"Shall I tell him you came by?"

"Don't bother. I'm sure I'll find him."

Gavin lost no time in heading for his grandfather's townhouse. Situated within view of the Marble Arch on fashionable Park Lane, its Palladian façade always struck Gavin as more like a public building than a private home. Ordinarily he avoided the place as he might avoid the plague. He had myriad memories of finishing out his adolescence there, at least on school holidays, but few of them could be called happy.

His grandfather's butler greeted him beneath the fanlight-crowned entrance. "Master Gavin, how nice to see you."

Stepping inside the foyer, Gavin was amazed at how the sterility of the place still stifled him. Marble busts of Greek and Roman philosophers were set in the recessed wall panels and the furniture and silver pieces polished to a high gloss.

"And you, Wentworth." The butler must be nearing seventy. Gavin remembered looking up to him as a boy but now the old man barely reached his shoulder. "Is my grandfather in?"

"He's only just returned home. He's in his study. Shall I inform him you're here?"

Gavin shook his head. "That won't be necessary. I am well acquainted with the way."

In his boyhood, he'd been summoned to his grandfather's sanctum often enough, usually to be dressed down for some supposed transgression, rarely to be praised. He vividly recalled a caning or two. Leaning over the desk with his trousers riding his ankles and his teeth gritted to keep from crying out, those episodes counted as the most humiliating of his life.

The door to the study stood ajar when he approached. He gave the perfunctory light rap and stepped inside.

Seated behind the mahogany desk, his grandfather looked up. "Given the turn our luncheon took, I hadn't thought to see you again this day or soon again."

Gavin doubted that very much. Not much took the old man by surprise and given the meddling mischief he'd been about, surely he couldn't be surprised to have his grandson turning up at his door.

Rather than play his grandfather's game, Gavin came directly to the point. "I've just come from Drury Lane Theater. I'm sure it will please you to know Miss Lake has rejected my marriage proposal."

"The devil she has." The old man must be something of an actor himself because the shocked expression on his gaunt face looked to be real.

"Forgive me if I admit to finding your reaction rather contrived, particularly when turning me down is precisely what you paid her to do."

For the first time in fifteen years, Gavin saw his grandfather hesitate. Moistening pale lips, he dropped his gaze to the desk blotter almost as if . . . as if he were ashamed to meet Gavin's eye. "Is that what she told you?"

"Yes."

"That is only half the truth. I did offer her money, a great deal of money, but she refused to accept so much as a penny from me."

For the first time since barging in, Gavin felt less than sure of his purpose. "But she said she took the money from you."

"If you don't believe me, then perhaps you'll believe the proof of your eyes." St. John reached into his coat pocket and pulled out two halves of what looked to be a bank note. He handed the torn pieces over to Gavin. "She rent this in front of me, consigned me to the Devil, and then tossed me out of her dressing room. Whatever else she is, she's quite a woman—a woman who must love you very much."

"A woman's who's lied to me." Gavin held off on adding "again" if only because whatever deception occurred in the past or present was between Daisy and he.

"By the by, you shall have my letter of resignation come Monday morning."

"I wish you'd reconsider."

"I can't be in business with a man who schemes to undermine me any more than I can marry a woman who lies to me."

His grandfather shook his grizzled head, and Gavin was again struck by how weary and frail he appeared. It was as if the tyrant of his youth had become an old man overnight. "We're none of us perfect, Gavin."

Rourke had said fair near the same to him the other night when he'd shown up drunk at his door. He dismissed it at the time, but lately he found himself giving the statement more and more thought. Did his high standards and perfectionist ways drive the people he cared for to lie rather than risk disappointing him—or losing his love?

"It may well be too late for you and I, but don't let your stubborn pride stand in the way of your happiness with Miss Lake. If you still wish to wed her, I won't stand in your way."

"Even if I were willing to debase myself by asking her yet again, it is obvious she'll do and say just about anything to be rid of me."

"Quite the contrary, she's been fighting to find her way back to you for the past fifteen years."

"What game are you playing at now, Grandfather?"

"Truth or consequences, I suppose you'd call it." St.

John drew open a desk drawer and slapped a bundle of letters atop the desk. "I should have shown these to you ere now. I only pray to God it isn't too late." He slid the string-tied letters across the desk to Gavin.

Heart pounding and palms perspiring, Gavin looked from the pile of post to his grandfather. "What's all this?"

"Letters Miss Lake, Daisy, wrote to you all those years ago."

Gavin felt a strange reluctance to touch them, knew a keen sense that to open so much as one would be akin to throwing up the lid on Pandora's Box—a life-altering experience, a deed from which there would be no turning back, not now, not ever. "Why didn't I ever receive them?"

"Believe me when I say I honestly had your best interest at heart."

Looking up, he said, "You kept them from me, didn't you?" It wasn't really a question.

Maximilian hesitated and then nodded. "When you went away to school, I left orders with the headmaster you were only to receive correspondence from a list of approved persons. Any letters from anyone else were to be remanded to me. I wanted to give you a fresh start, to give you a chance to purge the bad memories from the past."

"Not all my memories were bad. Apart from those of the fire, most of them were bloody good."

"But I didn't know that. After I brought you home here, many a night I'd be working in this study when your screams would reach me from above. I knew you were dreaming of the past, the fire. You'd suffered so much already, I couldn't stand by and see you suffer any more, not if I could prevent it."

"I suffered when you took me away from my friends. They were the only comfort, the only family, I'd known for more than a year, and yet you tore them from me much as you might tear off a limb."

"I see that now though I didn't then. For what it's worth, I am sorry, Gavin. I was only trying to protect you."

"You were thinking of one person and one person only, the same person who remains uppermost in your mind and your heart: yourself. You as good as killed my mother with your heartlessness and your rigid, unbending rules, and you've spent the past fifteen years doing your damnedest to break me as well. Well, you're not going to get away with it, Grandfather, not any longer. You and this firm can go to the Devil. I'd sooner hawk fish on Fleet Bridge than take a single more case to benefit you and your highbrow friends."

"Gavin, wait, don't leave like this . . . please."

"Go to the devil, Grandfather."

Gavin picked up the packet of letters and walked out into the twilight.

CHAPTER TWENTY

"We that are true lovers run into strange capers;
but as all is mortal in nature, so is all nature
in love mortal in folly."
—WILLIAM SHAKESPEARE, Touchstone,
As You Like It

The day of Daisy's theatrical debut dawned crisp and clear. Such fine weather constituted a good omen that Flora exclaimed she felt in her bones, but then her adoptive mother's anatomy was partial to the warmer, dryer weather. Owing to the split with Gavin, Daisy had a bad time of it the night before. It would take more than sunshine burning the fog away to lift her spirits. A good, long cry in private had been a given but afterward she'd been determined to pull herself together. Not only did she have a child and aging parents to support but the theater company was counting on her as well. Sir Augustus had confided that box office receipts had not been as sound as he might care to see. He was counting on her winning rave reviews to pack the house for the remainder of the play's run.

She reminded herself that her time with Gavin was never intended to be permanent, at least not on her part. In another few days, the agreed-upon month would have concluded anyway. Over the past week, she let herself be lulled into thinking they might have a future together, but the interview with Gavin's grandfather had confirmed that could never be. She'd met her month's promise to him and a lovely month it had been. She would cherish the gift of their time together as adults for the rest of her days but for the present, this day especially, it was time to move on.

Even with such a fine resolution floating about in her head, it had taken her a long while to fall asleep. When she finally did, she slept in snatches, dropping in and out of restless dreams in which she was both herself and her character of Rosalind. Like the latter, she was wandering about the forest only instead of searching for food and safe haven, she was searching for Gavin. All at once, the fictitious forest transformed into the busy London streets. Gavin stood on the other side of Catherine Street across from the theater. Every time she tried stepping out into the traffic to reach him, another stream of vehicles rolled by. In another version of the dream, she stood on the ledge atop the theater. Gavin was below her, orchestrating her rescue with a fire truck and an enormous circus-style net stretched just above the street to catch her when she leapt.

He called up to her. "Let go and come to me, Daisy."

"I can't," she called back. "I want to but I can't."

He looked up at her for a long, sad moment and then all at once the scene below her faded into fog, stealing her view of the street and Gavin with it. She was alone on the ledge and this time when her feet slipped out from beneath her there was no net, and no Gavin, to catch her.

Both times she woke drenched in an icy sweat, the bedcovers a damp tangle. Smoothing a hand over the empty side of mattress, Gavin's side, the irony of her situation wasn't lost on her. She who'd been so resolute in never letting a man spend the night in her bed suddenly couldn't sleep without one. But she was missing more than merely the feel of a warm, hard body pressed against hers. She was missing a particular man. She was missing Gavin.

She finally gave up on independence and slipped into bed beside Freddie. The cot was scarcely wide enough for one but holding her precious child against her, she finally found peace enough to fall asleep.

Morning had come early. Awaking tired and puffy-eyed, she scarcely felt at her best but as someone once said, the show must go on. Cups of hot tea got her through the dicier parts of the day and once she made it to the theater and was absorbed into the flurry of preparations and general mayhem, she felt her energy returning.

She'd just walked through the final wardrobe check along with the location of props. Scarce minutes before the curtain went up, she was left with nothing really to do beyond hold down her panic and wait. She lifted the curtain and peaked out onto the house. It wasn't a sell-out but there was a respectable crowd. Her practiced eye reckoned that close to three-quarters of the theater's three thousand-odd seats were sold out, not a bad showing for a first night's performance of Shakespeare with an unknown actress in the lead. Her gaze went to Gavin's box. Harry and an attractive brunette who must be his wife, Callie, were seated inside along with Rourke albeit without the elusive heiress he hoped would accompany him. Lady Katherine had so far proven herself a worthy adversary in fending off his romantic advances though Daisy suspected the stubborn Scot would mount another onslaught before long. The Lakes had brought Freddie, whom Daisy said might stay up late in honor of the special occasion. Her daughter looked pretty as a picture in the new celestial blue frock Daisy had bought to match her eyes, blue ribbons woven into her shiny black curls. Everyone she loved, everyone who loved her, had turned out to wish her well—except Gavin.

He had sent her flowers, though not the customary field daisies but a lovely bouquet of passion red roses. She liked to think the color signified there might be some hope for them yet, but the enclosed card bore no message beyond his name.

And yet what right had she to expect more than that when she had done everything she could to drive him away? Without him in her life, she could turn her attention to her career. She should be happy, elated even. Isn't this what she always wanted?

Even among comedies, *As You Like It* was such a *happy* play. The witty quips and easily brought about happy ending struck her as bordering on annoying. Who knew but despite her background with Paris's *opera-comiques* perhaps with her current experience she would find herself better suited to tragedy after all. Hers and Gavin's relationship seemed more akin to Romeo and Juliet than to Rosalind and Orlando. *Oh, Gavin!*

She felt a tap on her shoulder and whirled about, half-wondering if she had the power to will him there.

Her heart dropped when she saw the theater manager instead. "Sir Augustus. I didn't expect to see you before the performance."

"I was in my box, but I couldn't resist coming backstage to check on a few last minute things including my play's leading lady. How are you getting on, my dear? Not too terribly nervous, I hope?"

Daisy swallowed hard, praying the grease paint and powder hid the dark circles rimming her eyes. "I'm all right."

She wished she might say the same of him. His

face wore a fine sheen of perspiration and he cracked his knuckles as though he were the one about to be called onstage to perform before an audience of thousands.

"Good, jolly good." He clicked his heels, gaze darting to the right and then the left. Apparently determining there was no one close enough by to overhear, he leaned in and whispered, "Don't disappoint me, Daisy. The future of Drury Lane may well be riding on the success, or failure, of tonight's performance."

The stage director chose that moment to stride up to them, the ubiquitous clipboard in hand. "The curtain goes up in five minutes, Daisy," he said without bothering to stop.

"Thank you." Rosalind didn't appear until the second scene of Act I. There was still time. She turned back to the theater manager. "I'll do my very best, sir."

"Of course you will, m'dear. I'd wish you luck but then again we theater folk are a superstitious lot. Break a leg, as the Americans say." Sir Augustus managed a thin smile. "Mind that for the next two-odd hours, you *are* Rosalind."

He turned and headed toward one of the exit doors. Watching him go, Daisy thought, *I don't know who I am any more: Daisy or Delilah or now Rosalind. I might as well be Rosalind. In the end, she at least gets her man.*

Once the curtain went up, Daisy threw herself into her role, not merely playing the plucky Rosalind but becoming her, drawing on her recent real life joys and pains to enrich the character. When as Rosalind she cried out to the actress playing her cousin, Celia, "O coz, coz . . . that thou didst know how many fathoms deep I am in love," real tears wet her cheeks. And when in the final act she and her onstage Orlando made their way to the bridal bower, it was Gavin she imagined kissing when she accepted the actor's light stage buss.

The final act segued to its mutual happy ending for all involved. The overhead lights dimmed, cloaking her fellow players and the painted scenery into smoky darkness. Daisy advanced toward the footlights in measured steps. Looking out into the audience, hoping Gavin might have come to see her after all, she envisioned his handsome face.

She took her bow to thunderous applause and shouts of "Brava" and "Encore, encore!" The houselights came on, and she looked out into the audience to see every man, woman, and child risen to their feet. Breathless, she backed up to form a queue with the company, clasping hands with the actor playing Orlando and the actress playing Celia. A second and then a third bow was called for before the curtain fell for the final time.

A champagne reception followed in the theater's Green Room. After the final curtain, Daisy rushed back to her dressing room where she washed the grease paint from her face, combed and rearranged her hair, and changed into the green silk dinner gown. An hour later she stood at the center of London's theatrical elite. Her flute of champagne growing warm in her hand, she accepted accolades from renowned luminaries of the stage she knew by reputation but had never thought to meet face to face, including the brilliant librettist, W.S. Gilbert, who couldn't seem to praise her enough.

Leaning in so that his white handlebar mustache tickled her cheek, Sir Gilbert whispered, "I don't suppose there's any way I might steal you away to play the lead role of Mabel in Sullivan's and my upcoming production of *Pirates of Penzance*?"

Daisy hesitated. "Sir Augustus has been good to me."

"Don't tell me you've gone and signed an exclusive contract with the fellow?" Mr. Gilbert looked stricken until Daisy admitted she had not. Smile returning, he said, "In that case, call on Sullivan and I at The Savoy at your earliest convenience. I assure you that whatever salary Drury Lane is offering, The Savoy is prepared to match it. To sweeten the pot, I'll even give you a percentage of the door provided you sign an exclusive contract with us."

"I heard that." Sir Augustus sidled up to them, a scowl on his face. "I see you've come poaching as usual, Gilbert."

Gilbert did not deny it. "Miss Lake is not only a gifted actress but a charming young woman. We were just discussing her future."

"Indeed, I knew the very moment I laid eyes on her she'd be splendid for Rosalind." Shifting his gaze to Daisy, Sir Augustus's expression lightened. "Your performance tonight has outshone even my vision. Brava, m'dear."

"Thank you, Sir Augustus, Mr. Gilbert. You are both very kind."

"It's not every actress who receives a standing ovation their first time out. After tonight, you'll be the known as the Darling of Drury Lane."

Mr. Gilbert poked his silvered head into their huddle. "Or the future Sweetheart of the Savoy perhaps."

Face reddening, Sir Augustus rounded on his rival. "Now see here, Gilbert . . ."

Watching them butt heads, Daisy could scarcely believe her great good fortune. Being fought over by the manager of Drury Lane and the great Gilbert of Gilbert and Sullivan was heady stuff. Practically speaking, it meant she would be in a position to take care of Freddie and the Lakes on her own as well as start saving to pay Gavin back the money he'd invested in her.

Gavin. At the thought of him, her heart gave a lurch. More so than anyone, he'd believed in her all along. Were it not for him, she would still be in her dirty, dark-lit dressing room at The Palace, calves aching from finishing her third and final show of the day. She owed him so much and had given him so little. Beyond the very great gratitude she felt, she quite simply wanted him with her.

Mr. Gilbert took his leave and Sir Augustus turned to her. "Where is Mr. Carmichael?" he asked as if reading her thoughts. "I would have thought he would be the very first to congratulate you."

Daisy hesitated. The situation was even more awkward than she thought. "Unfortunately, he is . . . otherwise engaged this evening."

"That is a pity. When I next see him at the Garrick, I shall be sure to give him a full report on how splendid you were."

Daisy wasn't certain what to say to that so she settled on "Thank you."

"There is a gentleman who has been waiting most patiently to meet you. A very influential gentleman," he added, gesturing to a tall, bespectacled man clicking his heels in the corner. Feeling in a daze, Daisy made her excuses to Sir Gilbert and let Sir August lead her away.

The "very influential gentleman" was the theatrical reviewer for *The London Times*. Daisy spent the next several minutes listening to him exclaim over her performance, his praise a highbrow version of the overblown announcements the music hall chairman had used to make before bringing her onstage. Scarcely a month had passed and yet what a long time ago that seemed, almost another life.

Attention wandering off, she found herself searching

the room's four corners for the one person from whom a single word of praise would have meant the world.

Gavin. I know I've had more second chances that any one person could possibly deserve but if only you could find it in your heart to give me just one more . . .

"*Maman, Maman!*" Like a tethered colt suddenly set free of its harness, Freddie broke away from the Lakes and rushed up to her.

Shooting the reviewer an apologetic look, Daisy bent to enfold her daughter in a hug. "My daughter, Freddie." she said and smiling he informed her he had four little ones of his own.

"Fredericka, leave off. Your mum is working the room." Out-of-breath, Flora rushed up to them.

"It's all right, Mum." Grateful for the feel of those strong little arms about her waist, Daisy combed back a wayward blue-black curl. "Did you like the play, precious?"

Freddie answered with an eager nod. "*Oui, Maman,* I liked it very much."

"What was your favorite part?"

Freddie thought for a moment, one small finger pressed to the side of her mouth. "I liked the end best when everything is sorted out and they all get married and live happily ever after."

Swallowing against the lump lodging in her throat, Daisy admitted, "That's my favorite part, too."

The happily paired onstage lovers had served as yet another bittersweet reminder of her sad situation. By the play's end, Audrey had her William, Phebe her Silvius, Celia her Oliver, and of course, Rosalind her Orlando, only in real life there would be no mythical Hymen to bring about a happy ending with her soul's mate.

She felt eyes upon her and looked up to find Flora sending her a sympathetic look. "I expect it's time a certain young miss was tucked into bed and her grandmother with her. You don't mind our taking off, do you love? It's been a long day and Bob is feeling a bit peckish."

Daisy looked over to her father, who'd subsided into a chair by the door. She set Freddie from her and straightened. "By all means, you three run along. Hopefully, I shan't be much longer. Bed will be most welcome tonight."

Not long ago she would have considered it a point of pride to stay out celebrating past dawn, but her month with Gavin had changed her in profound ways, including teaching her the difference between false gaiety and genuine happiness.

Flora took hold of Freddie's hand and led her away. Though Freddie protested she wasn't a bit sleepy, her heavy-lidded eyes said otherwise. Daisy glanced down to the half-finished glass of champagne growing warm in her hand. The wine must be making her maudlin because going through the motions of celebrating her success was challenging her acting abilities far more than playing Rosalind had.

Rourke sidled up to her side, a glass of champagne in

hand. Without asking, he reached for her flute and replaced it with a fresh one. Setting the other aside, he said, "You look as though you could do with something stronger, but I dinna think passing you my whiskey flask in the midst of this hobnobbing crowd would go o'er too well."

"Probably not but this will do. Thank you." She took a small sip of the chilled sparkling wine to loosen the lump in her throat.

He took a step back and studied her. "If you don't mind my saying so, you don't look like a woman who's just brought the theatrical world to its knees."

On the brink of tears, Daisy shook her head. "Oh, Patrick, I'm afraid I may have made a terrible mistake and I don't know how to fix it."

"Gavin?"

She gave a miserable nod. "He didn't come tonight, and the very worst part is I can't blame him. I've made a hash of everything and what should have been the happiest night of my life has turned out to be anything but."

All at once, it was as if the dam of her reserve burst. Tears spilled down her cheeks. Cursing beneath her breath she reached for a handkerchief merely to realize she left her reticule back in her dressing room.

"There, there, lass, dinna fash." He pulled a plaid handkerchief from his pocket and discretely handed it to her. "Let's get you some fresh air, shall we? Or better yet, let's get you out of here entirely."

"Really?"

"Aye, you know we Highlanders. We get antsy if we're cooped up over long."

Leave it to Rourke to help her find her smile in the midst of crying. "You grew up in London and then in Kent. Unless your memory reaches back to the womb, until recently when you purchased that castle of yours, you didn't know any more of Scotland than I do."

"Why, Daisy, that's just geography," he answered with a wink.

Dabbing at her eyes, she nodded. "In that case, I accept. I only need to say my goodnights to one or two persons and stop back at my dressing room to collect my things."

Bidding goodnight to Sir Augustus and some of her fellow cast members took longer than she anticipated, but on this instance Rourke was the soul of patience. Eventually she broke away and led the way to back to her dressing room and then out a side door. Rourke pointed to a shiny black lacquer carriage parked by the street lamp on Russell Street. "Here we are."

Glancing up at the handsome coachman seated on the box, she blinked and then turned to Rourke. "Whatever is Harry doing driving your carriage?" she asked, thinking the evening had taken a queer turn indeed.

The Scot finished lowering the carriage steps before answering, "'Tis a fine night for a jaunt and he had a mind to drive. He's a fair hand at the ribbons though dinna tell him I said so." He opened the carriage door and gave her a gentle nudge.

Harry's wife, Callie, was seated inside. They met earlier in the evening but only for a minute. "Good evening, Daisy."

"Callie." Wondering what was going on, Daisy hesitated and then slipped into the opposite seat.

Callie greeted her with her customary serene smile. "Brilliant rendition of Rosalind. I would have congratulated you on it earlier but that reception was such a crush, I couldn't make my way near you."

"It was good of you to attend."

Callie shrugged. "Not at all. *As You Like It* has always been a particular favorite of mine."

"Are you certain you don't prefer *The Taming of the Shrew*, darling," Harry called down from the box, tone teasing.

"Quite." Callie made a face and, pulling back the curtain, ducked her head out the open window. Settling back inside, she said, "I've always adored the character of Rosalind. Though the play is hundreds of years old, there's something quite refreshingly modern about her, don't you think?"

Wondering where the conversation might be leading, Daisy agreed it was so.

"But you've lent something quite unique and special to her character. I've never seen her played quite so well."

Rourke joined them inside and drew the carriage

door closed. Daisy wondered why they were all traveling home together. She knew from Gavin's saying so that Harry and Callie lived in Mayfair, which was in the West End of town. Daisy's Whitechapel lodgings were in the East End, the opposite direction entirely.

Looking between the sheepish-faced pair, Daisy said, "I think it's time one of you told me what's really going on, don't you?"

Callie turned to Rourke and shook her head. "I told you she was too smart by half. When will you men learn to stop underestimating women?"

"You tell her then."

Turning back to Daisy, Callie admitted, "To put it quite simply, we're kidnapping you, my dear."

"Kidnapping me!" Daisy looked from Rourke to Callie, scarcely able to credit the evidence of her ears.

"Kidnapping is one of the oldest courtship rituals known to mankind—and womankind, for that matter." Callie punctuated the pronouncement with a smile.

"Aye," Rourke piped up. "Bride theft was practiced by the Highland clans right up to the previous century. If I have to attend one bloody more ball or soiree, I may give serious thought to bringing back the practice myself."

Brows snapping together, Callie said, "Patrick, you know I adore you, but I think it's time you joined

Hadrian on the box."

He hesitated and then shrugged. "Verra well, I'll leave you two to your woman's prattle."

Rather than reprimand him, Callie tossed back her head and laughed, clearly used to being baited by not only her husband but his friends as well. "Very magnanimous of you, and I'm sure neither Daisy nor I would wish to burden you with our *prattle*, not when you and my husband must have so many more lofty topics to discuss, such as the outcome of the latest wrestling match at Wapping or the horserace at Epsom Downs."

Rourke made a show of yanking an invisible knife from his heart and then opened the carriage door and climbed out, but not before Daisy caught his sideways grin. Responding to the lighthearted banter, she relaxed back against the plush leather squabs.

The carriage jolted forward and Callie continued, "On principle, I disapprove of such primeval tactics, but Rourke and Hadrian persuaded me to go along. Every rule has its exception, after all, and in your circumstances there's such a great deal at stake."

Daisy liked Harry's wife well enough but even so she felt herself bristling. "It is very kind of you to concern yourself, Caledonia, but if you'll pardon my saying so I can't help but question what a woman such as you would know much about either me or my . . . circumstances."

Callie arched one perfect half-moon eyebrow and regarded her. *Noblesse oblige,* Daisy thought it was called, this attitude that one's high birth obligated them to behave with a certain selfless virtue. The same action committed by a common person would be called meddling.

Just when the standoff inside the carriage was bordering on unbearable, Callie ended the silence by saying, "I'd rather you call me Callie. All my friends do. As to your circumstances, when it comes to matters of the heart, it might surprise you to learn we're not so very different. Not long ago, I came close to turning my back on happiness by holding on to a rigid and rather self-defeating belief. In my case, someone I'd foolishly trusted with my heart when I was very young made some cutting comments about my appearance." A shadow crossed Callie's face as though the hurtful memory hadn't entirely lost its sting. "For years, a full decade actually, I was left with the surety I was undesirable, too ugly and awkward to ever attract a man's passion let alone win his heart."

Daisy shook her head. "You'll pardon me, but I find that difficult to believe."

Earlier that evening, she'd seen Callie navigate the packed reception room with the poise of one born to such social situations. Though she might not be a beauty in the classical sense, the statuesque brunette looked luscious in a low-cut ebony evening dress with jeweled straps that accentuated her smooth shoulders and generous "charms." From her time in Paris, Daisy recognized the gown as a copy of the one worn by "Madame X" in the Sargent painting.

Callie graced her with a gentle smile. "It's the bald truth. But then Hadrian, or Harry if you prefer, came along and made me see myself not only through the eye of his camera but through his eyes as well. I'd just started to believe him when . . . when things fell apart."

Daisy had heard about the scandal from Gavin. Apparently a high-ranking Member of Parliament had approached Harry to take a nude photograph of Callie in order to discredit both her and the women's suffrage movement she represented. In desperate need of funds, he agreed, never anticipating that he'd fall in love with the famous suffragette. Before he could destroy the photograph, it was stolen from his studio and leaked to the Fleet Street press. Some women confronted with such an embarrassment would have retreated, never to show their faces in public again, but it was evident Callie was made of sterner stuff. She'd moved about the green room earlier that evening chatting with apparent ease as though half of London hadn't seen her in only her knickers. Mulling the situation over, Daisy conceded that perhaps she and Harry's highborn wife weren't so very different after all.

Callie leaned in. "Perhaps it's time you faced your inner demon, whatever belief that holds you back from letting love in?"

Daisy's customary response would have been to tell Callie to shove off but in this case one confidence invited another. Beside that, hadn't she spent the last twenty-four hours asking fair near the same question? Gavin's heated words rushed back to her yet again. *What are you so afraid of? That we might be happy? That I might actually love you?* What *was* she so afraid of that she was willing to sign up for a lifetime of loneliness rather than confront it?

Her heart picked up pace and the inside of her mouth felt as dry as cotton. Just using the word *love* in a conversation had her feeling panicky. "It's as though Gavin holds this image of me in his mind that no one could possibly live up to, certainly not me. At times when I'm with him, I feel as though I'm competing for his affections with another woman only that other woman is me, or rather the girl I used to be. I'm not making any sense, am I?"

Leaning in, Callie looked to be listening intently. "On the contrary, you're making a great deal of sense. Go on."

Daisy dropped her gaze to the beaded reticule in her lap. "The day his grandfather fetched him from the orphanage to bring him to London, Gavin came to the attic where I was hiding. It was our special place where the four of us, Gavin, Rourke, Harry, and me could steal away and create our own private world. We even held monthly club meetings with an oath of allegiance we used to take turns repeating. That must sound silly to you." She ventured an upward glance at Callie.

Regarding her with kind eyes, Callie shook her

head. "Not at all."

"I begged him to bring me along. He couldn't, of course. I didn't understand why not at the time, but having met Mr. St. John I suppose I should be glad he didn't. Gavin swore to write me, swore that somehow, someday he'd arrange it so we could be together again, but once his grandfather brought him to London, he forgot all about me. Worse than forgot, he ignored me. For two years, I wrote him, letter upon letter, but he never answered them, not a one."

Callie frowned as if trying to put together a puzzle whose final few pieces were missing. "I haven't known Gavin for very long, but from the bits and pieces of your time together at Roxbury House that Hadrian has shared with me and from what I've seen of him myself, I can't believe he wouldn't have written you back. As for forgetting you, that simply isn't the case. From what Hadrian tells me, this past year he's spent what amounts to a small fortune on a private detective to find you."

Daisy jerked her head upright. "Gavin's been paying someone to search for me? Are you quite certain?"

Callie's effusive nod left no room for doubting. "The detective managed to trace you to Dover, but after that he came up empty. The news brought Gavin's spirits quite low. Hadrian and Rourke dragged him out to the supper club that night, hoping a bit of fun might take his mind off you."

Gavin had been searching for her all along, could it

be? If so, then her life was akin to the farfetched scenario in the penny dreadfuls she read upon occasion where a case of mistaken identity or the machinations of a devious villain tore the lovers apart for years only to see them reunited in the end. In their story, however, the person Gavin had found again wasn't the sweetly innocent girl of his memory but a tart-up music hall performer prancing half-naked about the stage. Small wonder he reacted as he had. It must have been quite a shock.

"Instead of the detective finding me, by some fluke Gavin found me himself."

Callie nodded. "Yes, but my personal belief is that there is no such thing as happenstance. You and Gavin coming together again after all this time is a gift from God. Regardless of what brought you two together again, don't waste this chance. Second chances are rare as four leaf clovers. Third chances, well, we don't often hear of those, now do we?"

Daisy shook her head, which had begun to throb and not because of the single glass of champagne she'd drunk. "Even if Gavin didn't, strictly speaking, abandon me, I'm not that girl any more and haven't been for almost fifteen years. How can we ever come together as we are? He's a respected barrister and I'm a showgirl . . . well, an actress now, I suppose, but still I'll always carry my past with me. As long as we stay in England, I don't see how I can ever be more to him than a mistress."

A few weeks before, that would have seemed like a

plumb deal but these past weeks with Gavin had changed
her perspective on many things, including relationships.
Now that she had a glimpse of how it could be between
a man and a woman, how caring and respect and compassion and, yes, love could carry physical intimacy to
new heights, she wanted more, so very much more. She
wanted it all—the picket fence framed cottage, the hap-
pily-ever-after fairytale, and, yes, the until-death-do-us-
part marriage vows—all the trappings of commitment
that set soul mates apart from casual lovers.

"Perhaps it's time to let go of that belief, time to take
a chance and trust again, hmm?"

Take a chance. Trust again. What was the worst
that could happen? She might be hurt but then the past
twenty-four hours since she turned Gavin away had been
the most hurtful period of her life.

Silence fell inside the carriage, not an awkward or
sullen silence where people either make a great show of
examining their fingernails or cast fuming stares out the
window but rather a still, companionable quiet in which
everything that must be said and heard has been so done,
freeing all parties to mull over not only the "what ifs" of
the situation but, more importantly, the "what nexts."

Daisy looked over to Callie, realizing she'd lost all
track of the time. It might be midnight or midmorning,
five minutes or fifty since she climbed inside the carriage.
"I don't suppose you're going to tell me where it is you lot
are kidnapping me to?"

The carriage lamp swinging overhead illuminated Callie's small, Mona Lisa-like smile. Lips twitching with suppressed laughter, she shook her head. "Not on your life. The destination is meant to be a surprise. Were I the one to spoil it after all the elaborate scheming that's been carried on, Hadrian and Rourke would have my head on a platter and rightly so. For now, lean back and don't fret about the destination. Just enjoy the ride."

CHAPTER TWENTY–ONE

"The sight of lovers feedeth those in love.
Bring us to this sight, and you shall say
I'll prove a busy actor in their play."
—WILLIAM SHAKESPEARE, Rosalind,
As You Like It

They were traveling eastward, Daisy gathered that much. The streets were becoming progressively narrower and more winding and the smells wafting in through the carriage window considerably less pleasant. The carriage rumbled to a halt. Looking out the window on her side, she saw they'd pulled off the main street. A single torch lit the entrance to a large timber-framed structure in the Tudor style. The building sat back from the street, the turnabout paved in cobbles, a sign it must be very old.

The carriage door opened and Rourke offered a hand to help Daisy out. She took it and then turned back to Callie. "Aren't you coming?"

The brunette shook her head. "This is your night, and your second chance. Good luck."

"Thank you." Daisy turned away to accept Rourke's outstretched hand. She stepped down and, lantern in hand, the Scot escorted her to the main door. Somehow she wasn't really surprised when he opened it without needing a key.

Stepping back, he said, "This is the final leg of the journey for me, but the first step for you."

"Thank you." She tried for a smile, but it felt as wobbly as the rest of her.

"You're most welcome, lass." Drawing back, he hesitated and then said, "He really loves you, you know."

"I know, or at least I do now. And I love him, too, with all my heart."

"Go to, then." He handed her the lantern and turned back down the path.

With a final wave to her friends, Daisy stepped inside. The ancient arched oak door groaned closed behind her. Inside she had no need of the lantern. Candles lit her way from the entrance foyer to the auditorium. She followed the candle-lit path down the center aisle between rows of low, backless benches to the pillared platform stage. The tattered stage curtain rose as she approached, revealing a cloth-covered table set for two. Next to it, a silver pedestal bucket stood within reach, holding what looked to be a bottle of champagne on ice.

Gavin, heart-stoppingly handsome in formal evening dress, strolled out onto the stage. "I was beginning to think Hadrian might have gotten you lost in the dark."

"Gavin, what is all this? Why did you go to the trouble of having our friends kidnap me from one theater only to bring me to another? A dusty one," she added, suppressing a sneeze.

He shrugged. "I wanted some time alone with you, a private celebration, and Hadrian and Rourke were good enough to step in as escort and driver." He reached down a hand and, taking it, she climbed the three steps up.

He released her and she said, "You mean step in as co-conspirators in a kidnapping?"

He shrugged, gaze stroking over her. "It was the only way I could be sure you'd come."

"You might have simply invited me."

He cocked a brow. "Would you have accepted?"

She thought about lying and then dismissed it. Far too many lies stood between them as it was. "I'm not certain."

"Have you dined yet?"

Daisy thought for a moment and then realized she hadn't eaten since breakfast. Though the lobster patties, French cheeses, and strawberries dipped in rich, dark chocolate served at the reception had looked tempting, she hadn't been able to summon much of an appetite.

She shook her head. "No." Feeling eyes upon her, she chanced to see Jamison poke his silver head out from the side curtain as if awaiting his cue. Apparently, Gavin's servant was yet another co-conspirator.

Following her gaze, Gavin said, "In that case, I've champagne chilling and a cold supper waiting in the wings, so you won't thirst or starve. The only stipulation is that you have to spend the next few hours here with me talking, just the two of us. Do you mind?"

Daisy had no inclination to play coy. "Mind? Mind! I spent the better part of the day and then the evening after the performance wishing you might materialize next to me."

She reached for him, but he held up a staying hand. "First we need to settle things between us, once and for all. We need to come to terms, an arrangement we can both live with, if you will."

All this talk of terms and arrangements made him sound more like the flinty barrister of his reputation than the tender lover she knew. She opened her mouth to say as much when it occurred to her what he was about to propose wasn't all that different from the no-nonsense business arrangement she'd insisted upon that first day at his flat.

If laying out their future in black-and-white terms was what it took to keep him, she was prepared to do so as well as to sign nearly anything he proposed. She wanted, needed, Gavin in her life. They were two halves of a single soul and though he was without doubt the better half, she wanted nothing so much as to spend the rest of her life working to make him happy, to complete him as he most certainly completed her.

Praying she wasn't too late, she confided, "Oh, Gavin, I've just had what was supposed to be the most glorious night of my life only . . . "

"Only?" He still held himself from her but his voice was gentle.

"Only it didn't mean a bloody thing without you there to share it."

"But I was there, for most of it. I left midway through the final act."

"But you weren't in your box. I . . . I looked for you." She felt embarrassment sting her cheeks and hoped it was too dark for him to see.

She couldn't tell. He rested his gaze on her face, expression unreadable. How she wished she might fathom his thoughts as easily as she had just a few days before, but his heart, which he'd worn on his sleeve until now, appeared to have been put away. "I stood in the back just behind the curtain. You couldn't see me, but I could see you. You were brilliant. Better than brilliant, you *were* Rosalind. Your performance tonight is certain to go down with the likes of Sara Siddons and Dorothy Jordan."

"Thank you but I fancy myself as more of a Nell Gwynne." She managed to get the words out over the lump lodged in her throat. Gavin's compliment was sweeter to her than any praise penned by the most lauded of London theater critics.

He turned to the ice bucket. "Champagne?"

She shouldn't, her head was reeling as it was, but she nodded her acceptance anyhow.

Watching him pour the frothy wine into two flutes, her gaze fell to his hands. She found herself remembering the feel of them moving over her, inside her, and shivered in a way that had nothing to do with the draft.

"You're cold. Here." He took off his dinner coat and tucked it around her shoulders. "This is where we came in, remember, with me tossing my dinner jacket about your very bare and very lovely shoulders. Did you think me mad?"

Daisy smiled. "Completely. And what of you, did you find me brazen?"

"Utterly shocking, but over these past weeks I've discovered that I rather fancy your brash ways so long as, like those lovely legs of yours, you display them in private, for me alone."

She couldn't think with him standing so close. Champagne in hand, she stepped away under pretense of examining the carved paneling on the side of the stage. Even coated in cobwebs and dust, the craftsmanship was exquisite. "Where are we, by the way?"

He stepped back, too. "An old, abandoned theater built in Shakespeare's day and last known as The

Parisian. The final play performed here was *The Misan-thrope* by Moliere. It's been vacant for a decade, longer perhaps."

"What a shame."

A slight smile played about his lips. "Yes, I thought so, too." A pause, this one longer than the last, and then he added, "Sometimes people abandon their dreams much like abandoning an old building. Because it's less trouble that way, because there isn't enough love to see it through."

The thinly veiled metaphor had her snapping up her head to meet his eyes. "I never said I didn't love you. I've always loved you. I never lied about that."

And yet she lied about so many other things. Now that she considered it, what a great lot of energy she expended needlessly when truth telling would have been so much simpler.

"Why didn't you tell me you'd written me all those years ago?

The question and the accusation underlying it took her aback. Shaking, she set her glass down on the table before it could slip through her fingers. "I assumed you knew."

"I didn't."

Even now she couldn't trust herself to believe him. "One unanswered letter I could have chalked up to mishap but, Gavin, I wrote you so many times. The last letter I sent was from Calais."

"I never received a single one, at least not until

today." He grimaced. "My grandfather left orders with the school that my correspondence be strictly monitored. He gave the headmaster a list of persons from whom I might receive letters. Everything else was to be sent on to him."

Daisy felt tears prick her eyes. "When you didn't answer, I thought you must not care to be bothered with me any longer, that your fancy new life hadn't room for a foundling without even a surname to recommend her. When I sent my last letter and a month went by and you still hadn't answered it, I told myself I had to face the fact you'd moved on—and that I had to move on, too."

"I didn't move on. I drifted. Wherever I went, whatever I did or saw, all I could think of was, 'How Daisy would love this' or 'I can't wait to tell Daisy about that.' When I got back to London, the first thing I did was hire a detective to find you, but it was too late. There wasn't a trace of you to be found, not in London and not in the counties, either. I never thought to look in France, let alone considered you might take a stage name. Foolish, foolish . . ." He shook his head.

"How *did* you find out about the letters after all this time? Did your detective uncover them somehow?"

He shook his head. "My grandfather confessed what he'd done and then gave them to me. Along with owning up to the business about the letters, he admitted to attempting to bribe you into breaking it off with me. He also told me you refused him flat out. He even showed me the torn bank note. Why did you lie to me, Daisy? Letting me think you had a lover was bad enough but then to lead me to believe you betrayed us for the proverbial fifty pieces of silver . . . Why would you do such a thing?"

She looked down at the dusty floorboards. "I couldn't have you ruining your life over me. I gathered your grandfather would cut you off if we married. I couldn't come back into your life only to destroy it."

He shook his head as though she were a careless child. "Had you but troubled yourself to come to me that day I would have told you I don't give a tinker's damn about my grandfather's money."

"You say that now but it's been a while since you were poor. It would be very hard to go back to that kind of life."

"Difficult, yes, but not unthinkable, and I would have done it, I would still do it without a second thought if it was the only way we could be together. As it happens, however, I have money of my own, independent of my grandfather's legacy. Not great riches, by any means, but enough to take proper care of you and Freddie and the Lakes, too. But of course you didn't come to me, did you, Daisy? Because despite everything we shared, you still didn't trust me enough, didn't love me enough, to believe we could work it out."

"Oh, Gavin, don't ever think that. If there was anyone I don't trust, or love enough, that person is me.

Pushing you away before I could hurt you seemed the kindest thing I could do, but now I see it was cowardly and . . . self-defeating. As badly as I hurt you, I hurt myself that much more. If I could step back in time a month, I'd go about it all so very differently, but I suppose it's a silly wish. It's too late now, isn't it?"

Rather than answer that, he said, "I almost forgot. I have something for you." He reached into his coat pocket and pulled out a slender, brown paper-wrapped package.

Taking it from him, she asked, "What is it?" Surely she was the very last person deserving of a gift.

Gaze trained on her face, he said, "Open it and find out."

She slipped off the string and tore through the paper. Unfolding the contents, she snapped up her head. "It's a deed. The deed to this theater . . . with my name on it. You bought me a theater, this theater!" Daisy had never owned a piece of property in her life, let alone a whole theater. Well and truly overwhelmed, she found herself speechless, drowning in the rush of love she felt.

He nodded. "I know it's not the Savoy—yet—but I've had a surveyor out to look about and he's assured me that the basic structure is sound. It's everything else that wants fixing, but it's yours if you want it, outright without obligation. You can take it and choose never to see me again. But I'd very much like to be a part of it, not just this theater but your life, yours and Freddie's, if you'll have me."

"Gavin, are you asking what I think you are?"

His answer was in his smile, that wonderful lopsided smile that reached his eyes and lit up the whole of his handsome face. "Marry me, Daisy. Marry me and let us both stop drifting. Marry me and let the three of us be a family."

"Oh, Gavin, I don't know what to say."

He set his champagne glass on the table and walked toward her. "Say yes. Say you'll marry me. No more delays, my dearest darling girl, and God help us, no more lying. Whatever difficulties arise in the future, we face them openly and honestly and above all, together. And as much as I love you, I don't want you to accept my suit for Freddie's sake or the Lakes', for that matter. If you accept me, it must be for myself alone. And I'm giving you fair warning, Daisy, I'll expect you to love me with all your heart and all your mind and, yes, all your body, for the rest of our lives. Can you promise that? Can you possibly want me that much?"

She swallowed hard. "I can and I do." She loved him so much she felt as though her heart were squeezing in on itself. "But, Gavin, are you certain you've thought it all through? I'm an actress and before that a dance hall girl— not exactly the best background for a barrister's wife."

"I'm certain I love you, Daisy. Beyond that, nothing else really matters. I don't care what outrageous stage name you take or what color you dye your hair. You can dress in purple taffeta and rooster feathers if that's your fancy, it doesn't matter because I love you. You're the woman I want to share my life, and I want you to share yours with me. I want to be a father to Freddie and to whatever other children God may grant us. I want to grow old with you, making love to you long after our bones have begun to rattle and creak. And when my time comes to die, I pray it comes before yours because I can't fathom a world, my world, without you in it. What do you say to that?"

In answer, Daisy wrapped both arms about his neck and, standing on tiptoe, kissed him with all the intensity, all the passion, and all the love she'd shored up for fifteen long years.

Resting a hand atop either of his shoulders, she tilted her face to the side and brushed her mouth across his. "Thank you for loving me," she said, almost a whisper.

"You're welcome." He slid a hand through the warm cinnamon of her hair and brought her face to his. His mouth hovering above hers, he asked, "You'll marry me, then?"

"Oh, Gavin." Holding his face between her hands, she brushed her lips over his brow, his jaw, his lips, trusting that her answer was reflected in her eyes and in her kiss and in her touch. Just in case, she drew back. Smiling up at him through the happy tears, she said, "I promise to love you through thick and thin, forever and ever. Come what may, we'll stay together . . . just like a real family."

EPILOGUE

"Wherever there is a playhouse,
the world will not go on amiss."
—William Hazlitt

Six Months Later

Who would have thunk it?

Sipping her post performance champagne
with a satisfied smile, Daisy cast her gaze across
the theater's freshly painted green room bursting at the
seams with the *crème de la crème* of the London theatrical
world as well as her and Gavin's family and dearest
friends. Even Gavin's grandfather had deigned to attend
their debut performance, *A Midsummer Night's Dream*
with a lovely older lady on his arm, Callie's aunt-by-mar-
riage, Lottie Rivers. Apparently the two had known

one another for decades and over the past six months romance had blossomed. Glancing to the pair clinking champagne flutes in the far corner, Daisy saw Mr. St. John was actually *smiling*. Astonishing.

Hadrian and Callie managed to arrive for the play's final act, but missing from their celebration was Rourke. The Scotsman had sent his regrets in a telegram along with some rather astounding news. He'd eloped with, some might say abducted, Lady Katherine Lindsey. The newlyweds were even now making their way north by train to his crumbling castle in the Scottish Highlands. According to Hadrian, who'd seen the place, Lady Kat would likely have to spend months working her soft, delicate hands to the bone to render it halfway to habitable. Daisy hardly thought a ruin the proper setting for wooing a reluctant bride, but when she said as much to Gavin earlier, he only winked at her and reminded her of where—and how—they spent their own honeymoon night. Thinking back on how they made love in every dusty nook and cranny of their yet-to-be-renovated theater had prompted them to repeat the experience all that morning and afternoon.

Catching sight of Gavin across the room carrying a sleepy Freddie, Daisy sent him a soft smile. He transferred the child into Flora's arms to be put to bed and walked up to her. "You're looking rather pleased with yourself, my love."

"I am. I was just thinking if we must make love in

dust and cobwebs, I'd rather it be in a grand old theater than a crumbling castle—or the *attic* of a grand old theater," she added with a wink.

She and Gavin had resumed their Roxbury House club meetings only this time they held the membership strictly to two and instead of peppermint sticks and lemon drops, they served champagne and decidedly grownup kisses.

"It's a good thing, too, because given the funds we've sunk into this place, the castle may be rather long in coming. As for the other . . . " The corners of his beautiful mouth kicked up. "Rourke wed to a blue-blooded shrew, there's a play in that as well as ample poetic justice."

"Why, darling, that brilliant mind of yours isn't only for legal matters, is it?" Catching his blank look, she elaborated, "As Shakespeare might say if he were still alive, the play's the thing. In this case, the play's already written and has been for several hundred years."

Gavin's gaze connected with hers and a broad smile broke over his face. "You don't mean *The Taming of the Shrew*, by any chance?"

She nodded. "Indeed. I'd say given the circumstances, a special wedding gift is in order, wouldn't you? You never know, but it might make for . . . *instructive* reading."

"That depends upon Rourke actually reading it. I've yet to see him pick up anything that wasn't a newspaper or railway financial report."

"You assume Lady Katherine is the one in need of

taming."

He sent her a tolerant smile. "In that case, I'll post it first thing in the morning."

He'd surrendered his champagne to ferry Freddie about, and she offered him hers. Holding the fluted rim to his beautiful lips, she felt her heart trip over itself and her skin heat. It never seemed to stop, this passion they shared, this connection of bodies and minds and souls that bound them together as surely as if they inhabited the same skin. Separate people but, together, part of something greater and grander. And though in so many ways this night represented the triumph of her career, she could hardly wait for the guests to leave so she could make love to her handsome husband yet again.

He caught her wrist and brought her palm to his lips, mouth hitting the spot he knew by now drove her mad. Through the satin sheathing of her glove, she felt the heat blaze a trail from her palm to her elbow. His light finger working across her mouth silenced her more effectively than any words could.

Eyes warm, he leaned in and whispered, "Have I told you yet this evening how lovely you look? Or how utterly besotted I am with you?"

He was so dear, so gallant . . . so Gavin, her husband, her lover and her very dearest friend. These past months she'd made a concerted effort to stop questioning how she'd ever gotten so lucky and accept her good fortune for what it was: happiness, pure and simple.

"I love you, too, with all my heart." *And all my mind. And all my body.*

Now that she'd finally gotten past her fears over saying the *l*-word, she couldn't seem to *stop* saying it. She loved him with all that she was and hoped to be. Once the room cleared of guests, she meant to spend the rest of the evening not only telling him but showing him just how very much he meant to her.

The twinkle in his eyes and his sudden smile told her he knew exactly what she was thinking if only because he was thinking the very same thing.

"I know you love me, Daisy. And I'm glad, so very glad."

—THE END—

VANQUISHED

HOPE TARR

A devil's bargain.

"The photograph must be damning, indisputably so. I mean to see Caledonia Rivers not only ruined but vanquished. Vanquished, St. Claire, I'll settle for nothing less."

Known as The Maid of Mayfair for her unassailable virtue, unwavering resolve, and quiet dignity, suffragette leader, Caledonia — Callie — Rivers is the perfect counter for detractors' portrayal of the women as rabble rousers, lunatics, even whores. But a high-ranking enemy within the government will stop at nothing to ensure that the Parliamentary bill to grant the vote to females dies in the Commons — including ruining the reputation of the Movement's chief spokeswoman.

After a streak of disastrous luck at the gaming tables threatens to land him at the bottom of the Thames, photographer Hadrian St. Claire reluctantly agrees to seduce the beautiful suffragist leader and then use his camera to capture her fall from grace. Posing as the photographer commissioned to make her portrait for the upcoming march on Parliament, Hadrian infiltrates Callie's inner circle. But lovely, soft-spoken Callie hardly fits his mental image of a dowdy, man-hating spinster. And as the passion between them flares from spark to full-on flame, Hadrian is the one in danger of being vanquished.

ISBN#1932815759
ISBN#9781932815757
Jewel Imprint: Sapphire
US $6.99 / CDN $8.99
Available Now
www.hopetarr.com

For more information
about other great titles from
Medallion Press, visit
www.medallionpress.com